A Southern Exposure

Alice Adams

A Southern Exposure

O48044

WHEELER
PUBLISHING, INC.
ROCKLAND, MA

★ AN AMERICAN COMPANY

Published in Large Print by arrangement with
Alfred A. Knopf, Inc.
in the United States and Canada.

Wheeler Large Print Book Series.

Set in 16 pt. Plantin.

Library of Congress Cataloging-in-Publication Data

Adams, Alice, 1926-
    A southern exposure / Alice Adams
        p.   cm.
    ISBN 1-56895-324-0 (softcover)
    1. City and town life—North Carolina—Fiction. 2. New Englanders—
North Carolina—Fiction. 3. Depression—North Carolina—Fiction.
4. Family—North Carolina—Fiction. 5. Large type books. I. Title.
[PS3551.D324S68 1996]
813'.54—dc20   95-10296
—   CIP

To Amanda Urban

With love

Part One

Chapter 1

On a fine blue summer afternoon, in the distant Thirties, one of those brief and hopeful years between the Depression and the war, a once-grand wood-panelled station wagon heads south, down all those winding white concrete miles, in flight from Connecticut. The small family enclosed in that hurrying car—Harry and Cynthia Baird, and Abigail, their daughter—does not have a fugitive look; they look like rich Yankees, or maybe even movie stars; the man at the filling station where they just bought gas thought they might be from the movies. Cynthia and Harry, had they known, would have very much liked this view; it is what they wish they were, a glamorous couple—an image they hope to recover, down South, where life is much cheaper, they have heard. That is their general plan, to regain some comfort and ease of living—and in certain specific ways they are, as they might have half-ironically put it to each other, on the lam.

Small, handsome, sandy-haired Harry's flight is perhaps the simplest in origin: he is fleeing a job as the manager of a country club in Connecticut, on the shore. Marginal work at best, involving details that were endlessly boring to Harry: the ordering of booze and food, scheduling events, and endless glad-handing; Harry has sometimes felt his smile was deforming his face. And his rebellion took predictably dangerous forms: he often drank too much; he allowed a few backseat intermission flirtations to get out of hand, so to

3

speak. There will be none of that in Pinehill, their destination, though, he thinks. In this pristine, uncharted region he and Cynthia will regain their innocence; once more they will be in love and rich again, as before the Crash, now almost ten years back, when Cynthia's golden money seemed an endless stream.

Cynthia Cromwell Baird, a green-eyed blonde, is a languid but sexy, observant, and imaginative woman. Her escape is both more furtive and more complex than Harry's. For one thing, she owes Lord & Taylor almost three hundred dollars. Can she and Harry somehow be traced down here? Will they send someone? How incredibly embarrassing; besides, she does not exactly have three hundred dollars available. In Cynthia's mind, which tends toward the novelistic, she and Harry are at a lovely cocktail party, perhaps out in someone's garden, among all their nice new Southern friends; they are wearing their beautiful best clothes, which no one there could recognize as old—when suddenly: "Mrs. Cynthia Cromwell Baird? We have a warrant, will you come with us?" Would they do that, turn her into some Public Enemy Number 32, or whatever?

Her other escape is from a handsome, bad (really low-class) man named Jack Morrissey, whom she "led on"; she knows she did, knowing all the while that she didn't actually, ever, want to go very far with him. She just liked the kissing and the excitement. In Pinehill, however, there will be none of that, unless Russell Byrd, the local poet, whom Cynthia has read obsessively, whom she will *meet*—unless James Russell Lowell Byrd is as sexy as he looks. But no, she will only be polite and admiring, and maybe let him know that she has memorized quite a few lines from his work.

Abigail Baird is a fair, deceptively stolid-looking child, who has combined her father's opportunistic energy with her mother's imagination—with some success. She is an interesting, secretive, plumpish child. Who does not remember the Crash, having been born shortly before it took place. But she has a certain bias against big wealth, since all the girls at her school, Miss Taylor's, were very rich, and Abigail loathed the school, and most of the girls. Her best friend was Benny Davis, the janitor's son. A Negro boy about her age but much taller. Abigail is tall for her age, with long blond hair in heavy braids, and a thick fringe of bangs across her forehead. She looks forward to going to the public school in Pinehill (no one has told her that there will not be Negro kids there).

Abigail's most hated person at Miss Taylor's was the chemistry teacher, Mr. Martindale. As all the girls there knew, his irritation threshold was very low; it was quite possible that he disliked them fully as much as they did him. But he was not supposed to dislike these nice rich young girls, of course he was not, and so Rocky Martindale (fresh out of Yale) disguised his rage with (to Abigail, at least) the most perfectly transparent smiles. So hateful!

But Abby took revenge: on an afternoon shortly before this trip South, she and Benny, with keys "borrowed" from Benny's father, Dan, the janitor, went into the chem. lab, and there, in an extremely tidy and methodical way, they switched about all the compounds, one fine white powder into another's box or bottle. So meticulous was their work that nothing would be noticed, they thought, until the first day of school next fall, when Mr. Martindale began some of his show-off experiments. None of which would work. Abigail has liked to imagine his smiles of purest rage.

Sometimes, though, on this long drive, she has had darker imaginings: perhaps an explosion— she hates Martindale but would not wish to injure him physically. Or could she and Benny possibly have left any fingerprints, anywhere? Would they send down the FBI?

Fugitives, then, these three, driving through the long shadowed green afternoon toward their fates, their new stories. The main point, on which Cynthia and Harry are agreed, is that they won't have to worry over money. They can make do, easily, on what they have left, the little dribbles from unscathed stock. It will be like being rich again, and ten years younger. Abigail dreams of a wonderful public school—no rich kids and no Mr. Martindale.

The road over which they are passing is two-lane, white concrete. On either side rise banks of eroded red clay, finely crumbling, in delicate long lines. On top of the banks begin fields of yellow-brown broomstraw, and waving dark green pines. Occasionally there are deep rich thickets, an impenetrable interweaving of branches and twigs and leaves; and sometimes flowers, wild, and promiscuously, beautifully flourishing there by the highway—ragged Queen Anne's lace, and tiny bluets. Unlikely roadside companions.

They cross a bridge, more white concrete, that spans a shallow brown creek, bordered by a narrow beach of dark, dirty-looking sand, and bursts of honeysuckle vines, thickly tangled, suggesting caves, and secrecy. Hiding places, away from the sun.

And then the road begins its long slow almost imperceptible climb toward the town, as the hills surrounding spread their wide green gentle waves. That vast and until recent years unpopulated countryside surrounding the town of Pinehill is some hundred or so miles inland from the Atlantic; it is said to have once been underneath the sea, in some prehistoric formation. And the infinitely slow, grand undulations of those green hills do indeed suggest a subaquatic history, to scientific minds as well as to poetic temperaments. The local poet, Russell Byrd, whom Cynthia plans to meet, has frequently been inspired by this notion, and both the geology and the botany departments of the local college are fond of field trips. There are even rumors of whale bones, though none have actually been found. There are the ghosts of whale bones, possibly.

To anyone living in these parts, except perhaps for Russell Byrd, this landscape is most ordinary. It is what you expected, driving through the South, along with the bare brown yards of lonely farmhouses, built up from the dirt on stilts, where chickens graze and half-naked babies or skinny-legged older children play and hide. But to the Baird family (the fugitives!) it is all as exotic as a dream terrain, or a movie.

"There's so much wide open land" is how Cynthia expresses it. Then, trying again, "I mean, I think of what we're used to, even in the suburbs, and then the Hoovervilles, all those people crowded in packing crates, under the George Washington Bridge." She sighs. "If only people could be redistributed some way."

"The Russians are trying that out," her husband, Harry, reminds her. "It's not working too well, I don't think. Their famous Five-Year Plans."

"I think it's really beautiful," from the backseat Abigail informs her parents, who often tend to forget that she is there. "Like a big green ocean," she adds.

"'Green prehistoric undulations,'" murmurs Cynthia, from one of the Byrd poems that she has learned by heart.

"What?"

She does not explain.

Chapter 2

Missing the hills of his homeland, the endless undulations of green and the small rise of Pinehill itself, which is now at least a thousand miles ahead, Russ Byrd (James Russell Lowell Byrd) in his over-sized Hollywood Cadillac drives fiercely across the flat scorched plains of western Kansas. He succeeds in blocking out the five screaming children (his) who are fighting on the backseat and on the car's wide floor, and in also blocking out the woman who sits beside him, Brett—his wife, whom he himself named, changing her from SallyJane Caldwell Byrd to Brett Byrd, a whole new person, a poet's wife and mother of five. Brett is of course the one to cope with the children. As best she knows how.

Russ is speeding toward Pinehill as fast as he can, at the very same moment as the Bairds, too, are approaching the town. Only, in Kansas it is still earlier in the day; the sun is higher and much hotter.

"I hate you, I wish you were dead."

"Dead—you too!"

"Anybody wanna buy a duck?"

"That's not funny, Joe Penner is not funny."

"You shut up, you damn fool."

"I'll cut off your head with scissors."

"Is everybody happy?"

"You look like Olive Oyl."

"You look like a dumbhead dodo."

"I hate you!"

"Children!"

Russ is thinking of home, is concentrating on that known loved landscape, but every now and then all those voices successfully intrude, and what he thinks then is: Damn them, there's not a scrap of poetry in a one of them, not even Melanctha and certainly not in my boys, Brett's boys (there is also a secret child of whom he never thinks). Lowell, Walker, Justin, Avery, Melanctha. None of these kids even look like Russ, they all favor fair fat Brett; they are bland and blond, with quick ugly tempers just beneath their peaceful surfaces. Only Melanctha has something about the eyes that makes people say, "Well, she surely does favor you, James Russell. Do you reckon that little old girl could be a poet too?"

Russ does not think so, nor does he see the link between his own famously intense, deep-set, dark blue eyes, and the small blue dots on either side of his daughter's tiny nose.

"Handsome" is not a word generally applied to Russ; certainly he does not see himself as a handsome man—thank Christ! he might have added. His face is extreme, is striking in its contrasts: very white skin and very dark, very thick curling brown hair, and those dark, dark intense blue eyes, so deep-set, so fierce. Wide thin red mouth, and deeply cleft sculptured white chin. A large, slow-moving man, Russell speaks slowly too, as though

9

imitating the farm boy he used to be, and still claims as his true self (Russ has in fact several accents, or modes of speaking), so that the wild darts, sometimes lethal, from his intelligence elicit shock. Did Russ Byrd actually say that, just when you thought he was sleepily inattentive, even not quite catching on? Yes, Russ did say that, and those who read his poetry with any care found, buried in those rural landscapes, some messages that were somber indeed.

With the part of her mind that is not occupied with her screaming children (a large part), and her distant-seeming husband, Brett (SallyJane) Byrd considers Kansas. She compares Kansas to Santa Monica, the house just left behind, and she easily decides that of the two she likes it better in Kansas. She hated California: Los Angeles, Santa Monica, Palm Springs—all that she saw out there she disliked. All those furry-mouthed refugee intellectuals, so-called, and the fast-talking New York types—impossible to understand a word that anyone said. And all those skinny dyed-blonde women hanging all over the men with their boobs hanging out of their pale pastel silk clothes. The weather was pale and pastelly too, no zip to it, never a bite or scent in the air from anything real.

Whereas Kansas looks real, as real as hell. The way-off little farms, dirt farms, and dirt poor they looked to be; and the just plain miles and miles of nobody's land, furze land, burned grassland. And every now and then on the highway a Model T, or an old-timey hauling wagon pulled along by a brace of mules. Sometimes whole families piled up on a wagon, with their beds and babies and everything, heading to California to pick grapes, probably. Like in that new book, Mr. Steinbeck's

Grapes of Wrath, that Russ made her read. A lot of it made her cry with sorrow for those folk.

Of course Russ is driving too fast; he must be hitting sixty, anyway, so it's hard to get a fix on anything she sees. She almost wishes that something would force them to stop, like an accident, or a vomiting child. She sighs as she thinks, Could I have wished that, wished sickness on one of the children? Oh, God will surely punish me for that. And then she smiles as she thinks, It's good I quit going to church when I did.

"You dumb fool!"

"Melanctha is Alice the goon!"

"Justin is a doodoo."

"Avery makes poopoo in his bed."

The shrieks are laughter now, not tears, though it hardly matters, and at least no one is throwing up. Not yet.

Russell likes Los Angeles, Hollywood, all that, although back in Pinehill he pretends that he hates it. He even pretends with Brett, alone. But she knows better, she sees his face when the telegrams come, and the long-distance phone calls, summoning him out there. She sees that farm-boy smile spread from his mouth to his eyes, and when he gets off the phone to tell her what the plan is, she can hear it in his voice, pure pleasure. The country boy who's won a prize at the fair. For his corn. (Brett snickers to herself at this very private joke.)

And the way he talks when they're out there; it's a scandal. His "ma'am"s and even "suh"s come as thick as summer rain, those mean little eyes of his opening wide and innocent, talking so slow and country it's a wonder anyone can understand.

"But don't you get worried at all? Russell meeting all those sex-queen movie stars and going to

11

parties, swimming with them and all?" Several of the dumber women in Pinehill have asked Brett that question, each phrasing it a little differently, but the message is always the same. Aren't you jealous, aren't you worried, and if you're not, why not?

"Because I know Russ" is what Brett would like to say, to the nosey, fake-sympathetic, censorious ladies of Pinehill, and to some of the men. I know Russ; he's scared to death of those real live movie stars. My Russ is a total coward when it comes to women. He was scared of me a long time ago, when I was the university president's daughter, over in Hilton, and he was the scholarship boy, what was then called a "self-help" student, meaning that he waited tables in the dorm and took odd jobs on weekends. Russ was scared to death of me. I had to do almost everything to get him to look; I used to lie out sunbathing when he came over to fix a fence in our back garden, my fat breasts spilling out of my bathing suit, usually, and then I'd trot out lemonade and cookies to him (now there's an original trick), and then it was me bought tickets and asked him to the May Frolics, and then the Sunday Germans. Pretty bold, I was, back then. But I really wanted Russell Byrd. I wanted a husband and a poet, and a father. I wanted Russ.

Russ is driving too fast. He is dying to get back home, Brett knows, just as when they're heading west, to L.A., he's dying to get out there. It's always the next place, with Russ. The thing ahead. The new poem. The unborn child.

Too fast.

Sometimes beside the road there are people walking along, bums with their clothes on a stick—or, less frequently, women with kids. Farm women, from the look of them; gaunt and bony-faced, maybe heading west for some fruit-or some cotton-picking. They all look up as the big car passes them in the wrong direction, and then, seeing all the kids, sometimes they smile. You've got your troubles too, is what Brett hopes they're thinking, not just ugly mad jealous thoughts about rich folks in too large cars. "We're not all that rich," is one thing Brett would like to say to them. "But here, here's what I've got in my bag"—and she imagines a flutter of dollar bills trailing after the car, a woman and child bending down to pick them up, and then going on walking to the next town for a couple of good big meals.

They now pass an enormous hay wagon, coming from the other direction, east. All the kids reach out; they believe that a piece of straw from a wagon like that brings luck. On the other side of the road, Brett's side, she glimpses a tall thin person, she thinks a woman, in big dark clothes, and beside her something small and dark and round. A very small child, probably.

In the next instant several things happen: Russ swerves just slightly to the right, to avoid the hay wagon, probably (Russ is allergic to hay, a secret fact), the car bumps into something heavy, and two horrendous shrieks burst into the air, one obviously a woman's, the other crazed, inhuman.

The car stops.

Russ opens the door, and in addition to the screams, which hardly stop, there is an explosion of foulness, a ghastly smell. Fecal—worse than fecal.

"Doodoo!" the kids all shout. "Throw up! I'm sick! Icky doodoo!"

"You kids just shut up!" shouts Brett, over all

their voices, even as she thinks, I'll cope with the kids, it's all I can do, and more. Russ can deal with whoever he's managed to kill.

It was not the woman. Brett now sees Russ rounding the front of the car, and the large dark woman moving toward confrontation, the woman no longer screaming but sobbing loud, holding a red bandana across her face—whether to catch tears or to keep out the horrible smell, no one can tell.

Oh Christ, good Christ, he's killed her child, thinks Brett. But why did the child smell so?

She can hear nothing of the interchange between Russell and the woman, can only see their impassioned pantomime; the anguished woman weeping still, implacable, so gaunt and tall—and Russ, in his gentle phase; Russ explaining, Russ very country charming. But his smile, is it possibly overdone? A dead child there in the road, and he smiles?

Another minute, and Russ walks around to the window on Brett's side, and motions her to roll it down.

He whispers, "It's her goddam pig." He has said this too loudly for the children not to hear. "I've killed her damn pig, that's pig shit you smell. Jesus Christ. Give me the money, will you."

"Pig shit!"

"Daddy said shit—"

"Oooh—smell—"

This chorus comes from behind her as Brett reaches into the voluminous cracked patent-leather handbag that she insists on hauling around, as Russ puts it, including to Hollywood poolside parties. She pulls out some bills, not looking at them, not counting.

"That's not enough. It's the only pig she had, and it was very big. Her husband's dead."

Brett hands him more bills. She is unable not to think, Suppose it had been a child?

Out in front of the car Russ is immersed in further colloquy with the woman, who has now stopped her weeping. Who even looks at Russ with a semi-smile. And Russ, smiling too, is backing off. Even from this distance, through the bug-spattered windshield, Brett sees that he is pale and upset. *Poets*, she thinks, as she sighs and turns back to face her children.

"Look, you kids. Daddy feels very bad that he ran over the lady's pig. He gave her some money to pay for the pig but he still feels very bad. So you kids just be quiet for a while, you hear?"

Melanctha, who, despite Russ's theories, does in fact have a sensibility quite similar to his own, a delicacy of spirit, along with his eyes—Melanctha begins to cry, very quietly.

"Okay, Melly, you come up here with me. You sit on my lap. Darling girl," her mother croons. "Don't you fuss. For all we know pigs go to heaven too."

"We'll stop at a tourist court," says Russ, getting back into the car.

"Really? I've always wanted to, I think they're, uh, sexy."

"Christ, Brett. Your mind. Or maybe we'll stop at some house. You know, the ones with the lights and little signs on the lawn."

"Tourist home. Overnight guests. Well, that's okay too," Brett tells him, thinking that it is considerably less than okay: in a tourist court the kids could have their own separate cabin, or maybe two cabins. And she and Russ could be—well,

15

alone, for the first time in months, it seems to her. In the Santa Monica house the bedrooms were all strung out along a balcony, nice sunshine and ocean views but no privacy, none at all, not ever.

"Ursula." Russ has said this name musingly, almost romantically.

"Who?"

"That was her name, the woman with the pig. Unusual, isn't it? Wasn't there an Ursula the Pig Woman in some play? Jacobean, I think. Maybe Johnson. *Bartholomew Fair?* "

"God, Russ, I don't know." Brett is experiencing a terrible and familiar sense of defeat.

That night in the large (six bedrooms) farmhouse that is now, in these hard times, a tourist home, Brett sleeps between Melanctha and Lowell, with Walker sprawled near their feet. Fitfully she thinks of home, of Pinehill, and their big spreading-out house. With the children off in their wing. Suppose the Depression got worse, and she and Russ had no money left, would they have to turn their house into a tourist home? Brett doubts it: "I'd rather dig ditches, I'd get me a job with the CCC" is what Russ would undoubtedly say. "No way strange folks are going to be sleeping over at our house."

But he seems to enjoy it very much when they stay in those places. Tonight he has spent an hour or so after dinner, down in the living room, making talk with Mr. and Mrs. Williston, their hosts, a plump and red-faced couple (they look much alike), who visibly hang on Russ's words, his stories. Not to mention all the time spent at the garage discussing their car; the pig had made serious dents in the right front fender, the garage was sending to Topeka for parts. And time visiting Ursula, the pig woman, from whatever play. Russ returns with stories of Ursula's childhood, her husband's death (TB), her seven children, all now grown. Her pig. Ursula is a fine brave woman, both Willistons confirm; they have known her always.

Indeed, Russ has seemed to settle into Kansas. Brett could easily imagine the two or three days becoming a week, and at that she thought, Oh good, I won't have to go to the Hightowers' party, and push off those stupid passes from Jimmy, and have those terrifying Hitler conversations with Esther.

Mostly, though, Brett is haunted by the child, the child who was not there but whom if he or she had been there, walking along with Ursula, instead of the pig, Russ could have—he would have killed. Changing everyone's life entirely. Irrevocably, for good. That nonexistent dead child is much more real to Brett than the vague seven live grownup children that Ursula actually has.

Instead of a dead child there was a big fender-bending shit-stinking pig.

Ursula the pig woman. Ursula the pig woman. A play of Depression Kansas. For the Group Theatre? Provincetown Players? Well, the thing is to write it, forget who for—for whom. And forget too the actual Ursula and her pig, and Kansas. A familiar but recently unavailable excitement trembles in Russ's blood, and his face involuntarily smiles as he thinks, I could, no reason why not. It's what they've wanted and kept saying I could do. An American classic. Folk but never folksy. I could do it.

He allows himself this moment of mindless excitement, of baseless confidence, silly joy—but only a moment, before he begins to think, But Jesus, the work, all the words, I'll never be able.

Next he wonders if he gave Ursula enough money. Fifty bucks is a lot for these days, but it wouldn't hurt to add a few bucks, maybe another twenty or so? What's money for, anyway?

And how can he sleep with these kids all over him? Disentangling his legs from the warm, insistent arms and legs, Russ creeps from that bed toward the door to the hall, down which is the bathroom and presumably other sleeping quarters. But just as he gets to the door there is Brett, suddenly beside him, her hand on his arm as she whispers, very softly, "There's another bed right next door. A nice big wide one. Want to meet me there?"

"But—" But he doesn't, for so many reasons: one, a ravishingly beautiful girl named Deirdre.

"They probably hoped they'd rent it late tonight. Just lucky for us they didn't."

"I guess—"

"Oh, Russ, come on."

He does.

Chapter 3

"And then there's the suite," says the clerk at the Pinehill Colonial Inn, after a pause during which Harry and Cynthia have considered other offerings—a double room, with two beds; two single rooms, connected; or a double room with a single room down the hall. None of which were very appealing. Also, Harry is already having trouble with what he takes to be the local accent. At first he thought this young man was kidding, dragging out his words that way and seeming to make fun of certain words even as he spoke them, but then Harry realized that this was how he, the clerk, talked: when he said " suite," in three or maybe four syllables, he may have been kidding the concept (Southerners, as the Bairds are soon to learn, are quick to knock pretense of any sort; anything that smacks of "airs" invites derision), but a suite is what this young man meant. " There's this sitting room and two—I think three—little bitty bedrooms, and then there's this sort of a breakfast room. And a kitchen. But I think y'all better take a look."

Their first "y'all." Harry and Cynthia exchange glances.

The " suite," reached at the end of a very long hall and up a small creaking flight of stairs, has turned out to be amazingly pretty. "Attractive," which is Cynthia's usual word, even uttered at its most intense, did not seem sufficient. It was Abigail who, standing on tiptoe to look out from a narrow window, turned back to gasp, " This is beautiful. We could stay here forever. Have people over all the time."

Abigail was right. The rooms were beautifully proportioned, and the furniture, instead of the anticipated shabby pseudo-Victorian, or some other bogus Sears antique, was very plain and comfortable. In fact it all looked handmade, beautiful wood all polished, and upholstered in obviously handwoven wool and linen of a remarkable spectrum of color, colors in amazing combination, as in a garden. A small fireplace had as its mantel some of the same plain dark and resinous wood. Next to the hearth were large unpainted clay pots, which Cynthia's ready imagination instantly filled with roses or, perhaps in another season, clusters of bright leaves.

"Well," said Cynthia and Harry, in almost identical tones, simultaneously. "It's really nice. We'll take it."

Cynthia in her mind has already peopled the room with a small dinner party, one of her elegant but unpretentious ventures. A simple French casserole, a little salad. Herself and Harry, in their elegant old clothes, last year's—but who would know? Some terribly nice new people, just two or three nice new couples. Mr. and Mrs. James Russell Lowell Byrd.

In Harry's mind a cocktail party has formed in that very same room, a good-sized crowd, on maybe a cold October football day, people all packed around the fire. Pretty women in tight sweaters. Lots to drink.

Abigail's fantasy removes all the grownups from the scene; she is there with a nice big group of brand-new friends, all girls from school. The grownups are all off at a party somewhere, and she brings out Cokes and cookies for the girls, and they laugh and tell secrets about the boys and the other, uninvited girls.

"...these here rooms are mainly Miz Bigelow's doing," the clerk is saying. "And she'll be real glad to hear that you folks approve. Mr. Duke, he's the owner, he just told her to go ahead and do any old thing she felt like doing in these rooms, and I don't think he's had any cause to regret it."

Daylight shifts and brightens the colors of those rooms, adding, from long windows, vistas of the town: church steeples and tree-lined streets, gravelled sidewalks, a two-story brick business area, small stores with offices above. And houses: everywhere, shyly glimpsed between those huge green trees, behind hedges there are houses. Large white clapboard houses with heavy front porches; small gray-shingled cottages, daintily decked out in vines. From this distance all the Depression shabbiness is quite invisible—no matter that new paint is needed everywhere, and repairs to those sagging porches, those broken flagstone steps.

Off to one side a cluster of large square pillared buildings, many overgrown with what must be Virginia creeper, now red-leafed, thick. This group is surely the local college, with its yellowed areas of grass, walled off in brick—and, at the moment, its uninhabited look: no school just yet, only here and there a stray professor or an eager freshman makes his way to the library, or the bulletin board at the Y.

In another direction darkly wooded hills rise up; there too small bits of houses can be seen, a peaked roof here, an ornamental cornice there. A grape arbor, a tennis court, and a twinkling blue swimming pool.

"Goddam place looks like a movie set" is Harry's comment, on their first morning.

"I can't wait to start looking at houses," Cynthia tells him.

"When can I get a bike?" asks Abigail. "I'm really going to need one here."

"I'll take you to Sears this afternoon," her father tells her. "Surely there is a Sears?"

His wife and daughter exhibit some surprise; it is not like Harry to be so instantly generous. What neither of them knows is the outcome of a conversation between Harry and the hotel's owner, Mr. Duke. The "suite," for reasons unfathomable to Harry, is so cheap (so reasonable, as he prefers

21

to think of it) that he seriously wonders if they should ever move. It is a little small for permanent living, that is true; on the other hand, if one thinks of it as a little *pied-à-terre*, it is perfect. And who knows just how long this Pinehill phase of their lives will last? "No rush to look at houses," he says to Cynthia. "Let's sort of settle ourselves in first."

Her look tells Harry a great deal; he could have described her expression as an essay in contempt, which he is all too able to read. Don't you understand anything? she soundlessly asks him. Don't you know that we came down here for a house, and new people to see, so that maybe we could begin to like ourselves again, with a new house and new people liking us? Not just to camp out in some *hotel*.

Interestingly (and Cynthia is interesting, and contradictory), what she says has quite another tone from her visible feelings. In a light voice she comments, "You're certainly dapper this morning. You're going out on the town?"

"Well, maybe I could do the shopping." He grins, not very nicely. "Maybe I'll pick up some new friends."

"Daddy, can I come too? Can we look for a Sears?"

He hesitates, looking for a bare fraction of a second at Cynthia, who is fingering her long fair hair in a tentative way.

Then, "Sure, Abby-pie," he says merrily. "Come along. We'll find Sears, and knock the natives dead."

Left alone, Cynthia is instantly cheered by the view, or views—by the sheer prettiness of where she is. The colors of the fabrics in the sunlight, and the throng of hopes within her own very pretty breast. Standing there, having happily kissed her husband and her child goodbye, for a while she simply relishes the moment—and her own luck: she has outwitted Lord & Taylor (so far); and it was she who found this attractive little town for them. And she who insisted on the Inn—Harry might have gone to some awful tourist camp.

It is she who is beautiful (still) and who has memorized a great deal of poetry by James Russell Lowell Byrd, whom any day now she will surely meet. Whom she will get to know.

And that is what she wants of Mr. Byrd, Cynthia in her more rational moments is aware—she is, on the whole, a highly rational woman; she wants, in a social, friendly, possibly even an intimate way to know J. Russell Lowell Byrd. She has wondered what his intimates call him. She hopes not "Jim." Even "Russ" would be, she feels, inappropriate for a great poet. But she wants him for a friend, to lay claim to him in that way.

Her encounters—whatever one might call them—those backseat or off-in-the-countryside (once in some actual bulrushes, so wet and terrible) with Jack Morrissey in Connecticut have been a lesson for Cynthia, she believes. A lesson in how desperately you can want something that turns out to be purely ugly, sordid. Like dousing a flame with mud. Thank God they never went further than they did, thank God they never actually did it. (Cynthia has no clear word for the sexual act, which she tends to think of in capitals, S E X.) Though God knows they came too close. "Affairs" (a word she likes) are best simply fantasized about; they should be left to novels, or poetry.

And so, if she meets—or, rather, when she

meets—James Russell Lowell Byrd, if he turns out to be as compellingly attractive as she has imagined, she can write a few poems, or maybe sometimes just close her eyes and think of him. With Harry she can pretend that he is Mr. Byrd. She pretends a lot with Harry, and the awful part is that it works; Harry adores her passion, believing himself to be its genesis, its source.

Sitting down, regarding the room around her, Cynthia is struck again by its extraordinary style. Someone knows what she is doing, thinks Cynthia. Or does she? Could this Mrs. Bigelow be some entirely natural, native, untutored talent? Maybe just a woman working there in the Inn—a Negro woman, maybe? It does not strike Cynthia, a Yankee, that in that case she would not have been referred to as Mrs. Bigelow. Certainly the use of color is highly original, those pink-mauve striped pillows on the rich purple easy chair. *Vogue* magazine, collectively, would go absolutely mad; in fact Cynthia at this moment determines to bring this about, somehow, this "discovery" of hers. To bring about a meeting between Mrs. Bigelow and the doyennes of New York taste. She is surely not about to waste this Mrs. Bigelow on Lord & Taylor, despite what she has heard about their decorating department.

But first they must meet Mrs. Bigelow, which in a town of this size should be easy enough. As Harry set off with Abigail, she even said to him, "Maybe you'll run into Mrs. Bigelow in the A&P. Keep your ears open."

Harry, however, had a much better idea. After settling Abigail into a chair in the lobby of the

Inn—as always, she carries a book; today it is *Five Cousins*—he goes over to the desk clerk.

"Afternoon."

"Afternoon."

They exchange bland smiles before the pause that precedes Harry's getting down to business.

He says, "You know that Mrs. Bigelow, the one you said did up our suite so pretty?" To his own ears, even, Harry's speech sounds odd, for Harry is an automatic mimic; having recovered from his initial shock at this desk clerk's diction, now quite unconsciously and uncontrollably he apes it, along with the general style of delivery.

"Yes sir, Dolly Bigelow. Husband Willard's head of the Greek department, or Latin, something along those lines. But Dolly, she's a newfangled unique lady. Unusual! She is—"

"Do you think she'd mind? I'd love to tell her how much I like—*we* like the things in our room."

"Why, she'd be just as pleased as punch! Just plum delighted. Here now, I can get you her phone number easy as pie, and the phones right over there."

"Mrs. Bigelow, we haven't met but my name's Harry Baird." (Harry himself is now pronouncing it "Baaad," in three syllables.) "And my wife and I are staying over to the Inn, in the suite, and I cannot tell you how much we admire your colors—it's just plain beautiful, what you've done."

"Well, Mr. Bad, I am just plain delighted to hear that. And you-all are the first folks bothered to call! Sometimes I've heard, you know, like *rumors*, but no one has actually—I think you must be an exceptionally nice person. And your wife too, I'm sure she's a lovely woman."

25

"Matter of fact, she is. And she is just crazy about those colors in that room. You must meet Cynthia. I know she'd be just so proud if she could meet you."

"Well, I'd rightly admire to meet her, you can tell her that."

A pause while both Harry and Dolly Bigelow consider options.

Mrs. Bigelow, with a decisively drawn breath, takes the initiative. "Well, I don't know if you are busy Sunday week, but Willard and I, we're having this little party—"

Chapter 4

In Kansas, at the Willistons' tourist home, Brett is sick. Very sick. Bleeding, cramps. A fever. She knows what is wrong but she cannot tell anyone. Russell takes the children over to see Ursula and her grandchildren, and that seems to work out. So that all day Brett lies there dozing, alone on the long sleeping porch, in bed, while outside late September heat weighs down the remaining leaves on the sycamore trees, presses grass to the ground. Stills breezes.

"But you have to see a doctor, I'll get one."

"No—"

"Brett, come on. Be sensible."

"I'm not sensible. I'm sick. I know it's all my fault."

"Don't give me that Presbyterian craziness. Forget your catechism."

"'And there is no health in us.'"

"That's right, that's what I meant. Brett, I'm bringing a doctor."

And so it is to the doctor, a mild bald man with silver spectacles, that she whispers, "I had an abortion. Two weeks ago in San Francisco."

Sitting on a bench on the Santa Monica pier, in the blazing, endless, and unnatural August sunshine, with her stupid white frilled parasol and her even more stupid hat (a white cloche) and dumb high white shoes, Brett knew from the quick rush of bile to her throat: she was pregnant. Well, of course she knew—after five? And never one miscarriage. The air smelled of dead fish, and candy, and gin; earlier they had all been drinking Pink Ladies from a shaker that someone had brought. Brett swallowed quickly and looked around, her first thought having been that no one should know. Her second, as improbable as the first, is that she will not have this child. (But of course eventually Russ will know, and they will have six children.)

"Darling Brett, what heaven." Flounced down on the bench beside her, suddenly, there is an apparition: Fleurette Fresnaye (née Edith Framer), an aspiring English actress, not doing too well, despite studio-ordered platinum hair and the nutty name. Lovely though weak large blue eyes, and a hopeless chin. Impossibly affected, but nevertheless somehow nice, Brett has felt. The two women instinctively like each other, perhaps in part because both feel themselves displaced, out there in California, in Hollywood, or Santa Monica.

"My darling, how are you?" croons Edith-Fleurette, nearsightedly peering at Brett. "My angel, you don't look well—"

"I don't feel—"

27

"Sweetheart, tell Fleurette. Or, better still, tell old Edith." Fleurette is fond of dividing herself in this way: Fleurette the vamp, and Edith the good old pal, whose accent is faintly cockney.

"I don't know, but I sort of think—"

"Oh Mary, mother of God—you're not, please don't tell me you're preggers."

"Well, I'm not at all sure—"

"Let me look at your eyes. Oh dear Lord God, you can't possibly want five children. Or would this make six?"

"Six. No, I—"

The next day on the telephone they talked again, and the next day and the next—by which time Fleurette had arranged for them to go to San Francisco.

Russ was surprisingly pleasant about the trip. "I've heard that drive is something amazing. You memorize it for me, hear? And I think it'll do you good, you've been looking a little peaked. You're not stopping off at San Simeon?"

Their California nanny, Suzanne, would take care of Russ and the children for the five days that Brett would be gone.

There was the magnificent Pacific. Miles and miles of winding coastal highway, above the sea, flat and brilliantly shimmering in the sunlight. Brett closed her eyes against the terrifying drama of this view, its intensity. She is not thinking, though, of any of her ordinary concerns, not of Russ or the children. Certainly not of the word she does not use, "abortion." Her mind is filled with the prospect just before her, what she will see as soon as she opens her eyes, and then tomorrow night San Francisco. A party in their hotel.

"There're just these rather fun people I happen to know up there," Fleurette has said. "They drink rather too much, but it's fun, and perfect to take your mind off things." After a small pause she adds, "And my mind too. I can't seem to stop dreading this bloody war, which of course most of you Yanks don't believe is going to happen."

The day after that, on the way home, more or less, they will "stop by," as Fleurette puts it, a little clinic out in the Sunset District ("Not quite as romantic as it sounds, sweetie pie. But there are some sand dunes, and more lovely views of the sea"). Their stay at the clinic should not take more than an hour; Brett can rest in the car as they slowly drive down to L.A., "and everything by then will be hunky-dory," said Fleurette happily, clearly looking forward to the trip.

That night, in a large suite in the Mark Hopkins Hotel—not her own suite, though hers is quite large enough—Brett tries to explain to a kindly older man just how she feels about the sea, and California. "There was absolutely nothing else in my mind," she tells him. "All emptied out, no room for anything but all that light and water, everything blue and shining." She realizes that she is a little drunk, her words spinning out of control, but realizes too that it doesn't really matter; this man doesn't matter, and then tomorrow the knife will possibly kill her (she had not really thought of this before).

The older man, whose name is Barney, owns theatres, movie houses. He lives up here because he likes it better than down there. He has heavy white hair and a reddish face, with narrow sad blue eyes. Brett has the crazy (drunken) thought that if he were younger they could make love—something about him, his height, perhaps, and the hard molded shape of his mouth, is vaguely exciting. What would he do if she simply leaned forward and placed her mouth against his?

As though he had read her mind, he moves slightly away from her, and he asks, "More champagne?" But then he says, "You do have the prettiest voice."

Brett smiles, and wishes that she had kissed him, after all. He did look sad, and the room is so crowded that she probably won't see him again at all.

There seem to be mostly women in the room. Shimmering lean satin thighs and bare smooth white backs, all very slightly undulating as, glimpsed between all that shimmer, that flesh, the dark suits of men can be seen to move toward drinks, or to crowd toward certain women.

Someone, not Barney, brings Brett a drink of something she does not want, something sweet and very strong. At which she obediently sips.

"You're a stranger here?" this new man asks her.

"Yes, actually just up from L.A."

"I thought so." He smiles amiably, his small eyes racing around the room.

"I guess I'm not the person you were supposed to get a drink for," says Brett. This has seemed the polite thing to say, but it came out somehow wrong.

"Say, that's quite an accent you've got. You pick that up in L.A.?"

"No, it's more from where I'm from."

"Well, you've done a great job. Sounds almost real. I've got a friend down there sells accents, can get you any kind you want. In case you want to change." He grins at her in a congratulatory way, so that Brett feels it would be rude to explain. Besides, she is suddenly too tired, too tired for anything.

"Well, my lady, did you think I'd got lost?"

It is Barney, returned with champagne—Barney who suddenly seems an old, old friend. He says, "You look very, very tired," as the other man smiles and goes away.

Barney leads her naturally out of that room and down the hall and into her own (but how did he know where, she later wonders? Did she give him the key? She must have). Like an old friend then he undresses her, touching her soothingly, slowly, as Brett half thinks, half feels, No harm can come of this. Not possibly.

Partly because of all the champagne, and because she was at first so tired, Brett finds it hard, later on, to reconstruct or to remember just what happened—or, rather, how; it was all so strange, so dream-or trance-like.

She lay naked between warm silk-smooth sheets and Barney lay beside her. He had only taken off his coat and shoes; so reassuring, no harm possible. But as he began to kiss her, at first very gently, at first just on her mouth, as he gently explored her body with his hands, new sensations of the most extreme intensity began to run all through her veins, and then to concentrate in the joining of her legs, in what she thought of as her place. As his hands and then his tongue touched her more and more deeply. She felt the familiar heat that she knew, or used to know with Russ,

31

but then more spasms, deeper, more entire, until she felt her whole body might burst. She could not, did not then or later, think of what he was actually doing to her, kissing her there; what she remembered was an endless, endless sensation, like a series of rooms, explosions of light.

"I have the most terrible hangover," she says to Fleurette, who calls to wake her early that next morning.

"Then don't drink any water—after champagne you'll just get drunk again."

"But I'm so thirsty…"

"Hold off for orange juice. Believe me. Just get down a couple of aspirin with as little water as possible."

The aspirin doesn't work—nor does the orange juice, or the coffee. She crosses the city with Fleurette dazed and miserable, unseeing.

The doctor, a chiropractor, is Chinese. Tall and thin, extremely polite, quick and nervous.

"Don't make noise," he says to her several times, in the course of the work he does on her body.

As though she would.

The pain is so severe (no anesthetic) that Brett has instantly recognized that if she makes the smallest whisper, if she gives in to it in any way, she is lost, gone—is mad.

On the drive south what looked so dazzlingly beautiful two days before now is ghastly, terrifying: the sheer drop to the sea, the dizzying curves of the road.

"Are you okay?" kind, solicitous (silly) Fleurette keeps asking.

And Brett murmurs, "Yes, yes, I'm okay."

By the time they get to Kansas, she knows that she is not okay. "I had an abortion," she whispers to the doctor. "You mustn't tell my husband."

Chapter 5

At the Bigelows' party, that hot September Sunday, the guests were all such very old friends and had been to so many parties together that it hardly mattered anymore who spoke what lines; anything uttered by anyone could as well have been said by another person. Even the presence of the new Yankees, the Bairds, and the stray comments that their stylish presence occasioned did not radically alter the general tone.

"Trust a Yankee to show up in black on the hottest day of the year."

"It *is* September."

"So smart of her to keep her hair so long. I always did like that old-style way."

"Such a lovely day for a party!"

"Did you see? Dolly must have been making these beaten biscuits for weeks. Her icebox must be just jam-packed with those things."

"Dolly. More likely Odessa."

"Her roses never seem to last through early September. I wonder how come mine always do."

"...lovely day for a party."

"So brave of Dolly to invite these brand-new people."

"You have to admit, he's real good-looking too."

This last was spoken in a slightly lowered voice as Harry approached the group.

"Oh, how do you do, Mr. Baird. We were just standing here admiring your wife's lovely dress."

"Well now, that's right kind of you ladies. I'll tell her what you-all said." Harry smiled a new Southern smile, to go with his new accent, and moved along; an expert party guest, he was rarely still.

"Are the Byrds really coming later on? I heard they had this terrible accident in Oklahoma." Paying no further attention to Harry for the moment as local talk again predominated.

"Look a there. Jimmy Hightower's actually drinking iced tea."

"Kansas. Not Oklahoma."

"I just love that dress. I was so sorry when they went out of style."

"They ran over some little child. Was that it?"

"Horrible!"

"Black attracts heat. We all know that down here. It's why in the tropics, English folk wear all that white."

"Well, you know Brett's handwriting. 'Indecipherable' is just the beginning. So God knows what they actually ran over."

"Yes, she does look a lot like Carole Lombard. Especially in that black dress."

"Wouldn't you say more Ginger Rogers?"

"Well, whatever they had the accident with, you can bet Russ will get a lot of new poems out of it."

"Oh, sometimes you're downright mean. Ginger Rogers! So cheap!"

"Speaking of beauties, have you all heard that Deirdre's coming back to town?"

"No! Deirdre Yates?"

"Well, of course, what other Deirdre is there around these parts? With her little brother. The one her mother died in California giving birth to."

These Yates events were both too confusing and too terrible to contemplate for long, and so attention shifted back to the Bairds—for a moment.

"How old is their little girl, these Bairds? Bads, whatever they call themselves."

"She's around here somewhere. They brought her to meet the boys. And the Lees brought their little Betsy, I think."

"Too bad the Byrd kids are all still out of town. Melanctha. Now isn't that some name?"

"Trust Russ Byrd to name a child after some colored girl in a book."

"For all we know, Brett meant ran over a pig."

"Well, if they do show up later we'll hear all about it."

"Harry darling, I'm not understanding a word that's said to me." Some private signals brought Cynthia and Harry to a small space beside a giant boxwood, where they could almost privately talk.

"It's okay, angel. You look beautiful."

"I don't know, I'm not sure this black was the best of all possible ideas."

"You're the most stylish woman for a thousand miles around, I'll bet on that."

"Oh, Harry, you're beginning to sound like one of these people. Do you think Abby's having fun with those boys?"

"I hope so, she could use some new friends."

"I'll go check in a little while. They're sort of cute, those twins."

"Yes, but Abby's not really interested in boys."

"Of course not, she's much too young. Besides, a girls' school."

"We hope."

"Just that little Negro boy she liked so much. That Benny."

"We played doctor in Connecticut but that was back when we were little kids." Feeling herself segregated with Betsy Lee and the Bigelow boys, Abby Baird's tone was superior, and bored—a voice she had heard from her mother, on occasion.

"Oh well, Betsy here's not exactly grown up."

The Bigelow boy, who had suggested playing doctor, now tried to push the project off on Betsy Lee.

"Archer Bigelow, I am not so little. I'm just as old as you are."

"What all did you play in Connecticut, now that you'd got so old?"

"Oh, the usual stuff. Monopoly and card games, a few kissing games at parties. And some of us liked to play tricks on our teachers."

"That sounds good, you know any real good tricks?"

"Well, this boy I knew, I told him I didn't like the chemistry teacher at all, and so he got into the lab in summer vacation and changed all the names around. The names of the chemical things, in those jars."

"Oh, bang! How many people killed? Much blood around?"

"Billy Bigelow, you are not the least bit funny."

"Then how come you laugh all the time?"

"Billy's practicing to be a doctor. He loves blood and all that stuff."

"My father told me he once saw a colored man's thing, and it was purple."

"That's silly. Negro boys' things are just sort of darker. No different. It's monkeys' that are purple."

A long pause followed this authoritative state-
ment. It was Betsy Lee who broke it, in a very
high voice, asking what was in all their minds: "You
mean you-all played doctor with colored kids, in
Connecticut?"

"Why sure, what's the difference? We were all
doing it, sometimes."

"If my mother heard a story like that, she would
absolutely, positively have a great big stroke. She
surely would." Betsy giggled, rather faintly.

"Well, don't tell her. Actually there was mostly
just this one Negro boy, and he was a friend of all
of ours. His father was the janitor in the school."

A long pause. A silence.

"Do you all plan on staying down here a long
time?" Archer Bigelow, a Southern boy to his core,
managed to ask this politely, at the same time with
the shadow of a threat.

"You mean at the Inn, or down here in
Pinehill?"

"I still think we should play some game.
This silly party could last all night. You know
how they get."

"We might as well do something."

"I honestly don't know."

"Archer's is crooked. Did you ever see such
a thing?" Billy laughed, mildly hysterical with
daring.

"Crooked Archer. That's really funny, I think."
Abby too laughed, more loudly.

"If you ever say that again—"

"Don't threaten me, little boy. Even if you have
got a crooked cock."

"Ooooh, some words you Yankee ladies use."

"Well, it's silly to call it a thing. I think."

"I'm going to tell my mother!"

"But if Deirdre comes will she stay this time, do you think?"

"Silly to come all the way from California if she isn't."

"Do you reckon, when they're all out there in California, that Russ and Brett and Deirdre ever get together?"

"Do they even know each other?"

"They wouldn't just run into each other. There's a whole bunch of miles between Hollywood and San Francisco."

"Is that where Deirdre's been? I never—"

"Deirdre's the most beautiful, most perfectly lovely young woman I ever laid my eyes on. Bar none."

"Jimmy, you better lay off that iced tea."

"Did you hear that Brett ran over this little child out in Texas?"

"She is just the worst driver ever. Ever!"

"But Russ was driving. You know Brett's always in back with the kids. Russ wouldn't have it any other way."

"Do you reckon Deirdre's as pretty as she was—what is it now, five years ago?"

"How could she be?"

"And it wasn't any child that Russ ran over, it was this little old pig, in Kansas."

"She's bringing her little brother, little Graham."

"I never could get the straight of that. Her brother?"

"It's simple. Sad and simple. You remember Emily Yates? Deirdre's mom. She died having that baby right after they moved to California. So sad. She had this idea about California being this real healthy place, and she talked Clarence into going out there, once he got her pregnant."

"What do you reckon the kids are doing down there, all this time?"

"Oh, you know kids. Just making friends, some way they've got of their own."

"Jimmy, where's Esther?"

"She's home, poor thing, with one of her migraines."

"Poor Esther. Hitler—"

"Yes, every time."

"Funny, her being from Oklahoma and all."

"Well, I guess she's more Jew than Oakie."

"Will you take a look at that dress on Miss Dolly?"

"She said she was whipping up a little something for today, but mercy sakes—"

"Esther thinks we should go to war with that Hitler. Stop how he's treating those Jews. A war!"

"Dolly, you are just the smartest thing. I don't know another person who could get away with colors like that. That purple with the pink."

"It's like the colors in our suite. I just can't tell you how *attractive* I think it is, I think my husband said—" Cynthia's attempt to join the group was tentative—and largely ignored.

"Such a lovely party, a perfect day."

"And no one's getting drunk, have you noticed?"

"That's partly because old Jimmy's not holding his end up. One way to put it."

"And poor Esther with those Hitler migraines of hers."

"Seriously, you think we're going to have to go to war with that terrible man?"

"Seriously I do, but don't you quote me on that or I'll say you're a liar."

"I declare, that Irene Lee's the prettiest thing this old town ever saw."

"Since Deirdre left."

"Well, Deirdre, but she's so young. Hardly counts when you're not even twenty yet."

"That Miz Baird, though. Even if pretty's not quite the word I'd use."

"Have you noticed? Yankees aren't hardly ever exactly what you'd call pretty, now, are they?"

"Well, come to think of it. But how about that debutante, that Brenda something? All over the rotogravure."

"Brenda Diana Duff Frazier. And you know she's not pretty, she's purely gorgeous. A raving, tearing beauty."

"But did you hear she'd had her legs fixed? Slimmed down by some old New York doctor?"

"Lord, it's so hard to know what to believe these days."

"Look, I guess the Bairds are going. Is that their little girl with them?"

"I guess so. Plump little thing. Looks mad."

"Oh, Yankee children."

Safely out of all that, in her parents' car, Abby burst out: "Did you know that Negro children go to different schools?"

"Well, I guess we did, but we just didn't think about it."

"Well, in that case I want to go to a Negro school."

"Abby, you know perfectly well that's impossible. Now calm down, we're going home now."

"One of those boys' things is crooked."

40

"Abigail!"

"Well, that's how they are. Those Bigelow twins. They don't know any games but doctor, I think they're dumb. God, I'd much rather go to the Negro school."

"Abby, I've told you, don't say God."

"Well, they're all dumb, those kids. I don't want to go to their school. One of them said Mr. Roosevelt was a Yankee Jew. Is that what they teach in their dumb old schools down here? Yankee Jew! Roosevelt! They're so *dumb*."

Chapter 6

From the low plateau on which the town of Pinehill is built many roads wind down, and down and out in various directions: toward the coast, or the western mountains, or north, up to New York, Boston, Canada, all that. Going east, the coastal direction, is a fairly new two-lane highway. (This state is famed for its highway system; much more money is spent on highways than on schools, as local professors are fond of pointing out, shaking heads and muttering of the future.) On both sides of this eastern drive are deep and seemingly infinite woods, pines and oaks and maples and poplars, and a rich, indistinguishable undergrowth of bushes and thick vines. Recently, a dirt road has been built that goes back into these woods. Not very far out of town. At the end of this road, in an old refurbished farmhouse, Russ Byrd and Brett and all those children live. A marvelous spread, which a great many people in town have never seen; the Byrds are known for anti-sociability.

Most people don't mind. That is how the Byrds

are, how it suits them to be. Too late to change, and besides, why should they?

Among those who do mind, in fact the single person who minds passionately, uncontrollably (especially when a little drunk), is Jimmy Hightower. One clear reason for this mania of disappointment being that he came to Pinehill, bought a lot on the road leading out to Russ Byrd's house, and built his own big fancy "modern" house there, purely and sheerly in the hope—well, the certainty—of getting to know Russ. Being friends. Drinking buddies, although an early, minor disappointment had been the news that Russ was not much of a drinker.

And, eventually, they were to be writing buddies.

For Jimmy wants to write, more than anything in the world, more than years ago he craved to make money he now wants to write. And not just to write, of course, but to publish books, have his picture in the paper, book reviews in the *Times* and the *Herald Tribune*.

All that time in the oil business—and he was good: Jimmy Hightower, the wildest wildcatter west of the Mississippi—all that time he was actually a writer, in his mind. Clean and famous. Sober, most of the time. With a big modern house in the country, near this nice little college town.

Near Russell Byrd.

Russell Byrd, who now, very occasionally, will wave from the big Hollywood Cadillac that he drives so fast on the narrow white dirt road, just barely slowing down, not to add a hello or anything like that to the wave, just to lower the dust, probably. Leaving Jimmy standing there staring, his tentative hand caught in a semi-wave. It felt like—and Jimmy suddenly but conclusively knew what it felt like, the acknowledgment almost felled him—it felt like being hot for a girl who couldn't see you for dust. Yes, that is how it feels. Some impossibly tall glamorous blonde girl from New York, in black summer clothes and dark sunglasses, out visiting in Tulsa, someone's college friend who could barely remember the little guy named Jimmy Hightower who had asked her to dance at a party (of course she'd said no, too busy). But watching Russell Byrd drive by, Jimmy is seized with the same fierce humiliated longing—for notice; he just wants Russell Byrd to acknowledge that he is there. A neighbor. Someone to talk to. All the stuff about writing could come much later on. Just as, with the New York girl, he wasn't so much dying to kiss her (he would not even have aspired to the thought of kissing) as to have her remember his name. At the next party to have her say, "Oh, Jimmy. Hi," in that easy cool Yankee way.

Jimmy hates this analogy. Russell Byrd and the New York girl of so long ago, but there it is, he has to face the truth of it. The intensity of his longing.

One of the only bits of advice about writing that Jimmy has ever heard, from a lowly instructor in English comp., went like this: Give a lot of thought to the things you don't want to think about at all. For whatever reasons, never mind the lowliness of the source, Jimmy took this dictum seriously; it was part of his writing credo, insofar as he had one. It makes him give a lot of thought to his Russell Byrd feelings as he vows, I'll be a writer if it kills me.

In his study Jimmy has a massive oval desk (several people have made remarks about Mussolini, which Jimmy does not find very funny), and in those drawers he has parts of a Western novel (80

43

pages of that) and a sex-and-oil novel (120 pages) and 30 pages of a newly started story, about a town somewhat like Pinehill, in which two very famous writers live and work, and are great friends.

In the meantime, "To hell with you," Jimmy mutters to the slowly settling clouds of dust above his jonquil bed at the end of his impressive lawn, and he goes back into his house. He is thinking by now less of Russell Byrd than of Cynthia Baird, the blonde, the new girl in town. He believes that Esther and his daughters have gone somewhere for the afternoon, but although he knows he was carefully told, he can't remember. There is too much in his head, he knows there is.

Where was Russ going, anyway? So fast, not looking anywhere. Could Russ have a lady somewhere, someone he drives off to see, on a secret afternoon? Who? Where?

This thought, today's thought, is entirely new to Jimmy, and he finds it exciting, both stimulating and scary. If Russ, the upright, the Boy Scout of American letters—if pious blue-eyed Russ has a girlfriend, then anything could happen, and probably will.

Esther is actually in New York, he suddenly, shockingly remembers—and the girls are over at a friend's for the afternoon. Esther has gone up for some of her committees and meetings. Joint Anti-Fascist Refugees, something like that. She always comes back sick with migraines and other strong emotional symptoms, and consumed with an urgency to tell Jimmy all about it, what the committees are doing, what the most recent news is from there, from Hitler's Germany, the land of poor Esther's nightmares.

Thoughts of Esther, of Hitler and Germany fill

Jimmy with an extraordinary if vague discomfort, a squirming unease. He wants so much to help her, to cheer her and make her happy again, but there is absolutely no possible way to make Esther happy until Hitler is gone. Defeated, dead. "We have to go to war with Germany," she whispers fiercely—to Jimmy alone; no one else will listen to much of this stuff, and of course no one else is married to Esther. "Roosevelt knows it too, he's just buying time." Her great dark Jewish eyes are huge, filled with all the sorrows of all Jews, forever.

However, remembering that Esther is in New York, and the girls off at their friend's house for the afternoon, Jimmy pauses in his over-sized, over-windowed living room; he stares at the new French telephone, and he thinks of Cynthia Baird.

"I thought if you had any free time this afternoon—I know you want to see some houses—a little drive?"

"Oh, divine! I'd love to. I've been deserted by both my husband and child."

Cynthia's legs are long and thin, a little too thin for Jimmy's special taste but they are pretty, very pretty legs, he has to admit. She stretches them out in Jimmy's new Buick's front seat, showing off her pale silk stockings and spectator pumps. "It's so interesting, the shape of this town, isn't it?" she comments.

"I guess."

Beside him there she chatters. Is she nervous, does he make her nervous, or is she always like this? Jimmy wonders, and decides to ask her later. When they know each other slightly better.

"It's a real plateau, isn't it?" Cynthia continues chattily. "With those interesting sideways wrinkles all around. Roads, and then places where there aren't any roads."

"This is my road," Jimmy tells her.

"Oh, how beautiful!—the woods."

Driving very slowly, approaching his own house, Jimmy is thinking that while it seems strange not to ask her in, it might seem stranger if he did. And stranger still if she should say to Esther, "Oh, I loved your house." But of course only a Southern woman would say a thing like that; a classy Yankee like Cynthia would surely know better.

Knowing that she will understand, he tells her, "And that's my house. Unfortunately, Esther is in New York this week."

"Oh, isn't it nice! So big, so nice and new and white."

She doesn't like it. Well, what the hell, no reason why she should. And suddenly, looking through Cynthia's stylish eyes, Jimmy doesn't much like his big house either. The touches of "moderne," so much glass brick, and the rounded corners, look pretentious and out of place in these woods. It looks frightened; only frightened people would live in such a defiantly new house, way out in the woods.

He drives on. "We're almost to the end of the road," he says.

"Where Russell Byrd lives?"

"That's right." But how did she know that? Are there tourist maps for sale these days, with famous houses—like Hollywood, homes of movie stars? Jimmy makes an effort to control this line of thought, and tells himself in a rational way that anyone, anyone at all, anyone at that fool party could have said to Cynthia, "And that's Jimmy Hightower, lives out on the road to Russ Byrd's."

But would that person have added: "So strange, there they are practically next-door neighbors, and I don't think they're any more friends than anyone." Strange indeed, thinks Jimmy, with somewhat more than his usual rancor.

"Is he home from California yet?" asks Cynthia next—no need to identify the "he." "Or Kansas, wherever he was."

"Yes. Just back," Jimmy tells her authoritatively.

"I suppose we'll meet sometime," says Cynthia vaguely, a vagueness that Jimmy recognizes as quite fake.

"I suppose you will," he tells her unpityingly. "It's a very small town."

"I've noticed." And then. "Oh, what a marvelous house! Is that his?"

"Well, it's theirs. He's got five kids, you know."

"Marvelous," Cynthia murmurs, clearly not concentrating on Russ's children.

It is a good house, Jimmy in his heart must admit that too. To an old low-lying farmhouse, the Byrds only added a wing here and there, the new imitating the old with great success. The house seemed to love the land on which it lay; it rested there affectionately, its small discreet windows suggesting self-containment, no need of the outside world. Suggesting Russ himself, of course. And, for that matter, Brett too—a very reclusive lady, in the town's view.

Jimmy's house had been built with an eye specifically to not imitating Russ's: a defiant newness, modernity had been the aim, and how often Jimmy has wondered, has questioned the wisdom of this defiance—but only to himself, never daring to broach this regret, not even to Esther, or perhaps especially not to Esther.

Sometime later, a mile or so after Russ Byrd's house, after a time of silence between them, just as Jimmy begins to slow the car, to turn and go back, Cynthia points and exclaims, "Look at that old road, almost overgrown. You can barely see it. Do you want to explore?"

"Funny thing, I never saw that road before," Jimmy mutters, half to her, half to himself. Aloud he says, "Oh, sure, why not?"

The road that they have been on, the Russ Byrd road (will anyone ever think of calling it the Hightower road?) simply ends, about five miles on, in a series of broomstraw meadows ringed with pines; Jimmy knows the place well. At one time he thought of buying it and putting his house there. Sometimes he wishes he had.

But this secret road, onto which he now turns, is beautiful. All over-arched with branches through which occasional streaks of sun now break, the trembling pale green leaves illuminated. The road, almost never used, enforces a silence, a tense slowness. Jimmy feels his breath tight, as though he feared to make noise, and beside him he can feel the tension in Cynthia.

This must be Russ's secret road, Jimmy instantly thinks, and does not say. This is how Russ escapes; he sometimes goes off into town or wherever, without passing the Hightower house. A great puzzle to Jimmy, watching.

It is impossible to drive more than about a mile an hour, and not to stop. Almost whispering, Jimmy asks Cynthia, "Want a cigarette?"

"Sure, I'd love one."

He gets them out, lights hers. As he does she cups his hand, for the tiniest instant only as, for that instant, a flicker of sexuality passes between them. They make no move, do not look at each other, but continue to smoke, indifferently. But they both have noticed.

Some minutes later they are stubbing out the cigarettes, and still in a whisper Cynthia asks him, "Does anyone ever use this road, do you guess?"

Meaning: does Russ? And so Jimmy answers her, "Russ does. Sometimes." He has spoken with authority, about his buddy. He starts up the car, his quiet Buick whose slightest noise he now resents.

Driving along, still quietly, still with the most infinite slowness, Jimmy's mind races; it is one of those times of lordly clarity—past, present, and future all spread before him. He sees that Cynthia brought herself and her small family to Pinehill for Russ, very much as he himself did; he sees this clearly, and just as he imagined an important friendship, himself and Russ, big literary buddies, so Cynthia, being a woman and a beauty at that, must have imagined some love affair with Russ. Dear God, maybe even some fantasy of bearing his child. And for all he knows, she too has some literary ideas, some little poems somewhere. But he, Jimmy, seeing and knowing everything at just this moment, as he is able to do—Jimmy knows that on certain scores at least she is wrong. For just as he and Russ are not even casual friends and will probably never be so, she and Russ will not be lovers, or anywhere near.

Whereas by the end of the fall, or somewhere in between, he, Jimmy, and she, Cynthia, will be kissing. Kissing each other in stolen places, as often as they can. He feels no hurry, though; he can wait (not knowing that every single one of his predictions is wrong).

The woods on the sides of this road begin to

thin out, a few small shacks appear: small boxes, high up on stilt foundations, above their bare mud-rutted yards. Then more houses, somewhat better, bigger houses—and now they are back in town. It is several minutes before Jimmy quite knows where they are, but then he recognizes the outskirts of Deaconville, the "colored" part of town, adjacent to Pinehill. Where people's maids live, and the men who work around town at odd jobs, the janitors, men who hose down the filling stations, men who stand around on street corners on Saturday nights with their cousins in from the country—all in their dusty bib-front overalls, their dusty shoes.

Between Deaconville and Pinehill there is no exact border—or perhaps in the county courthouse there is, but otherwise the distinction is unclear. There is, for example, a row of old brick houses, none now in good shape, but all once handsome and upright and trim. Are these houses in Pinehill or Deaconville? No one knows, but since all the inhabitants are white—not exactly poor whites but people more or less down on their luck, widows who take in boarders, that kind—the block is thought of as being in Pinehill.

"What nice old houses," Cynthia now remarks, as she and Jimmy Hightower pass them by.

"They're in pretty bad shape," he tells her. "You don't want to buy one out here."

"But couldn't they be fixed up? You know, that's exactly what I'd really like to do. Buy something old and just terrifically shabby and make it all grand again. And I'll bet I could."

"Maybe you could, but you'd have a job of work cut out for you with those."

"But that's what I'd like. And a woman I

50

know in Connecticut made a really lot of money that way."

"I reckon somebody around here will do that exact same thing sometime. Probably after the war." (Jimmy and Esther, unlike almost anyone else in Pinehill, are convinced that there will be a war; they both speak of it as a certainty.)

Concentrating on the gears, which stick, Jimmy does not quite hear Cynthia's next exclamation, "...what an incredibly beautiful girl—oh, I wonder if she lives around here."

At which Jimmy does look up, but sees no one. "Worse luck, I missed her." He laughs. "I guess I'll just have to look at you."

"Oh, Jimmy. That girl looked like a movie star, she really did. This long dark hair, and her figure—!"

Chapter 7

There was indeed a most beautiful young woman who was just going into one of the old decrepit brick houses as Cynthia and Jimmy Hightower drove by, and if Jimmy had not been preoccupied with his clutch, he would have seen that it was Deirdre Yates, the town beauty, away for five years, but everyone still speaks of her in that way. Deirdre is back, with her little brother Graham, and she is about to take possession of this house, the sale of which has been negotiated in great secrecy; details will never be entirely clear to the town, despite the most avid interest and inquiry.

Deirdre, who is tall and dark, clear-skinned, green-blue-eyed, full-breasted, has no special sense of her own beauty, except at moments. It is something for which she has accepted the word of other people, a fact of her somewhat complicated life. Smarter people than she is (Deirdre is considerably smarter than she knows) say that her beauty is very great indeed, and so she thinks, Well, maybe. Maybe I am what they say.

So far her beauty has been quite as much an inconvenience as an asset. Visible breasts at twelve made her shy, the subject of whistles and not-so-furtive jokes. "Remarks" from the boys in school, and sometimes not-so-kind teasing from the girls. "Well, Deirdre, it's nice to *see* you again. All of you." It was all very well for her anxious mother to say that the girls were jealous and the boys just plain silly; still, Deirdre did not feel that her looks made anyone like her better, made no one love her. And Deirdre so wanted to be liked; she yearned so desperately for love that she could put no name to that yearning.

Town-gown feelings ran strong in Pinehill in those days, and Clarence Yates, father of Deirdre, owned and ran a filling station, about as tacky as anyone could get, never mind that he was handsome, and that Deirdre's mother *and* her grandmother had come out at the St. Cecilia Ball, in Charleston. No one knew why she had married Clarence, and in a social way no one "knew" the Yateses; they only spoke at accidental encounters in the A&P or somewhere else downtown. Emily and Clarence Yates seemed to have no friends, they had only Deirdre.

Deirdre in high school felt herself a real non-success; the girls for the most part kept their distance, and all the boys who called her on the phone sounded as if they were calling on a dare, like the notes they wrote in study hall, which were mostly unsigned. With her heavy breasts, and her paper-white skin that could stand no sun at all, her long long legs and her big eyes neither green nor blue but some sea combination of the two, Deirdre was mostly uncomfortable. She derived no pleasure from the fact of being herself.

Until the day in the post office, when she saw the famous poet.

How did she know who he was? She could not remember, she just did, she always had, but at the same time she was sure that she had never seen him before.

But there he was, standing in the line right next to her line, with his packages to mail. Just like anyone else—but not at all like anyone else, ever, anywhere, really. His blue eyes deeper and darker, hair livelier and stronger. His mouth. His hands. His shoulders in the old torn brown sweater. She couldn't not look at him. Unconscious that she stared, after a moment or two she realized what she was doing, and she blushed. She saw that he was slightly smiling at her. Just the smallest smile that said, I know you. Hello.

Did Deirdre smile back? Later she could not remember, although Russ always swore that she did. "You smiled so beautifully," he always told her.

I am in love with that man, that poet, is how Deirdre phrased what she felt, to herself, that afternoon at home, after the post office. She thought, So that's what it's all about, that's how people feel when they say "in love." All those songs and poems.

She was happy at this recognition; she was peacefully entranced, and confident. Of course they would meet again, and sometime, eventually, something would happen.

She took to walking around the town alone, after school, exploring its edges. Sometimes she would come across a bunch of kids from school, on their way to the ice-cream parlor or maybe to some game, but these days, with her mind and heart so taken up with the poet, Mr. Byrd, she didn't care much about whom she saw; she could say "Hi," or say nothing, with almost perfect indifference.

This all took place in a long cool smokey November. Deirdre had a bright red scarf that year, with a hat and gloves that matched. Wearing that red, she felt that she was sending out signals. Surely he would see, and remember, and recognize her again.

And of course he did. Once, near the entrance to the back road, near the row of old brick houses where later Deirdre was to come and live—one day just by those houses his car stopped at the sight of Deirdre. He rolled down his window and he asked her, "Can I give you a ride somewhere? You're a pretty long way from home."

He knew where she lived? But of course he did; in those days everyone knew everything about each other, and everyone knew that Clarence, who owned the filling station, lived in the cluster of very small frame houses in back of the elementary school. With Emily, his wife, and his daughter, Deirdre.

Not wanting to get into the car with him—and not knowing why, it just didn't seem right—Deirdre smiled, and she told him, "I'm just taking a walk. But thank you."

"Well, it's a nice day for walking. I like November about the best of the months, do you?"

"Oh yes. The smells, and the leaves—"

His eyes had never left her face, her eyes; their gazes seemed unable to separate. But then they did separate, and Deirdre and Russ both were saying, or murmuring, "Goodbye." Not, of course, shaking hands. No touch.

In those Depression years there were no paved sidewalks in the town, except for a couple of blocks in the business district and in front of the Baptist church. Deirdre walked home over the hard white rutted dirt, never looking and never stumbling either. But dazed. Bedazzled.

A week or so later it occurred to Deirdre that she could walk down that road, the one he had driven up from, out of. Why not? A walk in the woods, on a bright November afternoon. His favorite month.

Before she saw or heard his car, she felt some emanation, as though she had known exactly when he would be there. As though he had known she would come.

He stopped when he saw her ahead of him, among the bare gray trees, and she walked down to the car. He opened the door for her, and for maybe half an hour they sat there, making aimless conversation that neither of them could remember later on. Their brief courtship. At some point he asked her, "Do you want a cigarette? Do you smoke?"

"No. I mean, no thanks." She added politely, "I guess I could learn."

"No, don't do that." They were staring at each other, they had been staring since she got into the car. He said, "Maybe we should walk for a while." (And later he was sure that he had intended only that, a small walk, some relief from the extreme tension between them.)

Blindly they got out and headed into the naked landscape, going toward nothing. Loudly snapping twigs and branches as they went. From some distant Negro cabin came the pungent, nostalgic scent of wood smoke. Russ pushed heavy branches aside, and suddenly they were in a small and densely sheltered clearing, with barely space to stand in.

Then, as they turned toward each other, Russ grasped her face. "Lovelier than anyone, than anything in the world," he said to her, his voice thick, and caught. "Do you know—?"

But she had moved closer, and raised her face, her mouth, to kiss. As though she had ever kissed or been kissed before.

In that way they met for several weeks of afternoons, now by design, until one afternoon they moved, with infinite slowness, down to the hard winter earth, to the dead leaves and slippery pine needles. Not exactly to remove but to push aside clothes, until they were lying together. But still Russ whispered, "Deirdre, we can't—"

"We have to—" And she guided his member inside her, as though she knew what to do.

Her body exploded. Again, and again. With his.

If anyone had noticed a new look on Deirdre's face, he or she would have remembered that Deirdre had always been beautiful, and was simply getting much more beautiful. And if someone who knew her well looked more closely and saw, unmistakably, *love*, the radiance imprinted on her eyes, in her slower smile, that person (her mother was the first) could well have concluded, as Mrs. Yates indeed did, She's got herself mixed up with someone. Some boy over at the high school, or maybe one of those college boys. She hoped it was not a college boy. Too old for Deirdre.

And as for Russ's face, which clearly too showed change, that also could be explained, as Brett did explain it, or she tried to: Russ had a new poem somewhere in his mind. He was lost in his poem.

The winter was hard on outdoor lovers, and meetings had more and more to be contrived. And so Russ, unbeknownst to anyone but his banker, bought one of those derelict old brick houses, on that row next to the Negro part of town. The banker was a deacon in the Presbyterian church, a man of monumental discretion. "It's a sort of investment," Russ said to Mr. Gwynn, the banker. "But Brett would think I was nuts."

"Very wise, I'm sure. Those were fine old houses, in their day. They could be made fine again."

"I don't plan on doing much to it."

And so doors were unlocked, keys given, and a minimal cleanup accomplished. And that is where Russ and Deirdre met, in an upstairs room in which there was a wide high bed, with some bedding sneaked in by Russ. From Sears.

No streetlights illuminated that part of town, back then. They saw each other as dark stretches of naked flesh. As eerily shadowed faces.

They never met in the daytime, nor did they meet by accident in the town.

Except once, on a side street near the post office; they meant to nod and pass but were unable to do so, and stood for an instant, smiling and staring, held together. They were unseen, except for one crucial person, passing in a car. Unseen by them, it was Brett. Of course it would be Brett.

They had so little time together, it seemed, as it

does to most lovers. Very little time to talk. Russ told her about his offers from Hollywood (this was before he had actually gone out there), how tempting and at the same time how disgusting. How he could not help being curious about the life out there. She told him about her aunt in San Francisco. "We could meet somewhere in between." They laughed, both fairly ignorant of the geography of California.

By the time Deirdre told Russ that she was pregnant, sparing him the news for several months (she was terrified of his reaction; would he love her still?), she had already made up her mind what she would do: she would go out to California, to her aunt, and have the baby there. It never occurred to either of them to somehow "get rid of it." Of course there were abortions then (Brett could have told them that), but usually not for white middle-class people like them. Their pregnancies were concealed in marriages, or in some complicated fictions—like the one that Russ and Deirdre eventually devised. More importantly, Deirdre really wanted this child, this child of Russ—and he did too, once he appreciated her great calm, her absolute lack of demands.

Deirdre told Russ none of the family hysteria, the threats and the weeping.

The whole Yates family drove to California; they were moving out there, it was said, and nothing was heard of them for many months. And then the news was indeed dramatic: Emily Yates had been pregnant, it seemed, and had given birth to a little boy, named Graham, in whose birth she had died (such a risk, trying to bear another child at her age, so selfish of Clarence). Clarence Yates had bought a new filling station in the San Fernando Valley, and was staying put. But Deirdre was coming back in a couple of years to live in Pinehill, the rumor went. To bring up her little brother there. Little Graham.

Having been passionately anxious to get Deirdre into the beautiful old brick house, having worked strenuously and paid a lot of money to that end, Russell gradually comes to realize something quite terrible and amazing. Which is simply that, once Deirdre is back here in town, he does not want, passionately, to see her. He does not long for her constantly, as in the old (five years ago) days. It is enough for him that she is here. And the boy.

He comes to see her at night, in the old, excited, frantic way—but even at their extreme moments he has a sense of staginess, of acting. And in Deirdre too he senses an unreality, as though part of her mind were always on her son, her "brother," rather than on Russ, her poet-lover. Pale and still, unsmiling, she lies beneath him, until at last she stirs, and she says, "It's a beautiful house, I really like it here."

"If you ever need anything, you'll tell me—you promise?" He bends down to kiss her eyelids, as he always does. "Or for the boy."

She says, "I don't reckon—" But the sentence is broken by a small cry from Graham's room. Getting up, she says to him, "I'll be right back."

Lying there alone in the dark, in the house that he bought for her, and for her son, their son, Russ experiences a sadness, a sorrow so profound that it comes close to madness.

He thinks, So it all comes to this. A very beautiful and intelligent (but so uneducated) young woman, in a pretty, secret house, with her little son. It is like a story already written, finished. Russ wants no further role in this play, which he knows, in his heart, that Deirdre would make extremely easy for him. His exit.

And he wonders, Was this all she ever wanted of him, after all? A house, and a son? And in that case, why him? Almost any man could have given her those things. Why the added presence of his fame, and poetry?

Perhaps, Russ is forced to conclude, that part of it was simply accidental. He was simply the man her eyes fell on at her own ripest moment for love.

He will never write again, Russ thinks, at that black moment, still waiting for Deirdre. His poems are fully as trashy as his life is. Of course they are.

He will go back to Hollywood. He will write bits of scripts about pigs.

He stays at home, and won't see anyone. Especially no local parties, or "gatherings," as they are called. Once, at the post office, he runs into that little fool from Oklahoma, that Jimmy Hightower, whatever he calls himself. Who tells Russ (as though he cared) that some new people have moved to town whom he, Russ, would probably like. In fact, the lady, Mrs. Baird, knows considerable of his poetry by heart. She is in fact an unusual lady, this Cynthia Baird is (Russ detects a just-controlled leer on the face of Jimmy Hightower).

Well, so much the worse for her, is what Russ would like to say. What he actually mumbles is "Well, maybe. One of these days."

He tells Brett not to bother him with the phone,

and asks if she would mind going to the post office from now on.

She wouldn't mind.

Chapter 8

Although Brett has been proclaimed "well" by her
doctor, and has no more overt, identifiable symptoms, she does not quite feel herself to be well.
She feels a pervasive sort of lassitude and a corre-
sponding lowness in her spirits. And her heart, or
something that is interior and important, seems
out of control; she feels wild flutterings, plus occasional stabs of pain. Not enough to tell a doctor
about, could she even find the words for whatever is wrong. She wonders about the Change;
she is much too young for that, isn't she? But—
could the operation in San Francisco (Brett does
not think, has never thought, the word "abortion")—could that have brought it on early? Or
done some other awful thing to her inside?

Very likely because of the way she is herself,
Russ seems strange to her. He seems to be acting
oddly, although perhaps he is not, is the same old
Russ. One night she dreams that Russ is having
some big illicit love affair, and she thinks, in the
dream, Well, that explains a lot. But in the morning she recalls that this is another symptom of the
Change, crazy, groundless jealousy, and so she tries
to put the dream out of her mind.

The afternoon (now years ago, before Deirdre
Yates went off to California and then came back),
the time that she saw them, caught in that moment like pinned butterflies, although her heart
jolts hard when she thinks of it, she tries to forget

that too. It was nothing, she tells herself; people run into each other like that all the time in Pinehill. It was slightly odd that Russ didn't say, "Guess who I ran into downtown today." But not significant. A meaningless encounter. However, it has stayed all this time in Brett's mind, it is vividly fixed there: those two faces, Deirdre's and Russ's, as they seemed to stare at each other.

Russ does not like having dinner with his children. Nor, when Brett was a child (when she was SallyJane), did her parents have dinner with her; she was always fed by her mother's succession of maids—Mrs. Caldwell "could not keep help," as the local ladies whispered behind her back, an awful indictment. Brett thus feels that she is continuing a tradition, doing as her parents did, and doing right by Russ in feeding the children first; she forgets, when she thinks along those lines, the difference between feeding one child and dinner for five, and although it is true that she has help (unlike her mother, Brett keeps any help forever), still the effort involved in those six-o'clock children's meals is large and often exhausting, increasingly so, for which Brett castigates herself, with no self-pity or even sympathy.

After the children have been fed and bathed and are settled, more or less, in bed, Russ and Brett have a drink together, usually in the kitchen, while she makes the preparations for their private dinner. This drink together is often interrupted by calls of need from the children's room: "I want a drink of water. A sandwich. I want *you*."

"Honey, you're much too lenient with them. You make them worse. They're getting spoiled," Russ complains.

But Brett is unable not to go in to them, at least for a minute, if only to say, "Now go to sleep, you've had your dinner, you don't need a sandwich now." Dimly she recalls childhood loneliness, old needs of her own, for which she never cried out. In a way she is pleased that her children ask for what they want, despite the inconvenience for grownups.

Lately, though, since Kansas, Brett has been too tired, really, for either the children or for Russ. The only thing that gets her through is the drink, or drinks. She has come to count on that—that big slug of bourbon over ice, with a little sugar and bitters so it qualifies, really, as an old-fashioned. A civilized cocktail that anyone might drink. Sometimes, to help her through the children's dinner, all that, she has a small private not-quite old-fashioned while she's cooking for them. Frying the chicken, broiling the hamburgers or hot dogs, whatever. And the bourbon helps. It dims the children's noise; it removes her somewhat from their passionate rages, their fights.

The only problem is that by the time that is all over and she has begun to drink in a serious way with Russ, and to fix his dinner, she is extremely tired—not drunk exactly, but just a little out of control. She burns things. She fears saying things that should not be said. Fears saying, "Do you love me?" Or saying, "Deirdre Yates?"

But she does not say either of those forbidden things. She says very little. She sometimes in a mild way complains to Russ of headaches, but she is not quite sure that he notices.

She continues to feel that he is somewhere else.

Chapter 9

Abigail hates the local school. "I can't understand anything anyone says, and I know it all anyway. We read those books last year. Some kids come in from the country on trucks, and they're all much older than we are because in the winter the trucks can't get into town and they have to stay home. Those kids seem dumb but I don't think they are."

Abby is in fact fascinated by those large children from out in the country; they are called "truck children." So large and mysterious—she cannot imagine their lives at home, where they live, but she thinks of large bare houses, babies crawling across cold linoleum, babies crying, and fathers in dirty overalls. The very size of some of these children is frightening. Seated at small tables, in the small chairs arranged for much younger children, their legs are thrust awkwardly aside. Some of the girls have breasts already; they cross their arms over their chests and duck their heads down shyly. They don't know the answers when the teacher calls on them, and the teacher seems to know they will not.

One of the largest, darkest, and by far the noisiest of the truck children (mostly they are quiet, shy) is a boy named Edward Jones. He teases Abby, seeming to regard her as someone alien, foreign, *wrong*. "Abby Talk-Funny," he mutters, just out of the teacher's hearing. "Say something in English, can't ya?" He jumps out at her from behind the stack of garbage cans in back of the school. "Gabby Abby, big and flabby," he chants. She is afraid of Edward Jones, with his black hair, his flashing black eyes, and his long, long legs.

Abby does not become friends right away with any of the children she met at the Bigelows' party.

"I want to go to the Negro school," she tells Cynthia and Harry. "Why can't I? These kids are just dopey jerks, I like Negroes better. I could have friends there. Is there some law that I have to go to an all-white school? I thought public school meant Negroes too."

"There probably is some law," her father tells her.

"Would you like to go to a boarding school?" asks Cynthia.

"I would if they had Negro children too."

Cynthia: "I can't exactly write to a school and ask if they have Negro students. Or can I?"

Harry: "I don't see why not. What I don't see is how we'd afford it."

"Well, there's that. But the real point is, she's too young to go away to school."

"True enough."

"But maybe one of those nice Quaker schools in Pennsylvania."

"Are Negroes ever Quakers?"

"I don't know. But you don't have to be a Quaker to go to those schools." Cynthia pauses, musing. "I think I'll write to one of them, just in case. Some girls I knew in Connecticut went to one."

"Cynthia, I tell you, we can't afford it."

"Maybe a scholarship? She has terrific grades."

"Even with a scholarship." Harry in his turn pauses. "We're still thinking about a house sometime, aren't we?"

"Oh yes, of course we are." Cynthia utters this semi-truth with enthusiasm. It is something she says quite a lot. "We're still thinking about a house," she and Harry say to each other earnestly, and "We're more or less looking at houses," they say to new friends, with equal conviction.

The truth is that they like it where they are. Or, to put it more accurately, where they are suits them very well indeed, both their stated and their unstated, perhaps half-conscious purposes. They are comfortable in "the suite," if just slightly crowded. But because of that very lack of ample space they are free of certain obligations that were strongly felt in Connecticut: new furniture, large parties. Also (this is the unspoken part), living as they do, as they are, allows both Harry and Cynthia a pleasant sense of privileged visiting; they do not really live in Pinehill, and are therefore subject to none of the local strictures or even customs. They could almost as well be living in Bermuda, or off on Capri.

Also, their life is much, much cheaper in that low-rent suite.

And it is rather sexy, hotel living.

Abigail feels this too, this lofty impermanence, but, unlike her parents, she both dislikes it and is able to articulate her discontent. "We live in a hotel," she accurately states. "We're not like a real family."

Exactly, thinks Cynthia. This is not a settled, domestic life that we're leading. I'm not exactly defined by being a wife and mother down here, and so—so whatever I do is okay.

What she is doing, at the moment, on a great many afternoons, is "looking for houses" with Jimmy Hightower. Very satisfactory. He is crazy about her, that is clear. He is so impressed, he never met anyone like her. Eventually, Cynthia supposes, some sort of payment will come due. He will make some pass, will want to kiss her, even to have an affair. And when that happens—well, she will or she won't, she can't tell yet. In the meantime he doesn't so much as touch her hands, except for the barest, tiniest, but sort of sexy instants, lighting her cigarettes. He is not, though, in the least attractive. Too short, and puffy. Red-faced, almost bald. Though God knows he is nice.

But he has not, has never introduced her to Russell Byrd. Cynthia has not, of course, come right out and said, "I'm dying to meet Russell Byrd." And is she? And if so, just what does she expect of this longed-for meeting? But Jimmy must have got the idea, at least, that she is interested in Russell Byrd. She knows a lot of his poetry; lines of it come into her head all the time down here. It must be the landscape, she thinks.

Sometimes, fairly often, Jimmy drives her out by Russell's house, as though that were available, a house to look at. Amazingly, for a family with five children, no one ever seems to be there. Or the famous big car, the Hollywood Cadillac, is there, but no people. Once, they caught a distant view of a woman—"Brett?"—off in the garden, a large woman with a hat and gardening shears who could, Jimmy said, be Brett. Or maybe not. But never Russ. No sign that he lived there. That he came and went on ordinary human errands—and perhaps he did not.

Cynthia on these Byrd excursions senses an excitement in Jimmy that is almost equal to her own. He's like a kid, she thinks, with a sort of crush on an older boy. Only Jimmy is older, isn't he?

"How old is Russell Byrd, would you say?" she asks Jimmy.

"Oh, maybe thirty-nine, forty." Actually, Jimmy knows the precise year and date of Russell's birth, but he chooses to make this information vague.

"Oh, that's older than I thought." And Jimmy must be a good deal older than forty, thinks Cynthia, who feels very young indeed at thirty-two.

"Don't you know any Byrd kids at school? I think there're five of them," says Cynthia to her daughter.

"Oh, yeah. Those dopey kids. Some dumb girl named Melanctha, and four dumb boys."

"What's dopey about them?"

"Oh, I don't know, nothing special. All the kids in the school are dopey, it looks like to me."

"Oh, Abby, now really."

"The Byrd kids come to school on a truck, but they're not really truck children. It has something to do with where they live."

Abigail's own major obsession, this golden Southern fall, has been Benny, Benny and the mixed-up substances in the chem. lab, and the teacher, Mr. Martindale. What happened? Any explosion? Anyone dead?

Every morning, at first with dread, her stomach tightening, breath short, she has scanned the local paper, half expecting the headline EXPLOSION IN CONNECTICUT SCHOOL. On Sundays she reads *The New York Times*, which is carried by the local drugstore; Harry by now has one reserved. Abigail even reads the "Week in Review" section. It might be there.

But no, it never is. Just all this other stuff about countries arming, troops marching.

After a few weeks of such anxiety she decides

that it is over; nothing worth putting in the paper happened, no cops or anyone will come down there after her, and Benny is not in any reform school. Probably.

She is not especially relieved by this realization. What she rather feels is a vast and terrible disappointment. She wanted to know what happened—and she badly wanted something to happen.

One afternoon, when both parents are out somewhere, the perfect solution comes to her: call Benny. Long distance. How simple, how perfect. How could she not have thought of it before?

"God, Abby, it was just the greatest thing that ever happened. Oh, if you'd been there! If I'd been there—I got all this poop from Muffy Montgomery, you remember her?—when I was over helping my dad last week. Anyway, she told me that old Martindale made his little speech, you know the one, the magic of chemistry. Our chemistry is going to defeat Hitler's chemistry because it's better. All that bull, you remember, only this year he got a lot fancier, according to Muffy. With the gestures, the cute smiles. And then, nothing worked. It was so great. Nothing happened like he said it was going to. No smells, no explosions. I guess we're sort of lucky that way, right? But it would have been fun if something had really gone bang, or if there'd been some great big stink he didn't plan."

"What did he say?" Abby asked him. Talking to Benny is so familiar an activity to Abby that she can hardly believe she is doing it.

"Oh, you know how he is. He thinks it's okay if you smile all the time, then no one will know that you're starting an ulcer. He smiled and smiled,

Muffy said, and he said he reckoned the summer heat wasn't beneficial, that's what he said, not beneficial for chemical compounds. What a pill he is. What a fake."

"God, I wish I'd been there." I wish I were there with you. I would wish you were here, except it's an awful place and I wouldn't wish it on a friend, especially if the friend is a Negro. Abby says none of this to Benny; she has begun to think of her father finding this call on his phone bill. "I guess I'd better go," she tells Benny. "This is long distance, and you know my dad."

"Thank you for calling me. I'll call you sometime when I get some dough. Say, I forgot to tell you, I'm applying for a scholarship to this school in New Hampshire. Exeter? The coach says they're really interested in good ballplayers."

"Do they take girls?"

"I doubt it. I don't know."

"Okay. Well, good luck if you want to go there. Any school would be better than the one I'm going to."

"That's too bad."

"It sure is. Well, bye."

Abby hangs up feeling mildly depressed. What was all that about Muffy, anyway? Whom of course Abigail remembers, this really icky black-haired girl, with all these curls. And dumb. Benny couldn't possibly like her. *Much.* And she is just a little depressed about Exeter, where she can't go. Her mother wants her to go to Vassar after high school, because Cynthia got married instead of going to college at all. But she's pretty sure Vassar does not take either boys or Negroes.

Abby's reference to Harry's supposed stinginess is somewhat unfair; he will only be surprised by a phone call to Connecticut not made by himself and not explained by Cynthia. With Abby he is a generous father, giving her a quarter a week, which is more allowance than most kids her age get, in Pinehill, that year.

Thus Abby, on her new bike from Sears, is able each afternoon to get a small sundae at the Darby Dairy Products, otherwise known as the ice-cream parlor. Other kids go there too, with their nickels and dimes; the place is really crowded with kids that Abby halfway knows, from school. To whom she pays no attention whatsoever. Looking at no one except the counter boy, she pays and takes her Dixie cup of ice cream and chocolate sauce outside, to eat quickly before getting back on her bike and continuing her ride around the outskirts of the town—of which she hates almost every inch.

Chapter 10

Unlike her daughter, Cynthia "adores" this new landscape, this climate. "I think I was born to be Southern," she tells Harry.

"Maybe in some other life you were."

"I really think so. Why not? Can't you see me in a hoopskirt, on a wide veranda, fanning away?"

"All too easily, my love."

"Harry, you know you're really mean. All this light irony—well, you add it all up and it's heavy. A great boulder of irony, really crushing. You make me feel terrible—"

"Cynthia, for God's sake. Just the tiniest teasing."

Cynthia smiles. She is sitting at her dresser, getting ready for a party, to which they are already late. Now, instead of answering Harry, she applies a great pouf of powder to her nose, indicating that she attaches no importance whatsoever to this semi-conversation. Which she does not. But this is how, customarily, they communicate. They simply say things to each other, mostly for the sound; they like the atmosphere of conversation thus created. And each grasps some shred of meaning, at least, from the tone, the sound of the other. Harry has understood that Cynthia is impatient with him; she wants just to get on to the party. But from watching her, and her more-than-usually anxious glances at the mirror, he understands how especially anxious she is to please. To be pleasing, and especially pretty for this party at the Hightowers'. "Sometimes I think October is my favorite month," she tells him.

He agrees. "It's been pretty."

"Beautiful."

Pretty or beautiful, all the days of this month have been warm and clear, so far. Golden days, clear blue days, and high against the sky the pine boughs sigh and sing, bright green, bedazzled with light. Golden poplar leaves rustle in the breeze, and in the long cool shadowed evenings there are more rustling leaves on the hard dirt sidewalks and paths of the town. Driving out that wooded road to the Hightower house, Cynthia is thinking, Tonight I'll meet him, he'll be there. Russell Byrd. And maybe we'll walk outside for a while in Esther's garden. Maybe. In the magic October night. She says, "It *is* my favorite month."

In the garden the acrid scent of dying chrysanthemums, mingled with the livelier smells of rich, moist loamy fall earth, fills the cooling night air.

Russell Byrd, who is unaccountably, uncharacteristically drunk, asks Cynthia Baird, whom he has just met, "Ma'am, you ever smell fresh-killed pig?"

Arriving about an hour after the late arrival of the Bairds, and alone, Russell was seized by Jimmy and introduced to Cynthia. Russell then muttered that he must have some air. The garden? Cynthia chose to take this as an invitation, although he did look a little unstable, and she followed along.

Politely she answers what she believes him to have said, although his very thick accent and the heaviness of his speech make it difficult. "Why, I don't believe I have," she says. "Have you? I mean, often?" It is her sense that if she stops talking he will talk about something she does not want to hear, not at all.

As he does.

"Stinks," says Russ. "Stinks terrible. A putrid god-awful unforgivable unforgettable stink that I can't get out of my nostrils, my whole goddam head, whatever. The rest of my life. I'm now condemned to writing pig-shit plays. Oh, pardon me, ma'am, I forgot."

"It's quite all right," Cynthia vaguely, distantly tells him. She turns slowly back toward the house, the party.

Esther Hightower, upstairs in her bedroom, also smells the dead chrysanthemums, the loamy earth; she even hears the drunken voice of Russell Byrd going on about pig excrement—but who on earth is he talking to? Esther imagines a beautiful, shocked woman—but these perceptions occupy only the smallest part of her consciousness. Her absence from the party has been explained by Jimmy, "a sick headache"; actually her headache is worse than sick, she is worse than sick, she is mad with fear, and pity. Demented. She is living in Germany, and what she smells is the scent of human panic from those boxcars going nowhere, and what she hears are words in German. Incomprehensible but terrifying. And she thinks, because she is one of them, of those thousands of terrified people. Those who wait for voices in the night, and the angry clomping footsteps on their stairs.

Esther sits there, in the cool October starry Southern night, in the dark, and she tells herself where she is: Pinehill, America—but this stops nothing that is happening there, in Germany, at this very moment. And in her mind.

Esther wonders: If she simply got up and went downstairs, could she pretend to be okay? Could wishing make it so? Could she successfully pretend to be just an ordinary (Jewish) woman from Oklahoma, with a lot of oil money and a husband who is a little crazy, who wants to write, who came here to write, who has nothing to do with Germany, with Hitler and Jews? Esther sighs, and she decides that no, she could never carry it off, such deception. No one would think that she was okay.

Steps.

At that moment she hears them on her stairs, the sound of footsteps. But certainly not boots, nothing heavy. And then her door is opened, and a light, small, but definite voice is saying, "Oh, I'm sorry, I'm so sorry, I guess I'm lost," and she adds, "I'm Cynthia Baird." And then, "Oh, Esther, it's you."

Does Esther not, then, look as she usually does, not look like herself? They have only met two or three times before, these two women, but still Esther knows that she would recognize Cynthia anywhere. Although they have never had a conversation.

Esther explains, "This is actually the guest room, but sometimes I—I had some sort of headache. It's better now."

"Oh good, but I didn't mean—"

"It's okay. Would you like to use the bathroom? It's right there."

"Oh, thank you."

The trail of Cynthia's perfume across the room has obliterated the ominous scents in Esther's mind: the dead flowers, the dirt. The fear.

Emerging from the bathroom, Cynthia asks, "You, you really feel any better? Can I get you something?"

"Oh no, thank you. I'm coming right down. I just—" She looks up at Cynthia, at perfect blonde beautiful Cynthia Baird, in her perfect black. Esther is about to explain, when to her horror, out of control, she bursts into tears. Her face tightens as her hands fly up to cover it, and then in a moment it is all over, and Esther sits there, still holding her face. Entirely humiliated. Feeling so ugly.

The perfume comes closer, and Esther hears the soft voice say, "Oh, Esther, I'm so sorry, is there anything I can do?"

Esther drops her hands from her face, and for no reason that she can later deduce, she says what she has actually said to no one before, "It's what's going on in Germany," she says. "What they're doing to Jews. I can't stand it. I keep thinking I'm there. I'm Jewish, you know."

"No, I didn't."

"But that's no excuse—lots of Jews don't act like this. My being so neurotic, so irrational is really no help to anyone. There's a place where I send money, to help some families that come over here. I sent a lot more than Jimmy knows about. But that's not enough. I just can't stop thinking—"

Cynthia says, "Oh, I know, I can't stand to read about those things. I read a novel, *This Mortal Storm?*—something like that—and afterwards I had nightmares…" Cynthia now has perched on the bedside chair, as though she would stay for as long as Esther needed her there.

Hesitantly, Esther tells her, "I'm so glad you came in. I feel better. I don't know why I have to get so, so crazy."

Surprisingly, Cynthia laughs, a light little rueful laugh. "Talk about crazy. I just had a sort of conversation with Russell Byrd that was really nuts."

"Oh? With Russ?"

"He was talking about dead pigs, and how they smell. Can you believe it? Really, so much for my romantic fantasies. Poets!"

Suddenly, as suddenly as Esther's tears came, the two women begin to laugh.

"Russ is such a damn fool," says Esther at last. "I know he's a genius, and a great poet and all that, but he's a fool too."

"He's pretty drunk, I think."

"That's unusual, he doesn't drink much usually." Esther looks at her watch, which is tiny and gold, on her narrow, blue-veined wrist. "Long about now poor Brett'll be taking him home," she says.

"She's not here, he came by himself."

"Oh, well, that's some of the problem. He hates to go out without Brett," explains Esther.

"Brett seems an odd name for a Southern woman, it sounds more sort of English."

"He gave it to her. Russ named her. When they got married, she got a whole new name. Brett Byrd. That was one of the first things I heard, when we moved back here. Some change, from SallyJane Caldwell." Esther has moved from her bed to the dressing table, where she sits and smooths down her lively black hair with a brush, and dabs powder on her nose. As she frowns, she thinks, I really hate my dark sad face, I wish I looked like Cynthia.

"Your hair is really beautiful," Cynthia at that moment says.

"Oh, but yours—"

"Mine is so flimsy."

They smile at each other, acknowledging, maybe, the tentative start of a friendship.

By the time the two women come downstairs together, the throng below has thinned out considerably. Russell Byrd is gone, and the Bigelows. Some eight or ten people are clustered around the bar, which is a long carved heavy antique table.

In fact, as Cynthia's practiced eye had noted when she and Harry first arrived, almost all the furniture in the Hightower house is antique, and really good antiques, the real stuff. And pictures: Hudson Valley oils, also real. Here and there are what look to be family photographs in heavy silver frames. From Oklahoma? All in all a puzzling house, so peculiarly "modern," and furnished so conservatively, off in the Southern woods. If she didn't know better, Cynthia thinks, she would guess that one of the Hightowers, probably Esther, came from what her mother calls "real money." What Mrs. Cromwell herself came from—for all the good that did her in the Crash.

Harry is quite obviously waiting to take her home. But he does wait until they are in the car to ask, "So? How was your walk with the poet?"

Cynthia giggles, she cannot help herself. "Oh, Harry, so funny. All he could talk about was pig shit—that's actually what he said."

"How romantic."

"Exactly." She giggles again, moving closer to Harry. At that moment she is extremely fond of him. "As you saw, I guess, he just said he needed some air. And you know I have been, uh, wanting to meet him."

"I know."

"I guess he was drunk, he must have been."

Sometimes, in fact quite often, Cynthia likes Harry better than anyone. When they talk, she always feels in him an echoing understanding. She tells him now, "I'm extremely worried about Esther Hightower."

"You are? How come?"

She tells him, and then she says, "Remember Anne Rothschild? That sort of secret pipeline she worked with, getting people out of Germany?"

"Yes, but Anne's a millionaire. Several times."

"I don't think Esther's exactly poor. I just wonder if she knows about it."

"Don't know. Surely wouldn't hurt to tell her."

As they pull into their parking slot and Harry stops the car, Cynthia moves over very close to him. Very softly she kisses his neck, but he turns and takes her in his arms, and kisses her mouth, then whispers, "Hold on, I'll meet you in bed."

Chapter 11

By early November, Abigail Baird feels that she has worn out the town, in terms of bicycle explorations, and so she takes to hiding her bike here and there, and taking off into the woods. Then, grudgingly, she begins to feel a sort of interest in the landscape, the rustle of thin dry leaves, the crackling twigs and dead needles as she walks. The smells of that earth become almost as familiar to her as the smells of Connecticut woods. This *could* be home.

One afternoon, past a thick, uneven slope of pine woods, she comes to a narrow dirt road, and then what must be a cornfield, ancient, abandoned; crumbling gray furrows and desiccated brown-gray stalks, with moldering leaves, like sad flags. Beyond this field is a dense growth of vines and trees that must mark the creek. Graham Creek. On maps it is seen to run past the town, on its long slow circuitous route to the Atlantic.

Abigail hurries across the cornfield, sometimes stumbling, aware of dirt in her shoes, and also aware of some odd expectation: something will happen, something interesting.

She comes first to a stand of poplars, peeling, their trunks as white as ghosts. And then past a small dirty sandbar, the swollen mud-brown creek, with its freight of leaves and sticks, of submerged and anonymous trash. The day has been mild; still, it is November, and much too cold for wading. Probably.

Sitting on the sand, which turns out to be damp and fairly cold, Abby peels off her shoes and socks, she reaches her toes toward the water.

Cold. It is terrifically cold. As cold as Connecticut water. Reluctantly, she decides not to wade. Brushing the sand from her feet as best she can, she starts to put her socks and her shoes back on.

"Hey, girl, you're not supposed to wade in that creek!"

Suddenly accosted by this shrill and childish voice, Abby turns, but she sees no child. And then there is a child, a pale little boy coming out from behind a paler poplar tree. With his tall dark beautiful mother.

Deirdre—for this is Deirdre and Graham, her son, who in Pinehill she must always pretend is her brother—Deirdre is as startled as Abby first was, to see this plump blonde girl on the dirty sand by the creek, where before she has only seen little colored boys with fishing poles.

"I'm not going wading," Abby tells them defiantly. "I'm just out for a walk and decided to take my shoes off."

Deirdre asks her, "You live around here?" She has recognized that Abby is not from here: her accent and her clothes are from somewhere else.

"No, we live at the Inn. My parents and I do."

"That must be nice. Graham, stay back from that water!"

"I am!"

"Graham's my brother. Uh, my name's Deirdre Yates."

"I'm Abby Baird. Is your brother named for the creek?"

"Well, sort of. He was born out in California."

"Deirdre, I saw a fish!"

"Oh, Graham, you did not. You're making stuff up."

"Well, it could have been a fish."

By now the girl and the woman are standing together on the bank, just back from the sand where the little boy stirs at the creek with a long bent stick. Each is aware, both Deirdre and Abby, of a strong surge of liking for the other. Deirdre thinks: What a funny little Yankee girl, with her blond bangs and braids, like a little Dutch girl. She's cute, but not cute, really, she's interesting. I wonder if her folks know Russ.

As Abby in her turn thinks, This older girl is really beautiful, and she's nice. But she's lonely-looking, and a little scared. Her little brother is probably a big pain in the neck. I'm glad I don't have one.

Abby has been acute in ascribing loneliness to Deirdre. This is a terrible, confused, and painful time of Deirdre's life, a time when nothing makes sense to her, least of all this move back to Pinehill, where she was never happy, even before she knew Russ, and got pregnant, all that. Before Russ, before Graham, and her mother dying and California. She supposes that she came back because Russ wrote and called and said that the house was hers now, and because she couldn't live anymore in California with her father; she had never got on with him, and he really never went along with the plan of claiming the child as his and Emily's, and after Emily's death he was worse than ever, mostly cross about the boy. The least thing, the smallest noise would set him off, but he was cross at Deirdre too, pushing at her to go out and get a job when everyone knew that almost the whole country was out of work. And now here is Deirdre in Pinehill, with some money to live on (Russ gives money for her to the bank). And a house. But nothing to do. And no friends. She never had friends back here, but now even the people she knew she feels that she has to avoid. Just earlier this afternoon she saw a boy she used to sort of like, but she didn't think he saw her; anyway they didn't speak.

And Russ. Deirdre has no words for what she perceives as the dark and mysterious death of love. For going from such a dazzling of all her senses— his slightest touch on her hand could make her tremble then—from that to not touching at all. To heavy guilty silences, and to barely seeing each other. To not wanting to see him either, and only doing it for the boy. Her son, their son. Her "brother." A lie that, in the way of old lies, has come to seem true. The terrible last months of her pregnancy were so linked, for Deirdre, with the terrible last months of her mother's sudden illness, that Graham does indeed seem to have risen from Emily. To be Emily's child. Except that Russ is all through him, in his dark blue deep-set eyes—and he even acts like a poet, or Deirdre's idea of a poet: Graham imagines things, he is self-ish and lives all alone in his own mind, not need-ing anyone. He is an unchildish child, whom Deirdre in an automatic way tends to treat as her brother, asking his advice about what to do next (ridiculous, a four-year-old), where to go for walks. What to have for dinner.

Sometimes he seems less like a brother than like some distinguished guest.

Deirdre is too unhappy, though, to think very clearly about these strange facts of her life. She gets through each day as best she can with household tasks and books, and walks, long walks through the town and out in the woods, with Graham, always with Graham. She cannot for the moment even think of her life taking off in some other direction. She does not think of Graham older, herself older, and maybe getting some kind of a job somewhere. Maybe even married. She does not imagine any change between herself and Russ, not thinking, as she used to, of the two of them in Hollywood or San Francisco, or Paris, or New York. Sometimes, simply and despairingly, she thinks of Russ: He doesn't love me anymore. But another part of her mind, her intelligence, knows that it is not that simple.

By now the three of them, Deirdre and Abby and the little boy, Graham, are walking companionably across the desiccated cornfield. In the distance, above a jagged lonely line of pines, an ember-red November sunset burns, and burns, and fades with infinite slowness.

Deirdre asks, "You go to school in town?"

"Yes, and I really hate it, it's awful."

Deirdre laughs, a little. "I went there, and all the way through I guess I pretty much hated it too. Poor Graham, he's got all that coming."

"The teachers seem really dumb, and mean. They're especially mean to those big kids that live out in the country. You know, the truck children."

"Lord, I used to think that too. They can't be all that dumb."

Abby is aware of an excitement in her chest, a surge of warmth. This is the happiest she has been since they moved down here; she recognizes happiness in her eagerness to go on talking. This beautiful older girl with the nice quiet little boy, who is very handsome, really, for a boy that age. She asks Deirdre, "Do you like to read?"

"Oh yes, I read all the time. It saves my life, I think."

"Oh, me too."

And they are off. Titles, favorite authors.

The Count of Monte Cristo? Lost Horizons? The Wind in the Willows? They both disliked *Little Women, The Five Little Peppers.*

"Did you ever, uh, read poetry?" Abby ventures.

"Well, not much. Sometimes."

"There's this man around here. My mother's just nuts about him. His poetry I mean, she doesn't know him very well. James Russell Lowell Byrd. Of all the ginky names. His kids go to my school. But I'm not going to read him, I don't care."

"No reason why you should," says Deirdre vaguely; she suddenly sounds much older.

They have reached the path that goes up the hill, through woods. Through ghost-gray trees, dead pine-needle floor. "Deirdre, hold my hand, this is scary," says Graham.

In her own mother's voice Abby hears herself say, "Maybe you'd come by where I live for a while? We could have Cokes."

"At the Inn? That's not so far from my house. Well, maybe. For just a little."

Cynthia, meeting the girl and the little boy whom Abby brought in, has several thoughts at once, the first perhaps being: That is the most beautiful girl I ever saw, her bones and her eyes and skin, her color, her breasts and legs—it's good she doesn't know how beautiful she is, probably—she is just astounding-looking. (Deirdre

84

is sitting edgily on the sofa, her lovely legs childishly crossed, one hand holding her glass of R.C. Cola, the other patting Graham, who sits nervously beside her.) Cynthia further thinks: That little boy looks so much like someone I know. But who?

Cynthia asks Deirdre, "You've always lived around here?"

"Mostly. But we moved to California just before my mom died, and I've just now come back. I thought for Graham—" This last seems an afterthought that she is unable to finish. Why, what for Graham? If she ever knew, Deirdre is no longer sure what she meant.

"It's an awfully nice town" is all that Cynthia can think of to say.

"Yes, ma'am."

Am I old enough to be called "ma'am"? wonders Cynthia. Well, compared to this dazzling young girl, I guess I am.

"California is more interesting, I think," puts in Graham helpfully, at that moment.

"Oh, I'll bet it is!" cries out Abby, who has been sitting on a stiff small chair, more nervously even than her guests. But now, unleashed, she goes on. "This is the most boring town. I'll bet California is just terrific. Mom, couldn't we move to California?"

Graham scowls. "It's not all that great in California."

But in the instant of his scowling Cynthia has seen it: Russell Byrd's face, on this child. This young woman's much younger brother. It has to be: no man and child could look so much alike without blood ties.

And so: the dead mother of Deirdre and Graham—Mrs. Yates was Russell's lover, his mistress?

Was she as beautiful as Deirdre is? Cynthia is consumed with a wish to know all about that woman, but who can tell her?

She wonders if this is a shared but well-guarded town secret, if everyone knows but no one talks about it. And how very Southern that would be, she thinks. Did Russell's wife know, the improbably named Brett? Does Jimmy Hightower know? She will ask him tomorrow; she is sure that if Jimmy does know he will tell her. (On the other hand, could Jimmy and Esther be too recent arrivals to be allowed to share in the town's most interesting secrets? That would be very Southern too.)

Most mysterious of all, does Deirdre herself know about her mother's lover, the father of this supposed little brother? Very likely not, Cynthia decides; but very likely the father, Mr. Yates, at least suspects, which would be a reason for Deirdre's return. He wouldn't want the child around.

The sheer interest of all this dark history is terrifically exciting to Cynthia: she is quite literally thrilled, it is better than a novel.

"Your little brother's very handsome," she says, with some mischief, to Deirdre. "Does he look like your mother or your father?"

This seems to be a question that Deirdre has heard, and for which she is prepared (she and Russ worked it out). "No'm, not either one, especially," she says (her voice unconsciously imitating Russ's country voice). "He sort of favors an uncle of my mother's, Uncle Rab, lives over to Memphis."

"Graham's named after the creek, Graham Creek," Abby supplies, rather proudly; these are, after all, her friends, it was she who brought them home.

And it is for just that reason a curious social situation. Cynthia thinks this: There are no contemporaries present, all the ages represented have wide gaps. Abby is so much older than Graham (at their ages four or five years seems enormous), Deirdre is much older than Abby is, and Cynthia herself is a great deal (she feels) older than Deirdre. No wonder Cynthia has such a sense of imbalance, of insecurity about what to say to whom. She finds herself strongly wishing that Harry would come home. His easy, foolish, graceful banter would save them all.

But just as she is thinking this Deirdre gets up to leave. "I like to feed him real early," she explains. "That way he sleeps better and I do too."

Cynthia, even as she gets up and smiles goodbye, has an instant glimpse of such solitude, a beautiful young woman all alone in her house with a little boy. A woman sleeping alone, every night.

"I want you to come to see me real soon," says Deirdre then—to Abby, to no one else. Not to Cynthia, although she smiles vaguely in Cynthia's direction and says, as vaguely, "I thank you for the Coke." But Deirdre clearly establishes that she feels her connection to be with Abby, and Abby only, by which Cynthia is both pleased for Abby and just slightly chagrined for herself. She would like to know Deirdre too, to make a friend of her. But mostly she is pleased for Abby, who is looking radiant.

Deirdre tells Abby where her house is. "We don't have a phone yet," she says. "I'm not even sure I want one. Who'd call?" She laughs, with a little sadness, but no self-pity; she is simply stating a fact.

Cynthia laughs too. "I hope you get one. After all, you could always call us, we'd love to hear from you. And to see you."

This earns blank looks both from Deirdre and from Abby: they want to be friends, with no intrusion from Cynthia, the grownup.

But Cynthia keeps trying. Once Deirdre is gone, "What a beautiful woman," she says to Abby.

"I guess."

"Would you like me to have them over for supper sometime, when Harry's here?"

"No, I don't think so." Abby pauses, seeming to meditate. "I think I'll go over there tomorrow," she tells her mother.

Chapter 12

"The rich get richer," says Esther to Jimmy Hightower, on a late November morning, in their kitchen. "Even in the middle of a Depression. But I never expected to be living proof of that fact myself," and she gives a small sad laugh.

Their kitchen table is covered with papers. Some are letters, some visibly legal documents. Large, steaming, just-filled blue coffee cups sit, so far untouched, a judicious distance from all the documents.

"Well, it couldn't happen to a more deserving lady." Gallant Jimmy, whom Esther had accused of getting more Southern all the time.

So that now she cries out at him, "Don't give me that Southern blather! Christ, Jimmy! Almost everyone deserves it more than I do. Needs it, is more to the point."

"Well—"

Dead seriously she tells him, "Listen, unless I do something really, really important with this money, I'm done for. Do you know what I mean?"

Very slowly he tells her, "I know what you're saying. I hear you."

They exchange a look of extreme intimacy. Of comprehension that is absolute.

This is what has happened. A great-aunt, one of Esther's enormous, labyrinthine, and variegated family, has died in Pawtucket, Rhode Island, and her bequest to her "admirable and beloved niece Esther Goldman Hightower" amounts to something over a million dollars—1930 dollars.

"I'll have to go and set myself up in New York," muses Esther.

"What?" And leave me here? Jimmy does not say this last, but he might as well have.

"You could rent out the house and then we'd have even more money." Esther has said this as a joke, with a small denying laugh: she does not mean it, but Jimmy takes it up. "How long would you go for?"

"A year?" Making this a question, as though asking his permission, Esther adds, "I don't see how I could get anything done in much less."

"You've got definite ideas about what you'd do?"

"Well, there's this group that Cynthia of all people told me about, and they sound really good. She said she'd write to this friend of hers for me. Some Rothschild."

She looks happier and younger than she has for years. It is odd that money should make that difference for Esther, Jimmy remarks to himself, and then he reflects that it isn't really the money that is so cheering her; it is the chance to advance in what he thinks of as her private war against Hitler. "If you take the girls, I could live in a smaller place," he tells Esther. "Less maintenance and work for me, and I'd contribute the difference to your cause."

"Ah, Jimmy, you're really good. But don't get such a small place that I can't come down to visit, you hear?" And then she says, "Gosh, we're talking like this was all done, and I haven't even begun."

Later, Jimmy reflects on the rapidity with which this was all, or almost all, settled. It seems to him that Esther has only been waiting for such a chance, has been wanting to go to New York to *do something*, something important, and that it was only a matter of time, as they say, until she found something. Or until something found her.

"Funny you should call, Jimmy, I was just going to call you," says Cynthia that same afternoon. "There're all these things I want to ask you."

"And I've got some things to ask you. A whole new idea."

"Well."

"What do you feel like, a drive or a walk?"

"Oh, let's walk, we always drive. My daughter goes for walks all the time, she puts me to shame."

Jimmy ponders this last as they arrange to meet in an hour, at the Inn. Cynthia seldom mentions Abigail, but then neither does he talk about his girls—or not often, Jimmy reflects. It is as though the two of them, Cynthia and himself, have been pretending to be childless.

And Cynthia and Esther carry on a quite separate friendship: they talk on the phone; sometimes they meet downtown, in the drugstore, for Cokes.

★ ★ ★

"Well, we won't get very far with you in those heels" is the first thing that Jimmy says to Cynthia that day.

She laughs, in her flirty Yankee way. "I thought more a town walk. We could go over to the campus?"

They do; they walk along the hard white rutted sidewalk, past low gray stone walls that are often broken, past wide green yards with their borders of fading, dying fall flowers, and sprawling houses with their generous broad porches. Dilapidated furniture. Peeling paint. Thinking of New York, and of Esther there, as he observes this town, Jimmy is more than ever aware of its general shabbiness, its air of genteel poverty. Its air of depression, of the Depression. It is worse than Oklahoma, in a way, where things are simply poor, the people down and out.

All of which only a war will cure. Various people have started to say this, all over, and unhappily it makes a certain sense.

"This Emily Yates, was she very beautiful?" Cynthia asks him this question, seemingly from nowhere.

"Who?" At first Jimmy truly cannot imagine whom she must mean.

"You know, the mother of that beautiful girl, that Deirdre. The one who died. The mother, I mean."

"Emily Yates," says Jimmy ruminatively. "No one really knew her, you know. Just to say hello to on the sidewalk downtown. She'd nod, some people said she was really snobbish and felt she'd married beneath her. But Deirdre Yates, what a looker! Even at thirteen or fourteen. I guess it must have embarrassed her a little, all that attention so young. But Emily Yates, a woman you'd hardly notice, unless I really missed something." He laughed. "How come you ask?"

Cynthia laughs too, but evasively. "It may just be a novel I'm writing in my head. But it is odd, don't you think? Two such ordinary people, as everyone describes them, producing such remarkable-looking children. Deirdre and that little Graham. And they don't even look alike. Not really like brother and sister." She laughs again, this time a girlish giggle.

They have reached the college library, a pillared brick building with broad steep steps leading up to its narrow and quite superfluous porch.

Automatically, because they have done so fairly often before, Jimmy and Cynthia sit down on the steps, and Cynthia stretches long silk legs, showing off her pretty, very impractical shoes. This is a place that they both like. Among the clusters of the college students who are also seated there, they feel themselves young by contagion, as it were; as young as the girls in their sweaters and pearls, their pleated skirts, their saddle shoes or loafers, and the boys in their cords or jeans, their letter sweaters or plain white shirts.

Jimmy speaks in a stern low voice to Cynthia. "Now look, dear girl. If you're manufacturing romances involving poor Emily Yates, just forget it. That poor dim lady. Condemned to dull Clarence for life, and then cursed with this freakishly ravishing daughter, whom she hadn't a clue what to do with." He adds, half-seriously, "Just leave the fiction to me, dear girl."

He has, actually, been thinking of a Deirdre Yates type in the Western novel that he is writing. A beautiful girl with no idea of how to use her beauty. A shy girl, more intelligent than anyone around her.

But there would be no Emily Yates. In his book the girl would hardly have a mother.

Cynthia frowns. "But—" And then she decides to leave it alone. Jimmy is simply not as observant as she thought he was; he probably won't be a writer, after all. Men in general are not very observant, she has noticed. And then a more subtle, interesting thought occurs to her, which is that Jimmy could be entirely in the know; in some way he could have found out about Mrs. Yates and Russ Byrd (easy enough, they live so close; he could have seen them), and for Boy Scout reasons of his own is protecting them—protecting Russ, his hero. Cynthia gives Jimmy a long, speculative look, and a smile of complicity—a look and a smile that Jimmy does not quite understand.

Eventually, Cynthia is sure, Jimmy can be persuaded to share this information with her, to tell her all he knows.

For the moment, though, she reverts to a more familiar theme. "I really love it more here every day," she says, sighing. "Don't you? I mean, when you and Esther first came, did you talk all the time about how great it was?"

"Not exactly all the time. But we liked it fine. We still do."

"I think New York makes more of a contrast than Oklahoma, probably. Even Connecticut. But I have some friends in Sneden's Landing, that's across from the George Washington Bridge, and every time we go across I look down and see all those people living in orange crates. I mean it, literally. I couldn't bear it. I mean, I know the colored people down here are really poor—"

"And a lot of white ones," Jimmy reminds her. "Drive out to Robertsville, you want to see poor whites. Or out on these farms, for God's sake. Shacks with broken outhouses, and no floors. Just red clay."

"Abby's always talking about these poor white kids from farms. 'Truck children,' she calls them. Abby, by the way, has struck up this great friendship with Deirdre Yates. It's too perplexing."

"Not really. Deirdre's always been a loner. I don't think she likes it around here very much. It's funny she came back, actually."

"And that's how Abby feels, so far. She's become a sort of loner too. She says she hates the kids at school."

Cynthia is actually thinking less of the loneliness of Abby than of her own innocent pleasure in being with Jimmy. In just this short time they have become true friends, she feels. At first there was some little, very minor flirting going on, but now that seems to have passed (she thinks), and they are quite simply the greatest friends. And eventually he will tell her everything.

As though reading her mind (almost), Jimmy leans toward her. "There's something I want to discuss with you." He laughs. "It's almost a proposition."

"Well, heaven knows I'm open to propositions. Pretty free for anything fancy."

They both laugh, sitting there in the November sunlight. Feeling young, as young as the college youth surrounding them on those steps.

"Seriously, though," Jimmy tells her, "I had an idea."

And he explains his plan, which goes like this: Esther and the girls will go to New York, and he, Jimmy, will be all alone in that big house. "Not that it isn't a comfortable house.

It is, extremely," he says. But he just won't need all that room.

So why don't he and Cynthia—and Harry and Abigail, of course—simply trade? He likes their little apartment, their suite at the Inn; it's in many ways perfect for him—though it must be getting to seem just a little small for the three of them? Cynthia admits that this is so.

They could have a year or so anyway to look around and enjoy life, to make decisions about whether to buy or build, all that. He gives her a short, oblique look. "And think of your neighbors," he says. "Your new ones, that is."

Of course he has hit on the very thing that Cynthia thought of first, at his suggestion: Russ Byrd, just down the road.

"But, Jimmy, that's too generous of you. We really couldn't—"

"It's not all that generous. I'll charge you some rent. How about making it the same as whatever you're paying at the Inn?"

"Of course I'll have to talk to Harry, but it sounds the most divine plan."

"Harry, it does sound the most divine plan."

"It's generous, all right. I hope Esther gets along with those Rothschilds of yours."

"Oh, she will. Pipsy Rothschild couldn't be more adorable. And Esther will get such a sense of doing good, it's just what she needs. And Pipsy will find them a place to live and a school for the girls, she's terrific at all that stuff."

He laughs at her. "And we'll give a lot of parties and assume our natural social role in Pinehill, and very subtly redecorate the Hightowers' house."

95

To the considerable surprise of her parents, Abby likes this new idea. "I'm tired of the Inn," she tells them, which is not a surprise. "And it's embarrassing telling people you live in a hotel. It makes us sound so rich. But the Hightowers' house will be good. I can go to school on the truck, and I know a sort of secret road between out there and into town."

"How on earth—?"

"Deirdre told me, and showed me where it is."

Chapter 13

"Dolly, it's Cynthia Baird. Well, we've been wanting to see you too. I don't know where this fall has gone."

She is beginning to sound like them, Cynthia thinks. She is as bad as Harry, imitating accents. Is it a sort of infection, Southern speech? Southern attitudes?

"Well, yes, a lot certainly has happened. We've been really busy. Especially this move. Yes, we love this house, just crazy about it. Esther and Jimmy really did themselves proud. But you know, this sounds a little crazy, I suppose, but we really miss our little old suite at the Inn. Yes, we really do. And it's most of all your colors that we miss. What you did there was just so beautiful....No, no, no, you're much too modest. Harry and I used to say to each other almost every day, 'That Dolly Bigelow is a genius, she purely is.' We still do say that, honestly we do. Anyway, we miss it, and that's what I wanted to talk to you about. We were just wondering if you could, just possibly, do a little something like that over here at the Hightower place. Maybe just some pillows, and some kind of a slipcover for the velvet sofa. You know, after all that color we're used to, this place just seems real dark. Maybe if you could just come over some morning and we'd have some coffee and maybe you'd just get some ideas.... Well, next Tuesday would be just wonderful, absolutely wonderful.... Well, no, I haven't got anyone in yet to help, but there's no need for you to bring Odessa, just for coffee.... Oh, I see. Oh yes. Well, if she actually can help you, of course, yes. Bring her along."

"I honestly don't get it," says Cynthia to Harry, later on; she notes that at least when she speaks to Harry it is not in a Southern voice. "She insists on bringing her maid, for coffee. I never heard of such a thing. So nineteenth century, ladies going about with maids. But whatever will I do with her while Dolly's here? Honestly, Southerners and what they call their help—it's too much for me."

It is late at night, and they are lying in their ex-tra-wide, custom-made bed. The Hightower bed.

"Sweetheart, why don't you just leave that to Dolly? Bringing Odessa was her idea, let her cope. They've got all this stuff worked out, they have for years." He adds, "The only trouble with this bed is that I can't find you. Oh, here, here's something that feels familiar."

Odessa is very tall, she must be six feet or over, a powerfully built woman with broad hips, broad shoulders, and long swinging arms. But her eyes are frightened. Coming into the Hightower house (will anyone ever think of it as the Baird house?) walking behind and to one side of Dolly Bigelow,

Odessa looks everywhere except at Cynthia, darting glances into corners, up at the ceiling. ("It was so hard to tell if she was just scared and shy—of me!—or just measuring things," Cynthia later tells Harry. "Maybe both" is his rather sensible answer. "In any case," Cynthia tells him, "she has the most ravishing skin.")

Odessa's skin is dark brown—to most people, Southern people, just that, a dark brown Negro skin. A darkie. Cynthia, though, less accustomed to such skin, is instantly aware of the shades and the rich subtleties within that brown, the complexity of its spectrum, and the velvet smooth look of the skin itself.

"I just wanted Odessa to have a look at you-all's living room," explains Dolly, as though Odessa needed explaining. "She just has the best ideas, and you know she's the one did most of my weaving for me. She and her sister have got this loom they set up. Odessa honey, you just look around everywhere you want to. Me and Miz Baird'll just be setting in here and talking, so you just take all the time you want to, and then you go on in the kitchen and heat yourself up some coffee."

As Dolly and Cynthia settle in the living room, Odessa, as she was bidden, looks carefully about, moving with a curious combination of directness and unease, moving jerkily. Dolly seems completely to ignore her, but Cynthia is unable to. After all, she is another person in the room. Hearing them talk. Presumably, reacting.

"...the most wonderful house for parties ever in this town," Dolly is saying. "And, speaking of social occasions, what is there so much worse about a woman getting drunk than a man who does the exact same thing, will you tell me that? It doesn't make sense, if you look at it just in a logical way, and maybe there's no logic to it, but I just have to say I can't stand the sight of a lady who's had a touch too much. Willard says the same. Of course you know who I'm talking about."

Actually, Cynthia does not know, she does not remember any conspicuously drunken lady at any recent party. On the other hand, there must be local parties to which she and Harry are not invited—yet. (Although they have done extremely well in that direction, as they frequently say to each other, laughing as they refer to their "Southern social climb.") But Cynthia makes a face, a sound to indicate, Of course I know who you mean. As she watches Odessa's broad shoulders move into the dining room. Does Odessa know who Dolly is talking about? Does she care, or are all white ladies just the same to her, mean and silly and incomprehensible?

"Of course I can't blame her for sometimes drinking more than a little too much," continues Dolly, in what is now an almost saccharine voice. "I was married to Russ Byrd, I think I'd have a few nips now and then myself."

Brett Byrd? Drunk? Cynthia finds this hard if not impossible to imagine. Shy, rather placid Brett, with her perfectly knotted golden hair, her calm blue eyes, and her soft dull voice, getting drunk? Behaving "conspicuously"? This was surely not a scene at which she, Cynthia, has been present.

Dolly seems also, then, to recall the absence of Cynthia at whatever party she was so vividly remembering. "Oh, I am just so forgetful! This was over to the Lees', and you-all don't even hardly know them. I'm so tacky, just a tacky forgetful old gossip I'm turning into. Just like my momma."

99

Cynthia laughs at her, as she is sure that she is supposed to do; Dolly enjoys this version of herself as a comic character. "In that case, you might as well tell me all about it," says Cynthia.

"Well." And Dolly settles in. "Some of us were over to the Lees' a few nights ago, you know, Clifton and Irene? She's the pretty one. I think Jimmy Hightower used to be a little sweet on her."

Of course Cynthia does remember the Lees, from that first Hightower party. She remembers an extremely pretty smallish woman, who drank a lot. With a big fleshy husband with whom, as Cynthia remembered the scene, Dolly was furiously flirting. Hardly thinking, she says, "I do remember Irene Lee. Very pretty, isn't she? It seems to me she was drinking quite a bit herself."

Dolly giggles in an agreeing way. "Well, she does have that tendency sometimes. I declare, poor old Clifton, I think it's downright embarrassing for him."

Out of some odd mixture of motives then, only half understood by herself, Cynthia chooses that moment to lash out (though mildly) at Dolly. "I just don't agree with you about women drinking," she declaims. "I think any messy drunk is unattractive, and God knows I've seen more messy men than women. Falling-down slobs. Actually I think I feel more sorry when women get drunk. I always think, Poor things, they must be really tired, or having their period, or some bad trouble with some man. I guess that isn't quite fair either, making allowances for women when I don't for men, but that's how I feel."

Somewhat surprisingly, Dolly agrees. "Oh, I'm glad to hear you say that! Really deep down I've always thought that too, but it's just like something you're not supposed to say, or even think. But you know whole lots of times at parties when some lady's had a little too much and everyone's muttering just exactly what I just now said, I'm secretly thinking the opposite, which is what you said. I'm thinking, Poor thing, I'll bet you've got the curse, or your husband is mean, or just plain cooling off, his mind gone to somewhere else. Or you're tired from your kids and all. And like you say, it's the slobby men are the worst drunks, no doubt about that."

There is a pause during which Cynthia considers this about-face—so interesting, as though Dolly had been waiting for some permission to have or to voice those subversive views. Nevertheless she asks her, "But what on earth do you think is wrong with Brett Byrd?"

"Just about everything, I'd imagine." Dolly stops to think, her plump legs pressed against the edge of the sofa, one foot lightly tapping. "Beginning and ending with James Russell Lowell Byrd himself."

Wanting badly to ask some very direct questions, Cynthia still does not. She has been down here long enough to realize that people just do not do that. She cannot ask Dolly, Did Brett Byrd know about Emily Yates? Is she upset, seeing that child around town?

Instead she only very mildly says, "He mustn't be too easy to be married to. Not that anyone is, I mean—" She laughs. "But a famous handsome poet, that would be really hard, I'd think."

"Brett lot of times just closes her eyes to things," says Dolly somewhat portentously. "And maybe sometimes it all gets too much and she has to take a couple of drinks to get those eyes back closed."

At that moment Odessa appears in a doorway, as though poised to swim back into the room—or, rather, to dive: head lowered, she seems to contemplate depths.

Turning, Dolly asks—actually, she states—"I'll just bet you've got every single color in your mind somewhere."

"Don't know about that, Miz Dolly," Odessa grins. "How 'bout some curtains in here too? Make a world of difference."

"Oh, draperies?" Dolly looks at Cynthia, eyebrows raised.

"Well, sure. Why not? The room is kind of stark." Cynthia turns and asks Odessa, "What color were you thinking of, Odessa?"

"Well, ma'am, maybe this real pale spring green? You know, like the first little shoots that come up, in April?"

"It was really the most bizarre conversation," Cynthia reports to Harry that night, as the three of them sit at dinner, in the grand (very grand for only three people) Hightower dining room. "The connection between Dolly and Odessa is really something, something from another world. They seem to have their own somewhat subterranean language. But I really think it's Odessa who does the work with the fabrics and all, and she's really the one with the ideas too."

"Smart of Dolly to give her her head, or whatever. To recognize the talent."

"Dolly's extremely smart. Though she tries to hide it. God, Southern women!"

"No one down here knows any Negro people at all," Abby puts in. "It's all so crazy. Deirdre told me it has a lot to do with sex."

Automatically, Harry and Cynthia glance at each other, quickly fearful: how much does Abby know, and what does she know? So far they have told her almost nothing, beyond the most basic biology—about which they are a little vague themselves.

Seeing their puzzlement, Abby tries to enlighten them. "You know, they're afraid that getting to know each other will lead to sex and babies. Sounds like a good idea to me," says Abby. And then she says, "Can I go to the pep rally tonight? It's Friday and Deirdre says there's a torchlight parade that's really neat. She wants to take Graham."

"For all our plans to sweep the town off its feet, it looks like that's more what's been done to us."

It is Cynthia who says this, but Harry agrees, quite as though he had thought of it too. "Yes, our daughter's been taken over by a very strange and beautiful young woman, and our housing all taken care of, one way or another."

Harry sighs. "If I take this job in Washington— I don't know. All our new best friends would miss me."

"Not nearly as much as I would, my darling."

"But wouldn't you come with me?"

"No, I don't think so. I like it here, remember? You'd have to commute."

"To Washington? You're nuts. But you're probably right, we should stay here. I don't need to work for the Navy. And think of the money we're not spending, living here. I think of it every day. Besides, living down here makes you think there's not even going to be a war."

Chapter 14

The pep rally begins with the torchlight parade; in the heavy November dark, a straggly crowd marches along, some singing, many carrying flaming torches that to Abby look dangerous; in fact, she finds the whole scene frightening, uncontrolled. The dark, and the wavering bright torches, the strong hoarse songs, and the shouts: "Beat Duke! Beat Duke! Who are we going to beat tomorrow? DUKE!"

Dragging along in the crowded dark, holding one of Graham's small hands while Deirdre holds the other, Abby thinks that they are in the wrong order; she and Graham, the two children, should be one on each side of Deirdre, the grownup. She's afraid. The shouting sounds like newsreels, wars, and the torches could set everything on fire, people's hair and their clothes, like burning cities in the Sunday papers, all over the world.

And it's dark, so dark, a dark black dark. She can't see anyone, can barely see Graham, just huge black shapes of people, and everything so loud. "BEAT DUKE—WHO?—BEAT DUKE, BEAT DUKE, BEAT BEAT BEAT BEAT DUKE!"

Then a large shape, black like all the others, is coming toward them from the opposite direction, and, like a policeman, or a Nazi, he has stopped Deirdre, standing in front of her, close, so that they all stop and now Abby can see his face from the torchlight. Brown curly hair, deep blue eyes, about the age of her father. But he looks like Graham, a huge blowup Graham, like a Disney cartoon, and at first Abby thinks he must be Deirdre and Graham's father, Mr. Yates, but then Deirdre is saying names: "...Russell Byrd, Abby Baird, you've met her parents, probably."

The man looks at Abby, but blindly, she could as well not be there; she hears him mutter, "...pleased..."

To Deirdre he is saying, "...somehow I'd find you here, what a chance—must see you."

Whatever Deirdre has said, if she has said anything, makes the man, Mr. Byrd, turn to go; he is gone, and Deirdre is changing their hands, keeping Graham's and taking one of Abby's, as Abby wanted it to be in the first place, and close to her ear Deirdre whispers, "This is awful, what say we go?"

Abby's frightened heart surges. She had not been able to imagine the relief of not being there; these present circumstances, the dark and torches and the shouting, had come to seem a permanent condition, she was caught in a newsreel that would go on forever.

"Besides, Graham's really tired," Deirdre continues unnecessarily. "We went for a very big walk this afternoon."

"No bigger than we always do," corrects Graham.

Deirdre does not say or explain what is clear to Abby, that she has to go and meet Mr. Byrd now—nor does she tell Abby not to mention Mr. Byrd to her parents, which Abby for whatever reasons of her own plans not to do.

In any case, having decided to leave, Deirdre seems nervous, very hurried. "We're not far from where I left my car, actually. I can drop you off at your house and then swing up that little road to mine." By now she is talking mostly to herself. Is she afraid of Mr. Russell Byrd? Afraid to be late to meet him?

BEAT DUKE, BEAT DUKE. BEAT DUKE.

The rhythm seems slower and stronger, the shouts come louder, even as they are moving away from the crowd, not stumbling or unsure but very definite as they make their escape. Abby is thinking of her bed and of a really good book. *Jane Eyre*, she has just started it. She thinks too about Deirdre and Mr. Byrd, and whatever it is they plan to do, so urgently. She has a vague, excited, and on the whole unpleasant sense of this, this urgency. It is something she knows that she should not know.

"I guess he's asleep," she whispers, letting him in the front door.

"I had to see you—"

"That really scared him. And I think Abby too."

"—so I knew you'd be there. You had to be—"

She laughs, very softly. "You sure do trust in your luck."

"We've had good luck all along, haven't we? In a way?"

"Graham?" She laughs again, softly. A little sadly.

"Yes, Graham too. Of course Graham too. He's—he's exquisite. Perfect. Our Pearl."

"Pearl?"

"I just meant he's perfect."

"He looks more and more like you. Someone's going to notice. If they already haven't."

"I suppose." Not thinking about it, not then, he tangles his hand in her hair, all that strong dark silk. He asks her, "You don't want to go back to California?"

"Well, sometimes I do. I feel scared here, I don't know—"

Since she must stay, she must—at that moment Russ feels that his life would be unbearable without her, his mind races toward a possible fictional explanation; it is true both that Graham looks much like him, and that this will be noticed. He wonders: Some distant blood relationship? But even as he thinks this, imagines saying it, Russ recoils: himself, a Byrd, related to a Yates? And then the irony of such an incredibly snobbish recoil strikes him; he is in fact in love with a Yates, his most beautiful son is a Yates. And as for families, his branch of the Byrds wasn't exactly such hot stuff either.

"Y'all do look a lot alike," says Deirdre. "Why don't you grow a beard, or something?"

"A beard? Like my grandfather had?" What an entirely crazy idea; no one wears beards but grandfathers these days. Maybe poets, though, it then occurs to Russ. Why not? He begins to laugh.

"Hush!" she whispers. "What's so funny?"

"You. You're so wonderful. You're my funny girl."

"I don't think I'm so funny."

"And beautiful. Lord have mercy. Every time I see you, the shock—"

Curiously, they are still standing there in the front hall, where they met to kiss, when Russ first tapped so gently at her door, when she said, "I guess he's asleep."

They are standing there still, half embracing, half talking, somehow unable to commit themselves to either.

Longing to make love to her, Russ in another part of his mind or heart thinks of Brett. At home.

The children. He reaches again to caress Deirdre's long hair.

Something in his gesture, something tentative, resolves Deirdre, and she tells him, "I think you'd better go now, you know?"

"My darling, you're right. Ah, how I love you—"

"I thought you didn't. Anymore." She has said this with a pure simplicity. No art, or design.

Russ is moved almost to tears, and later, recalling her tone and her words, he is moved again. (Is the phrase, he wonders, "crying into your beard"? But no, for God's sake; it's into your beer. Good old masculine beer.)

"I think I will grow a beard," he tells Deirdre. "Ah, you're so sweet—"

She says, very sweetly, and seriously, "I think it might work, for a while."

They begin to kiss, again.

"Abby, darling, how nice and early you're home."

"Uh, yes'm."

"Abby! For heaven's sake. Are you saying 'ma'am' to me?"

"It just, it just came out that way." Feeling weak, Abby laughs.

"If you're going to talk like that, I'll have to take you home to Connecticut." Cynthia laughs too, a little.

"The point is," Harry now puts in with a frown, "how was the famous pep rally?"

"Well, it was sort of noisy. But all those torches, it was sort of neat."

Abby can find no acceptable (to herself) reasons for not having liked the rally, and so she feels that she must lie and say that she did like it, that it was neat. She cannot say, The whole thing scared me a lot, and then Mr. Byrd came along, and he scared me too, but Deirdre had to do what he said, and go home to meet him there.

"Well, isn't it nice you're home so early. Actually your father and I were just going off to bed, so we'll all have an early night."

"I guess so."

"Well, good night, my darling. Sweet dreams!"

For the second time that night, Abby feels herself thrust aside, thrust out of the way of grownups who are themselves impelled by violent and incomprehensible forces. She sighs as she gets into bed. Where she does not have sweet dreams, but rather newsreel nightmares, in which a man who seems to be a combination of Hitler and Russell Byrd is shouting "BEAT DUKE!"

Chapter 15

"I just can't believe a thing that's happening these days. Harry Baird off to Washington, to the Navy—"

"And Cynthia all alone in this beautiful house. I just can't believe—"

"Do you think old Jimmy's planning to move back in with her?"

"Oh, you're terrible, that's a terrible idea. Jimmy wouldn't—and with Esther—"

"Are Russ and Brett coming over, do you know?"

"Someone saw him downtown—in the post office, I think—and they told me he's growing a beard."

"Lord, Russ with a *beard?*"

"I just can't believe the job that Dolly did on this house."

"Of course she says it was all Odessa, that's her little joke."

"Well, maybe it was."

"I just can't believe that Odessa—"

"Where's their little girl, that Abby?"

"Is that really Deirdre Yates across the room?"

"Isn't she just the most beautiful thing? You ever see such skin?"

"Irene, you're looking real, real pretty. How's Clifton?"

"Well, of course there's going to be a war. I don't care what Mr. Roosevelt says. Or her either."

"Isn't it nice that Cynthia's wearing that lovely dress again."

"Just what is a 'defense plant'? Does anyone know?"

"But Harry's not going to Washington to fight. Just the Navy in Washington. A desk job, they call it."

"Harry says Japan's the country to worry about. Not so much Germany."

"Japan! We were there on our honeymoon."

"Deirdre Yates, if you aren't the prettiest thing in the world? Now tell me, how's your daddy doing out there in California?"

"I don't think Russell and Brett are coming, after all. I'll make you a little bet."

"I just can't believe Odessa made all these things."

"But Dolly says—"

"Deirdre, how's your little baby brother? We're all just dying to get a look at him."

"Cynthia says he's here but he's gone upstairs with Abby."

"Maybe old Jimmy will move up to New York with Esther and the girls."

"Oh no, Jimmy'd never live up there with Yankees. It's different for Esther, she's more Jew—"

"Can you imagine Russ Byrd with a beard?"

"Well, he is a poet."

"That Harry's going to be the handsomest thing in the Navy."

"Deirdre, I tried to get them to come downstairs, but Abby just won't. I don't know—"

"It could be just as well, don't you think?"

"There's going to be these defense plants all over, everyone says."

"Well, at least it'll do a lot for unemployment."

"But I'm dead sure that's not the same dress."

"It's the colors that make all the difference. Poor Esther, I'm not sure she knows a whole lot about color."

"But will she like it, if she ever comes back down here?"

"Has anyone heard what Russ is working on now?"

"Some goddam thing about those goddam pigs, I'll bet."

"Clifton Lee, is that any way to talk at a party?"

"Well, it's all he talks about since they were to Kansas. Goddam dead pig."

"Oh, sometimes I just wonder how Brett bears it!"

"Oh look, Jimmy's trying to make up to Irene again."

"But it looks like Harry Baird's cutting him right out."

"Come on, he's just trying to be a good host. Even Yankees know to do that. Sometimes."

"He's going to be mighty cute in that old sailor suit."

"Come on now, Harry's a grownup man. They're not going to put him in any sailor suit."

"Oh look, there's Abby now, with the darlingest little boy."

"Do we know that child? Some way he looks like we do."

"Just looks like a plain little old boy to me."

"Oh, he must be Deirdre's brother. Look, he's running to her."

"Yep, hiding his face. Must be real shy, poor little fellow."

"And Cynthia didn't like that one bit, his hiding in his sister's lap. Cynthia had it in mind to introduce him all around."

"But he's not having any of that. No, not that kid."

"Look a there, heading right back up the stairs again. Going up there fast, sky winding."

"Do you think Russ and Brett are going to show up, after all?"

"That little old boy sure did remind me of someone."

"Just plain boy, that's all. Maybe a little on the pretty side, but then take a look at his sister."

"These beaten biscuits of Odessa's, I declare, they do beat all."

"How comes Odessa did these? She working for Cynthia now?"

"Lord no, you know Dolly'd never in a month of Sundays let her go. She just lends her out sometimes."

"And this funny thing about Cynthia, she likes to do for herself. No help at all."

"Well, there's just the two of them. The three, with Abby."

"And just the two when Harry goes off to D.C."

"I just think *Rebecca* is about the loveliest book I ever did read."

"Oh, I'll take *The Yearling* any day. Although I reckon the literary folk over to the college would call it sentimental."

"You know what Russ keeps saying, that old William Faulkner from Mississippi's the only writer worth talking about."

"You'd better eat some more, Jimmy. And looks like you need another drink."

"Oh look, there's Odessa! Looks grand in that white apron, don't you think?"

"Is that apron a tad too small? That's a mighty big woman, you give her a real good look."

"Funny, always looks to be swimming when she walks."

"But colored don't go swimming ever, do they?"

"Well, of course they do, at their places in the creek and all."

"Russ don't even think much of our own Thomas Wolfe."

"I think they were to the university about the same time, and they didn't hit it off too good."

"And how about this colored fellow Russ thinks is such a writer. Richard Wright?"

"A Communist too, I heard."

"What's Esther been up to in New York City, Jimmy? Apart from her work, that is."

"Well, the Pulitzer folk seem to think *The Yearling* is good enough for them."

"You know how Russ is about prizes."

"Esther saw *Our Town* and she said it was truly wonderful, she thinks that Thornton Wilder's some kind of genius."

"Oh, I've heard."

"And she's trying to get tickets to some show, *Pins and Needles*. Supposed to be a hit."

"Heard of that too."

"Supposed to be real funny. She could use some cheering up."

"Have you heard the new Eleanor story? Well, it seems like she—"

"Harry darling, it's a terrific party, don't you think?"

"The best, but you always carry it off."

"Have you noticed how Southerners get more and more Southern as they drink? So interesting."

"Yes, I have."

"Did I tell you I wrote to Lord & Taylor? Well, I owed them just this tiny amount, and then when I got that birthday check from Daddy—"

"You didn't tell me."

"Well, it was really about Odessa. My letter to Lord & Taylor, I mean. I told them how—"

"Seems like we're going to have an early frost this year."

"Might snow?"

"Of course Dolly's going to be absolutely furious."

"Don't you-all ever get tired of all those Eleanor stories? I personally think she's just a first-rate lady. I don't care what anyone says."

"*Well!*"

"*Well.*"

"But so far it's been the warmest winter we've had, oh, forever."

"But the leaves, the leaves have been just, just unreal. The color."

"Have you heard that he's really dying, Mr. Roosevelt? Can't walk one single step unaided?"

"If Russ and Brett do come, they're going to be mighty late."

"Yes, even for them."

"Looks like old Jimmy's really hitting the bottle again. Thought he went on the wagon."

"Misses Esther and the girls, most likely."

"No man really likes to be a bachelor, do you think? Not past a certain point."

"Well, I had this uncle, but he was just not the marrying kind, you know what I mean?"

"Oh, I surely do. My husband's brother, he was like that. Poor thing, he got drunk one night and shot himself."

"Why on earth would Russ Byrd be growing a beard, at this time of life?"

"Whatever do you mean, time of life? Russ is young yet. Talented young poet and playwright. That's what they all say. They still say."

"Wonder how Brett feels about the beard."

"Tell you what, doesn't matter a tad what Brett feels. You know that as well as I do."

"Have you heard about this new doctor, down to Southern Pines? A psychiatrist is I guess what he is. Cures drinking problems, and all like that. Name of Clyde Drake, or Duck, or something like that."

"Sounds expensive, right off. Rich Yankee place."

"Drinking problems. What I'd like to know is, who hasn't had a touch of that, one time or another?"

"No one from round here, that's for damn sure, now, isn't it? The men I mean to say."

Laughter all around.

"That Jimmy looks drunk as a skunk, or drunker."

"Boiled as an owl. But how come they say that about owls, will you tell me that? A sober-looking bird, I would have thought."

"Speaking of birds, you think that Russ and Brett—?"

"Harry, you've got to hold off on the drinks a little bit. Everyone's getting really plastered, look around you. God, you'd never know most of these people are professors."

"Not to hear them talk you wouldn't. Isn't it funny how the most educated people down here all imitate the ones that aren't."

"Darling, that's really profound."

"I try to be."

"Oh, Deirdre, do you really have to go. I'm so sorry—we've hardly—Graham, I hope you'll come again, Abby would love—"

"That little old boy's a pretty fellow, but he doesn't much favor his mother, do you think?"

"Pity that little Baird girl didn't get her mother's looks."

"She'll do all right, you mark my words."

"Well, look a there, coming up the walk. If it isn't Mr. and Mrs. James Russell Lowell Byrd."

"Walking funny. Could they be drunk, the both of them?"

"Oh we're so terribly late, we're so sorry. It's all my fault, I said to Russ—"

"Brett, for God's sake—"

"My name is not Brett. Not anymore ever. It's SallyJane."

"I suppose everyone's practically gone home."

"No, only person you missed so far is Deirdre Yates. She just left with that little brother."

"Oh."

"Oh, how is Deirdre?"

116

"If Russ isn't plastered, Brett is for certain sure. You hear what she just now said about her name?"

"Well, high time for that, is what I say. How come she ever let Russ stick a new name on her in the first place. Like he was God, or at the very least her father?"

"Well, will you look over there? There's Russ and Jimmy all over each other like long-lost brothers. Can you beat that?"

"It's what Jimmy's always wanted."

"Well, Russell and Brett, I'm just so glad to see you."

"My name is SallyJane."

"Honey, of course it is. But you mean for us all to call you that all the time?"

"I said my name is SallyJane."

"Well, of course, but you know it'll take some getting used to."

"Russ, old man, what you need is a good stiff drink."

"Well, Jimmy, my boy, I'm not sure you're right about what I need, but I surely would like one."

"My name is SallyJane."

"Goodbye, Odessa, I can't thank you enough for coming along to help out. Here's a little something for your trouble. And I'll let you know about you-know-what. In New York."

"Mmm. Ma'am."

"Well, darling, was that a good party?"

"Oh it was, but everyone got so drunk! Did we do something wrong?"

"I don't think so, they always get drunk. It only seemed worse than usual today. I don't know why."

"So odd, Russ and Brett—SallyJane—showing up just after Deirdre Yates left."

"Coincidence. What do you imagine, they sat in their house and waited for her car to pass?"

"Oh, Harry."

"I think you over-planned that one, my love."

"Harry Baird, whatever do you mean?"

"Come on, Cynthia. Don't give me that Southern stuff. You know perfectly well that you were doing some arranging there."

"Well, of course I did want to see what they'd all look like together."

"And what on earth are you cooking up with Odessa?"

"Oh, never mind, just an idea."

"Dolly Bigelow will kill you, you know that?"

"Oh, Harry, whatever will I do with you off in Washington? Sometimes I think there's really something wrong with people down here."

Chapter 16

In the days and weeks that follow Harry Baird's departure for Washington—he was quite unexpectedly and urgently summoned just after the first of the year, in early January—Cynthia observes very strange and quite new moods within herself. Unanticipated. Having imagined a lowness of spirits, she had planned to keep very active to combat this. And having expected depression, a sagging and heavy heart, she had also planned activities, diversions.

But instead she finds her heart as light as a very young girl's (a pretty, spoiled girl, as she herself used to be). She feels energetic, and warmly affectionate toward the world. In a word, she is happy, is happier in fact than she has been for years. Each day seems a possible fresh adventure, to which she wakens with pleasure and enthusiasm.

But how very alarming! Does this mean that she and Harry are supposed to separate—to, finally, divorce? How terrible! She does not want to be a "divorced woman," with all the sleazy, tacky (a new favorite word), and needy connotations of that phrase. She thinks with dread, with fear and a little pity of the several (maybe three) such women she knew in Connecticut, and the awful condescension with which everyone else—all the safely married or respectably widowed folk—viewed these strays, these derelicts.

It is only when such vivid thoughts occur that Cynthia's warm happiness is chilled, a black cloud across the sun—so that she wonders if she is as happy as she thinks she is living apart from Harry.

Which is not to say that she does not miss Harry, for she does; but as she herself might put it, almost "only in one way." She misses Harry in bed, his mouth and his knowing, expert hands. Making love to her, over and over (they are both very greedy in that way)—that is what she most misses.

And not just at night. Some midmorning, with Abby safely off at school, Harry might look at her, in his way, and he might say, "How about it? Don't you really think the smallest nap, about now?" So delicious, so wicked-feeling, lying there afterwards in the full sunlight, entangled in sheets, sea-smelling.

Also, Cynthia read somewhere, in some magazine, that it is bad for you not to do it, once you're used to a lot of sex. Bad for your body and your emotions too. But did she actually read that, or did she make it up? Or is it something that Harry once told her, trying to talk her into doing it more often? Not that she has ever needed a lot of persuading along those lines. As she sees it, she has been all too eager, once they got married and started in. Never hard to get, as she read somewhere else that even wives are supposed to be, sometimes. "Play hard to get occasionally," this article said (at least she is sure that this was not something made up by Harry). "Your husband will appreciate you more." But even if she wanted to play hard to get with Harry, Cynthia is not at all sure how she would go about it. They know each other too well—Harry knows when she is as eager as he.

Cynthia has many times thought how nice it would be if women ever discussed these things among themselves. If she could talk to some other woman, say, a woman who thought she loved her husband but found herself very happy—in fact especially happy—when he was away. And who finds herself mostly thinking of sex. She could never have had such a conversation with any of the women she knew in Connecticut, not with Pipsy or Pol or Sudie or Amanda, and most certainly not—especially not—with anyone she has met down here. For one thing, she does not know them well enough, and for another, Southern women are different from other women, she thinks. In ways that she has not yet been able to formulate. Maybe, possibly, they're just like other women only more so? In any case, there are a lot of subjects that one would simply never bring up with any of them.

She wonders about somewhat younger women, and thinks of Deirdre. But an intimate conversation with Deirdre Yates? This is unthinkable. Out of the question.

The idea of discussing sex with Southern women is as bad as that of discussing race, the Negroes—another out-of-the-question topic. With any Southerners. Aside from their endless stock of funny-maid or dim-witted yard-help stories. As she and Harry have said to each other, if an educated, smart, middle-class family of Negroes showed up, the Southerners would not know what to do with them.

Cynthia misses Harry in that way too, their talking. Making jokes. But mostly it is sex that she misses, and she notices that its lack in her life has driven her to embarrassing fantasies and dreams of other men. As though her mind were an open book, to be read by casual observers, when she sees Russell Byrd in the A&P, for example, she feels a warm blush on her face, as though he could tell what she dreamed the night before. What he did in her dream.

"Have you heard the terrible news about poor little old Brett?" It is Dolly Bigelow who asks this of Cynthia, one morning on the phone. "Well, it was just a few days after you-all's party, I guess. One morning Russ just told her to pack up a little bag, and he put her into that big old Cadillac, and he drove her right straight down to Southern Pines. To that place. That sanatorium, whatever they call it. Some Dr. Drake that I guess Russ has been talking to a lot on the phone, long distance. And I guess that Dr. Drake just finally said, Well, I guess you better just bring her on down. Not anything I can do for her from here. So Russ took her on down there. Place just full of alcoholics, I under-

121

stand. And some real depressed folks. They've got this new treatment, call it electric shock, sounds just plain terrible to me, but I understand it works real well. Come to think of it, poor Brett is depressed a lot of the time, along with the drinking, but I hope they don't use any of that shock on her. If she could just quit the drinking, for good and all, it would do her a world of good. But anyhow that's where she is. SallyJane, her old name, she wants us to call her now, Russ said. Your neighbor. I hear this Dr. Drake is real handsome, too."

"Oh, that's terrible. Poor Brett. SallyJane. I've heard of electric shock. Oh, poor SallyJane. It is a nicer name, don't you think?" But even as she is saying all this, and meaning it, another voice, small and evil and insistent, is silently saying, Well, there's Russ Byrd all alone now, and just up the road.

"How's Odessa doing?" Cynthia asks Dolly, to her own ears sounding somewhat pious.

"Oh, 'bout the same as ever, I reckon. Now don't you be turning her head, though, with all that New York talk. A plain old colored woman like Odessa. 'New York' doesn't mean anything to her. It's like with a child."

"But if they sent her money—"

"Money!" Dolly laughs unamusedly. "Real grownup money wouldn't mean a thing to Odessa, anymore'n it would to a little child. Every week I give her these dollar bills and I can tell you, it's a lot more than many folks around here give theirs. But she's like a little girl with an allowance."

"But, Dolly, come on, she's got those children to buy food for, and you said no husband. She's got to have some sense of money, what you can buy. Food prices."

"I have to tell you, darlin' Cynthia. I don't think any people from Connecticut *or* New York understand our colored friends." As she said this, Dolly pursed her lips and raised her chin: she had spoken.

And Cynthia felt herself too cowardly at that moment to pursue it. Also, what Dolly said was true: she did not understand the people whom they all called "Nigras." The word itself was a puzzle: were they consciously not saying "nigger," a word she had never heard used in these parts, or was "Nigra" simply what their accents made of "Negro"?

She has sent samples of Odessa's woven work to the decorating department at Lord & Taylor, and she is waiting to hear.

And now Russ is living down the road, with just those children. And the maid. And she is living alone with Abby.

One morning late in January—it is a Sunday, and Abby has spent the night with Betsy, daughter of Irene and Clifton Lee—Cynthia awakens to a silence more profound, more serious than any winter silence she has known. As though she were still asleep and wrapped in dreams, dreams of her childhood in Connecticut, perhaps—Cynthia goes back to sleep, and she dreams of snow, of waking to such magic silences, long ago. Dreaming, she remembers the Fifth Avenue of her grandmother's house, in New York, horses clopping through snow, the smell of violets, and horses, and snow.

Waking again to the same thick silence, through the parted curtains she sees—yes!—snow. Everywhere white. Pristine, with a diamond sparkle from the early sunlight. Boughs heavily laden. Telephone wires sagging down. A few dark tiny birds on what was the lawn, hopping about, directionless. And the sky, as though reflecting snow, is pale and bright, barely blue.

Even before she takes the receiver off the hook and listens for a moment, she knows that the phone will be dead, and indeed it is: no way for her to call anyone, nor for anyone to reach her. This notion of complete inaccessibility makes her smile; she lies back luxuriously in her warm sheets, against the silk-soft pillows, a princess who must be rescued. Someone will have to come for her, she is sure of that. She feels happy and vaguely excited.

At last, in a pretty pink robe, she goes downstairs to make coffee, only regretting that of course there will be no Sunday papers.

Abby will be fine at the Lees', and eventually they will bring her home.

And then, as she is finishing her second cup of coffee, when she had almost given him up, there he is: Russ Byrd, her hero, her rescuer, trudging his way up her drive.

But there are two of him. Another man is following Russ, a smaller, wider man. Cynthia watches as Russ turns to grin and wave at Jimmy Hightower, who has stopped to wipe his glasses, but then he too is trudging on, toward her front door. Since there are two of them, it is all right to be in her robe, Cynthia decides—all right to open the door to them, to laugh at the whole situation, everyone more or less stranded in the snow, and she not dressed. At almost eleven on a Sunday morning.

"Had to come and see how you're doing, neighbor!" Folksy Russ, who does not quite look at her.

"Cynthia, is there anything you need?" Jimmy looks around. "Where's Abby?"

Cynthia explains about Abby, and explains too that she stocked up at the A&P on Friday. "Almost as though I'd known." She laughs, tosses her hair.

Russ looks amazingly young and—well, fit. The weather becomes him, the skin above what is now a glossy full brown beard is smooth and clear and flushed with cold; his mouth, somehow more noticeable above the beard, is softly, beautifully curved. Cynthia closes her fingers against a sudden strong desire to touch his face, his cheeks and his forehead and his lovely strong mouth.

"Well, how're you doing, anyway?" asks Jimmy. "How's the single life?"

"I don't think I know quite yet, but it seems okay." Saying this, Cynthia risks a sidelong look at Russ: should she mention Brett—SallyJane; should she say she's sorry or something?

"Come to think of it, that makes three of us," Jimmy continues, headlong. "Although Russ here has already got another lady moved in," he says insensitively.

A wave of shock goes through Cynthia, so that she can hardly hear Russ's hurried, not-quite-coherent explanation: "…Ursula, you know, the pig woman from Kansas. You know, I killed her pig and then we stayed on in Kansas. Poor Brett, I mean SallyJane, was so sick, and then she seemed to like it there, and she and Ursula wrote, and then Ursula just suddenly arrived. To take care of me for SallyJane, she said."

"How nice of her."

"Two days on the train. On the day coach."

She must be crazy about you, Cynthia does not say. But this seems a possible time to ask, "How is Brett, I mean SallyJane doing?"

"Her doctor's not the most articulate man in the world, I have to say," says Russ, with a small pained frown. "So it's hard to get any real information. I don't know, I guess—I hope it's the right place for her. She seems to like it there fine, and she liked the doctor."

"You'll have to meet Ursula." Jimmy grins at Cynthia guilelessly—or is he in some way teasing? Cynthia can't tell.

"She's a big help with the kids," Russ tells Cynthia earnestly. But is that just an excuse for having this Ursula there? "And it lets me get out of the house more often. I really have to, sometimes," he adds.

"You'll have to bring her over for dinner sometime," Cynthia tells Russ. "And, Jimmy, you come too." But as she says this she is thinking: God, it'll be like a double date. How ghastly! She asks, "Will you-all have some coffee?"

"You-all," teases Jimmy. "Never thought I'd hear the local lingo from Mrs. Baird."

In a good-sport way, Cynthia laughs as she reaches for coffee cups, spoons, sugar. "I guess it's really happening to me," she says. "I'm going native at last." She is laughing to conceal the desolating loss that she has felt at the announcement of Ursula's presence in Russ's house. She asks, "Do you think the snow will melt soon, you-all?"

By early afternoon the snow is melting fast, in the brilliant sunlight. Water drips steadily from eaves, and from the trees. From pine needles and from the bare branches of oaks and beeches, maples.

126

Watching from her window, listening to the steady tap, tap, tap of melted snow, Cynthia feels as though she were weeping internally—and for what? For Russ, whom she barely knows?

Chapter 17

Dr. Clyde Drake has the saddest dark blue eyes that SallyJane, formerly Brett Byrd, has ever seen. The deepest-sea eyes, such depths of sorrow there. Does he care so much for his patients, SallyJane wonders? Does he, can he take on all their human pain, like Christ? But what of his own life, the ordinary and killing private troubles of all private lives, once you know the least little bit about them. Which of course she does not know about Dr. Drake. Not the simplest thing, like is he married? Children? Where did he go to school? SallyJane feels it would help her to know all this, but maybe not, and she is sure that you're not meant to ask.

The nurse, Miss Effington, tells her, "Now, Miz Byrd, the doctors' lives aren't any concern of the patients, I can tell you that. But since you ask, and you don't look to me to be anywhere near as sick as most, I'll just tell you that Dr. Clyde Drake is married to one of the most lovely women you would ever want to see, Norris Drake, and they have these absolutely beautiful children." But Miss Effington's voice, as she said all these nice, praising things, was a furious voice, high and shrill.

Why does Miss Effington hate this Norris Drake so violently? Might she kill her? Come up on her at the golf course, or the country club, or the Dunes Club, with some poison or a knife? The hatred in her voice was dangerous, palpable, and chilling. SallyJane shivers. She knows that she could not bear to hear about a murder, at close hand. Nor could she bear such a loss for Dr. Drake, such further infinite sorrow for his face.

"Dr. Drake, he sure looks sad," says SallyJane to Carrie, one of the maids.

"He do," agrees Carrie. "Everything a man could want, and sometimes more." She laughs and rolls her eyes, the way colored people are supposed to do but usually don't, in SallyJane's experience.

"More?" queries SallyJane, in her white-lady way.

"Doctors be mens as much as they be doctors," says Carrie mysteriously, in her not-mysterious voice.

"Oh."

"You notice he a mighty handsome man?"

"Uh, yes. I guess I noticed."

But all these messages about his family and then about his life, though fairly specific, came through only vaguely to SallyJane, who could no longer deal with specifics, so overwhelming were her own feelings of helplessness and grief, of intractable guilt and loss.

She thought sometimes of a strong and competent woman, herself, who took good care of five children and a moody, hard-to-please, and often-unloving husband. Herself, as Brett. She found it impossible to believe that she could ever have done all that—and knew that she never could again. Never not cry when anyone said anything to hurt her, never kiss anyone when they were hurt and murmur to them, "Don't cry, I'm here, I love you."

She needed all that now herself, but she knew that she was too old for comfort, that none would ever be forthcoming. Drinking had been at least a

128

temporary comfort, though she had never really liked it very much. But it seemed to work for other people, lots of their friends: why not for her? Other people drank and got cheerful and silly and fun (especially men, like Jimmy Hightower, Clifton Lee), but not SallyJane; it made her cry. Almost everything made her cry, she could never stop.

She has not told Dr. Drake about what happened to her in San Francisco, not any of it. She will never tell anyone about all that.

And now Ursula is up there with Russ, out from Kansas, and taking care of everything, the way she took care of SallyJane after San Francisco. How wonderful of Ursula. Too bad they have no pigs for her to take care of too. Maybe Ursula and Russ will take to raising pigs? Along with all those children; her children, raised like pigs?

Such thoughts as these, which do not stop, make SallyJane think that she is really crazy. That she really needs the shock that Dr. Drake has mentioned.

Sometimes Dr. Drake thinks so too.

She sees him for about an hour, every other day. Not enough.

She never quite knows what to wear, not to mention what to say. He never says much at all. And there is so much that she cannot say. Cannot allow him to know. She says as little as possible to Dr. Drake.

San Francisco.

She just says, "It seems so unfair to Russ, being married. To me. He should just be having a love affair with someone very young and beautiful. Like Deirdre Yates. Once I saw her in the post office with this little boy, I guess her brother, and he looked more like Russ than our boys do, and so I thought, Oh-ho (no one would think those silly syllables but I did think, Ah-ha). I thought, So that's what you've been up to, Russell Byrd. But it doesn't make much sense, does it, if that little boy is her brother?"

"No."

"Of course that was around the time when I started getting sick, so I guess probably you might say that thinking that little boy looked like Russ was a delusion." She is somehow proud of this admission, but she wishes she was wearing a prettier, cleaner dress, maybe something flowing, with flowers.

"Yes, probably." His sea eyes are deeper and sadder than ever, his voice very soft, and sad.

Meeting his eyes seems to SallyJane an intrusion, and yet if she does not meet them with her own, will he think her really sick? Will he not like her? Give her shock treatment?

"I guess wives just sometimes have these ideas about their husbands, don't you think?" She needs to cry as she says this, but she manages not to.

He only says "Yes," but she feels the smallest frown.

And then she won't see him again for another two days.

It is very much like a hotel, this building she is in, but because a lot of people are there at the moment, SallyJane has a room on the ground floor, away from the others—who seem to be Northern, and rich, mostly. Rich Yankees, with red drinker faces and harsh, hoarse voices. The men wear knickers to play golf, and the women wear practical seersucker dresses, or light flannel skirts and cotton shirts and little golfing caps.

130

Her room, SallyJane's room, is fairly bleak and bare, and she didn't think to bring anything from home to put in there, to cheer it up. "Don't you want me to bring you anything?" Russ asks her on his visits, and she always says no, not wanting to be a bother, while all the time she would really like more clothes, some pretty new sweater sets and all her best jewelry, her pearls and things, though she might look a little silly, all dressed up just to see her psychiatrist; besides, there's a rule against jewelry.

Lying in bed at night and trying to sleep, SallyJane also tries to think, although she knows that she should stop thinking and count sheep or something, maybe pigs, and then go to sleep. But instead she thinks, and sometimes she thinks very rationally. Or, fairly rationally: how can she tell?

She thinks that if she and Dr. Drake were friends she would be all right. Being his friend would be a proof that she is okay, since he would obviously not like a crazy person, not have one as a friend. And she wonders if this could not be possible: he and Russ would probably get along, both quiet men with sad blue eyes. And of course Dr. Drake is supposed to have this terrific wife, Miss Effington said so. But that could work out too; Russ might like the terrific wife, and she, SallyJane, would cook something wonderful for all of them, everyone getting along, all friends. And no one, certainly not the shining hostess, SallyJane Caldwell Byrd, no one crazy. Broken down. The Drakes would not have broken-down friends.

At darker, more sleepless times, SallyJane thinks, He must love me, he must come to me and take me in his arms. If he doesn't love me, I will die, I know I will die, and I may die anyway.

131

Sometimes she can hear Dr. Drake late at night in his office, only just down the corridor from her room—being also on the first floor, naturally. Sometimes, she thinks, she hears patients weeping toward him—led by Miss Effington, she thinks.

If she were perfectly better, then she thinks that they could be friends. Or, if she were terribly worse, led weeping down the hall, then mightn't he take her in his arms at last?—in love?

One night, quite certain that she hears unusual sounds (she is often not quite certain of what she hears), very bravely SallyJane gets out of bed, and she creeps to her door. With great caution she opens it, one tiny crack. And just down the hall, just outside his own door, which is open, there indeed is Dr. Drake. With someone in his arms. The light shining on them. Just as SallyJane has imagined, he is holding some weeping patient; some patient who is desperate for love, or warmth or simply sleep. SallyJane can't stop looking, though, as she stands there, and in a minute she sees (or believes that she sees; later she is to be uncertain on that score) that it is not a patient; it is the nurse, Miss Effington, and he is not just comforting her but violently kissing, his hands moving fast up and down, all over her body.

In an instant, with no sound at all, SallyJane has closed her door and crept back into her bed, where her heart pounds wildly as she begins, already, to doubt what she just saw. Could that have been Miss Effington, actually?

Very likely not, she decides. It was probably some patient, and she, SallyJane, only thought that they were kissing.

Chapter 18

Odessa lives a couple of miles out of town, down a winding white concrete highway that passes scattered small high wood-frame houses, next to eroded clay fields; now, in January, the broomstraw is frozen, the mud puddles frosted over. Cynthia, with directions from Dolly, goes past a narrow bridge that is high across the brown trickle of creek; she drives between more wet red clay banks, gray winter meadows, and stands of pine. Bare oaks, and peeling poplar trees.

She comes easily enough to the sharp left bend in the road, and the small lane that goes down and then out to the gray shack that must be Odessa's.

This is Odessa's day off; she gets every third Thursday to herself, and every second Sunday. ("It must be hard to keep track of all that." "No, we mark it down on the calendar, it's fun," says Dolly.)

There is no firm reason for Cynthia's visit; she could have talked to Odessa at Dolly's on Friday, the very next day, and besides, it was not as though she had remarkable news to report. Lord & Taylor had in effect said no, despite admiration. The truth is, as Cynthia is finally forced to admit to herself, she wanted to see what she had been unable to imagine: Odessa's house.

The lane off the highway is deeply rutted, almost impassable. Clearly no one ever comes out here in a car—of course not: very few Negroes have cars at all, and the school bus would just stop on the highway, assuming the bus for colored schools even comes out here.

A very large, spreading oak stands just next to Odessa's house; in the spring and summer its leaves would provide cool and shelter, but now, in the dead of winter, its bare twigs and bare black limbs all contribute to the barren poverty of the scene: the leaning, weathered gray shack, the hard frozen earth of the yard around it.

Pulling up, and stopping the car, Cynthia begins to understand what she has done. ("Absolutely mad to go out there," as she later puts it to Harry. "What did I think she would do, ask me in for coffee?") She has no idea what to do next: to knock on the door, to wait for Odessa to see that someone is outside in a car, or (this is the strongest impulse of all) to start up again and drive off, drive anywhere. Away.

It is Odessa who decides, however, by opening her own door and then walking deliberately to the car, as though Cynthia were an expected person. ("God, she behaved so much better than I did," Cynthia said to Dolly, later that afternoon.)

Cynthia gets out of the car, and begins to chatter. "Oh, Odessa, I just wanted to see you, I got this letter from Lord & Taylor—you know, the store in New York where I sent some samples of your material? Anyway they love what you do, they especially mentioned the lovely colors, I knew they would, but they just wondered how much you could produce. I mean, if they wanted any at all, they'd needs yards and yards of it, you see? Mass production, I mean, everything they do is for lots and lots of people."

"That so" is Odessa's neutral comment. In the strong winter light her skin is especially, markedly fine, opaque dark brown silk.

"Mmm. Do you have any idea how many yards you do in a day, say, when you and your sister have the time to work?"

"Don't do in yards," Odessa attempts to explain. "Miz Dolly, she measure out with a tape what she want, and then us try. But it's Miz Dolly do the measuring and the cutting."

Behind Odessa the door to the shack stands ajar, but Cynthia can hardly see into its darkness. Is it possible that the floor is bare? Is only hard dirt? She decides that it is, and decides too that her errand is insane, as was the early impulse that led her to try to connect Odessa with Lord & Taylor. And no use in telling herself that she meant well; everyone usually does, Cynthia believes. But she has absolutely no imagination, she decides. No true sensitivity.

Odessa is wearing one of her regular old flowered cotton dresses, and over it she has put on a man's old tattered cardigan sweater, dark gray wool, out at the elbows. Now, obviously cold, she clutches her arms around herself; she looks at Cynthia with an expression that Cynthia can only read as hostile. Why did you come out here bothering me, you rich white lady? Odessa is mutely asking this quite reasonable question. To which there is no answer.

And so Cynthia responds, "I'm really sorry to have bothered you about this. But I wanted to say—and I thought I'd said—"

"Ain't no bother," Odessa mutters politely, but her eyes are no less angry.

"Well, I'll go along then, and I'll see you soon, and we'll talk…" Cynthia says all this as she heads back around her car, her voice rising on the final, meaningless note. She leans out to wave as she backs up and heads toward the highway, but Odessa has turned her back and is walking fast into the house.

The gray winter landscape through which Cynthia now drives windingly up the hill and back to town looks infinitely sad, all frozen and barren. Hopeless. Cynthia has no idea how long the winter lasts down here. Forever, she could at the moment believe, thinking of Odessa back in that shack, with its leaning walls and the cold hard bare floor. No spring ever, no green vines and delicate buds and soft warm winds. No shielding leaves on Odessa's oak tree.

"I feel as though I'd made a bad situation much worse," Cynthia says to Harry, on the phone. "I mean the whole situation—all these Negroes down here whom no one knows and no one cares about, really. Oh I know, of course I didn't really make it worse, not the whole thing, but you know what I mean. Oh, Harry, I do miss you."

Cynthia to Dolly: "I know I had no business going out there, Dolly, I know. But listen, I've been thinking about it, and I may have come up with a good idea....Yes, I do miss Harry. And what it's doing to our phone bill!"

Jimmy Hightower is a frequent visitor. Cynthia gathers that their period of courtship, of flirtation or whatever it was is over; Jimmy is seriously lonely now and he wants to be friends. It occurs to Cynthia that he may be interested in someone else, maybe even having a real affair, but if so, who? Irene Lee? That is almost too obvious; if they were

136

having an affair, they'd make more of a secret of it—or so Cynthia believes.

In any case, Jimmy calls and asks if he can bring some barbecue over for supper, or sometimes he just drops by.

Cynthia has observed that he talks a great deal about Russ.

Ursula from Kansas has gone, Jimmy says; he met her several times before she left. A very nice, good woman, according to Jimmy. "Just crazy about old Russ, of course. No, I don't think he returns the favor. She's a little bit on the heavy side, and after all she's quite a bit older than Russ." And that is all that Cynthia is to hear of Kansas Ursula for quite a while.

One night, having dropped by fairly late with a bottle of brandy, Jimmy announces good news. "Brett"—SallyJane is well, and is coming home. "That fellow Drake is driving her up tomorrow. Russ said he'd gladly make the trip, of course he would, but Drake more or less insisted, said it was right on his way to somewhere he had to go for some meetings."

Catching something in his voice, Cynthia agrees. "It does sound a little odd, the psychiatrist bringing her home, but maybe not."

"I've been reading some of Dr. Freud," allows Jimmy. "Interesting fellow. Makes a lot of sense to me. Poor man, I understand he's mortally ill in London, though at least he got out of that Austria. But I gather he doesn't approve of doctors having any truck with their patients. Of any nature. However, one time when Russ and I went down to see, uh, SallyJane, I brought up Dr. Freud and Dr. Drake didn't seem to think too highly of him.

So there we are, I guess. A different school of thought."

"Well, the main thing is if SallyJane feels better." But Cynthia too is uneasy. All along she has had some sense, some vague suspicion, in regard to Dr. Drake. Possibly because the first thing she hears about him was how handsome he was, but surely that is unfair? It's really all right for men to be handsome too? However, isn't he married, and if so, how come he's driving SallyJane home alone, assuming that to be the case? She is unable not to ask Jimmy, "His wife's coming too?"

Jimmy hesitates. "I don't rightly know. Seems like she's not around very much. We all know he has a wife, but she's not much there. I think she plays a lot of golf. I got the idea from somewhere that she's the really rich one."

"Poor SallyJane," says Cynthia reflectively, and then, mainly out of a feeling of fondness for Jimmy, and because it has been so very much on her mind, she begins to tell him about her meeting with Odessa. Going out to her house.

"I don't know what I was thinking of," says Cynthia. "I've never felt like such an intruder. And that's how she felt about it, I know. She really resented my coming. Of course she was perfectly polite, but I could see in her eyes, she was furious, and sort of afraid of me too. Afraid I'd march right past her and into her house. Which of course was what I really wanted to do."

"It's very hard," Jimmy agrees. "Of course all the folks around here think they have some handle on it. According to them, they're all great with 'our colored friends'—some of them even say that. And they think we just don't understand."

"They think you're a Yankee too?" That was hard

to believe, with Jimmy's Oklahoma twang, which was Southern to Cynthia's ears.

"Sure. Oklahoma's more west than south to them, and oil is not a Southern occupation. They don't think Texas is Southern at all."

They both laugh.

"It's much more a Southern than a college town, isn't it?" Cynthia comments. "I wasn't exactly ready for that. I guess I didn't think about it much."

"Same mistake I made, in a way," Jimmy tells her. "To me it was purely a writers' town. Russ Byrd's town, is the truth of it." After a somewhat heavy pause he adds, "It can't be easy for SallyJane, being married to such a complicated fellow."

"Marriage is always complicated, I think," says Cynthia, who had never thought of this before. What she is really thinking is that she is very lonely, she wishes Jimmy would stay with her. Not necessarily for sex; if he would just stay and hold her in his arms all night, as Harry sometimes does. "I really miss Harry a lot," she says, and she hopes that Jimmy could not have read her mind. "Don't you? Miss Esther?"

"Well, Russ and I've been so goddam busy, I haven't had much time for missing anyone. And I think Esther's really happy. That's the main thing," he piously adds.

Cynthia asks, "Oh really? Busy how?"

Jimmy leans back, a satisfied expression on his face, which Cynthia now recognizes as having been there for weeks. "It's supposed to be a secret," he says. "But I know you're a very discreet gal. Russ's helping me along with my novel. It's wonderful, it's the most wonderful thing ever happened to me."

"Oh, that *is* wonderful!" exclaims Cynthia as her whole heart sinks. "How marvelous for both of you—I mean so kind of Russ, and it must be such a help to you."

"Oh, it is! Just the greatest! Russ is a wonderful teacher."

Later, lying in bed and fighting sleeplessness, Cynthia is aware that she overdid the enthusiasm with Jimmy; she babbled, she knows she did, but at the moment she could not help herself. For all the time he was talking she was inwardly crying out, Why? Why Jimmy? Russ and I could be involved in that way, I could be writing something and we could be talking about it, he could be teaching me.

And the terrible answering voice, the sleep-preventing voice, which is always right, responds: You read a lot, and you think about writing, but you never do it. Jimmy does. You just want time alone with Russ. Romantically.

And now SallyJane is coming back.

And Harry might fall in love with someone in Washington, and never come back.

And you may never sleep, not again in your life.

Chapter 19

SallyJane, formerly Brett, is perfectly happy just now. Perfectly. On this day, which is the day before she is to drive up to Pinehill with Dr. Drake. With "Clyde"? Does she call him Clyde now that he is coming to her house, more or less as a friend?

The drive will take about four hours, which seems to SallyJane infinite, an infinite gift of time. So much can be said in those four hours. "Unless we hit bad weather," he ("Clyde") has warned.

"Then, of course, it could take a little longer."

And so SallyJane prays for rain. But she dreams of snow. A heavy fall of snow, maybe beginning just as they leave the sanatorium, beginning with light innocuous-seeming flakes, nothing to deter them, and then gradually increasing, slowly turning into heavy, blinding snow; they are gradually forced off the road, perhaps into a small sheltering grove of pines, the boughs becoming laden. Bent down and huge, enclosing.

She imagines their conversation, in the closed-in car, in the snow.

"Are you warm enough?"

"Well—"

"I have this brandy, just in case."

"But I'm not supposed to drink, remember?"

"Well, as of right now you're not a patient, you're just a good friend, and may I say a lovely woman? Whom I'm lucky enough to have along on this trip."

That last surely has the sound of Dr. Drake, SallyJane notes; she feels that she is good at this.

And she wonders if this is what Russ does. Does he think of someone and then just listen to the words that come out of that mouth? She doubts that that is how it works with Russ, for how could he think of large dark fat silent Ursula, from Kansas, and hear poetry?

After the conversation, in the car, she imagines a lot of kissing with Dr. Drake—with Clyde, and she hopes she has not had enough brandy to make her sick; sometimes that is not a good combination, sex and booze, she knows that from some of the parties in California, when she was so nervous that she drank a lot, and then, surprisingly, Russ, in bed, would want to do it.

But Clyde is a doctor; she could tell him how she feels. Although she never would, of course not. Especially when she is with him as not-a-patient.

In the meantime, in the real world, like a young girl she washes and brushes her hair; she does her nails and rubs heavy cold cream into her face and neck. Her fair skin tends to be dry, especially in winter, and like everything else this condition gets worse with age.

She is getting more boring too, with age, SallyJane believes. She does not know how Dr. Drake bears it, listening to her for those couple of hours a week. She talks sometimes about her parents (because she has read that she is supposed to). She talks about growing up over there in Hilton, a long time ago. The president's daughter, and always such a disgrace to him, as she now seems disgraceful to Russ, she supposes. Such a rude, aggressive, assertive little girl. Never "sweet" like all the other little girls her parents often saw, the daughters of their friends. "We saw little Ruthie last night, the sweetest prettiest little thing, so adorable, so polite." Privately, SallyJane has concluded that this is not good for children, these constant and invariably unfavorable comparisons—she would never do such a thing with Melanctha, nor with the boys. But she has not mentioned these child-rearing ideas of hers to Dr. Drake; he would probably agree with everyone else that her parents were only acting for the best. And look at her kids: they're not exactly models of wonderful behavior either, and no one would ever call Melanctha "sweet."

Just thinking of her own parents, even now, fills SallyJane, literally *fills* her, with a heavy, familiar, hard-to-name, and quite intolerable emotion. "Terror" and "guilt" are the words that come closest, although she has never really tried to describe what she feels. Certainly not to Dr. Drake, and never to Russ. She thinks of her mother's tears, her wild, wild sobs, and her streaked red hating face, of her mother's ugly sagging dark aging body—and of her father's remote sad elegance. How terribly unhappy she made them both.

Curiously, it does not occur to SallyJane that her parents made her even unhappier than they themselves were—and that they were the stronger, powerful ones.

Talking about her parents does not seem to get her far with Dr. Drake, even when she tries to.

And talking about Russ is not a great deal better, although at least she can tell that Drake is interested. He seems curious, and he asks a lot of questions, some of which SallyJane is unable to answer. How many poems does Russ usually write each month? How much does he usually get paid for a Hollywood script? And so at last SallyJane tells him, "I just don't know too much about Russ's work. But you could ask him if you wanted to. I know he'd love to talk to you." She does not know this at all, but she believes that her saying it had something to do with Dr. Drake's decision to drive her up to Pinehill.

She does not talk much about her delusion-suspicion about Russ and Deirdre Yates, and that boy looking so much like Russ. She does not want to appear a jealous wife. Delusional. It is all she can do to admit unhappiness. And she does not do

143

that very well. She does not, cannot make it interesting. Russ. Five children. A too large house. Cooking. The weather. Does all that make a normal person unhappy? She is quite sure that it does not. Would not.

Of course the next day it does not snow, how could it? It is a beautiful clear sunny day. All over Southern Pines the sand is bright white, and all the pine needles glistening green.

The first thing that Dr. Drake says to SallyJane (never Brett, not anymore) is about her hair. "Your hair in the sunlight," he says. "It's so—so bright. Spun gold."

So pleased that she is unable to respond (how lucky she washed her hair!), SallyJane smiles, and she gets into his car with him, as, smiling, he nods and opens the door for her. "This is great," he says. "You know, I feel like a boy on a date. Or maybe a kid just let out of school."

A good start! (Too good?) But, riding along, SallyJane is almost instantly queasy. Dear God, she may throw up. Carsick, as she was as a child, so often. And how angry they were about that, all her family. As Dr. Drake will be, she knows, if she manages to spoil his day; that was what her mother always said, or sometimes her father, about her spoiling their days. Always about "managing," as though she had intended to be sick.

SallyJane puts her head close to the window, breathes deeply of fresh air.

"You're not going to be carsick, are you?" Dr. Drake laughs, as though this were impossible, such a childish thing: grownups don't get carsick. But he adds, "I can't have you spoiling my day." Incredible: the very words.

144

He must have read them in her mind.

Happily he then points out the rolling green golf course where he plays, some men in white knickers, a couple of women in sweaters and skirts and socks and little hats. He asks her, "You ever try golf?"

"No, I never did. There's no course in Pinehill, and back in Hilton—"

"How about your husband? He much of a sport?"

"No, Russ walks a lot, in fact he's always walking. These very long walks. He likes to walk at night—"

"Walks at night, oh, does he?"

Is he saying, You goddam fool, don't you know your husband must be off with some beautiful young woman? What a fool you are!

"I think he composes poetry as he walks," SallyJane tells the doctor, as though to compound her stupidity. She imagines him thinking: Lord, this woman will believe anything. No wonder she's gone crazy.

"Poets sure are a different type of folk," remarks Dr. Drake.

It occurs to SallyJane that Russ would find that sentence really funny, but she's not at all sure she should save it for telling Russ; it might make him think Dr. Drake was sort of silly, not worth his money.

Dr. Drake grew up in a really small town just north of Hilton, he now tells SallyJane. He says the name and she remembers that once a shabby-looking football team from there came down to play Hilton's slightly better equipped team. He talks a lot that day about his town, his folks, as he puts it, "two of the nicest old people you'd ever want to meet. Can't figure out how I came out so crazy, one more living disproof of the theories of Dr. Freud."

Does he really think he's crazy? SallyJane is almost reeling from this as she concentrates, still, on not being sick. She decides that he does not at all mean "crazy" in the way that she does when she feels crazy; he means a sort of amiable eccentricity. He likes himself quite well.

The land they are passing now is less flat, less sandy than that around Southern Pines. The narrow white highway surmounts small hills; it cuts through low eroded red clay embankments. It crosses small creeks, brown and swollen with winter rains.

And Clyde Drake goes on talking.

SallyJane manages not to be actively sick. Manages not to spoil his day.

But when she thinks of her fantasies, how she imagined this trip would be—Lord, even imagining snow!—she is so acutely embarrassed, humiliated, that she is sure he must be aware of her feelings. Aren't psychiatrists supposed to be able to do that, to read minds, or almost? However, today for Dr. Drake seems a holiday from psychiatry.

As he talks on, SallyJane finds her own mind wandering from the car, her thoughts straying out to the fields and the small clapboard houses that they pass, little square boxes up on stilts—she supposes to keep them from the mud and rain in wintertime. Poor colored people mostly live around here; little children and a few stray skinny chickens, a yellow dog, a striped scrawny cat, emerge from the yards—and SallyJane considers the terrible accidents of birth. Born colored and poor, in one of these little houses, what earthly chance do you have? Whereas she, SallyJane Caldwell Byrd, born tall and blonde and passably smart (though she has never been sure of that, despite all those IQ tests and the way the teachers at school talked to her parents), she has messed up everything, her marriage and all her children, she believes. Certainly she has messed herself up, so that she has to go down to a very expensive resort, to a sanatorium for rich alcoholics, where it soon turns out that she is not even alcoholic. Just "undisciplined," and unhappy.

And what is her unhappiness, compared to that of the woman who is sitting on that porch, say, as they pass? A skinny old woman with enormous dark sunken eyes, with little children all around her, and probably a husband off somewhere looking for work. Unfair beyond words, or thoughts. It makes SallyJane feel crazy, just trying to comprehend this unfairness. And how very crazy anyone else would think she was if she should try to explain these thoughts.

"Well, Russ Byrd, what a really great place you have here! All the feel of an old country house, but so comfortable!"

Standing there in the parking area with her husband and her doctor, the very familiarity of it all is so intense that SallyJane could faint: the sounds of pine boughs, smells of pine and clay, the sunlight on the dark brown shingles of her house.

It has been explained to her—Russ explained— that the children are all off playing somewhere. But as he said this SallyJane suddenly realized how clearly she had expected them to be there. How

147

much she had purely wanted to see them, especially—oh, especially all five of them! Her children. Hurt, without them she feels that she has no function with these two men, and in a listless way she follows Russ, who is carrying her bags into the house.

"...like to lie down for a while—put your feet up?" Russ is asking her hopefully.

And although this is the very last thing she would like, to be alone in her own room for a while, with her own thoughts but without her husband and children, or her doctor, SallyJane says, "Sure, I'll just go put my feet up for a while."

She lies rigidly on her bed, listening to the men downstairs, who talk, and talk. Whatever about? Not about her, she is quite sure of that; they are not all that interested in her. But what is the point of this visit, after all? Why is she at home? She was much more comfortable at the sanatorium, SallyJane now thinks. That had become more like home.

So tensely she is waiting, so unrestfully lying there, it is almost as though she were afraid to see her children.

She is tensely braced against whatever will happen next.

Chapter 20

"Esther will love her house the way you all have it fixed up," Dolly Bigelow reassures Cynthia.

Cynthia, very distressed, has just confided the fact that Esther is coming over for a visit. "Not to inspect, of course, but it feels like an inspection, you know?"

"It'll cheer her up," Dolly insists. "She can't help but love all this color." Rather ambiguously she adds, "Of course, Esther never did have what you might call taste."

"Oh come on, Dolly, the house wasn't all that bad."

Cynthia and Dolly have progressed in friendly intimacy sufficiently for Cynthia to feel that small corrections, little disagreements are all right. However, she has noticed that they are never quite all right with Dolly. And she thinks, for the thousandth time, that "Southern" is a language that she cannot possibly ever learn.

"I never said a thing that it was bad." Dolly draws herself up, though she still smiles. "It never was real pretty. Not homey."

"But maybe that was the way she wanted it, and she won't like what I've done." Carefully, Cynthia does not say, "we've done," nor does she dare to mention Odessa.

Esther is briefly in town for a visit to Jimmy, and to her friends, and she has, according to Jimmy, expressed a desire to see their house, ostensibly just to pick up a few things that she left locked up in a downstairs closet. Cynthia of course has said that that was fine with her, perfectly fine—but as she has confided to Harry on the phone, she is scared. "It's like an inspection at boarding school," she told him, for no reason whispering into the phone. "Have a big stiff drink before she comes" is Harry's advice. "Come on, she's a very nice woman," he reminds her.

"How's Odessa doing?" Cynthia now dares to ask Dolly, knowing that this is a dangerous topic these days.

"Oh, uppity as ever. You know what Clifton Lee says is just sure to happen? All the Nigras in town will start working over to the defense plant, and then none of us will have any help at all, and they'll all just get drunk with their money and have their Saturday night razor cuttings and beating up."

"I can't imagine Odessa—" Cynthia begins.

"Oh, can't you now. Well, you just don't know that woman the way I do. She's got a temper—who-eee. And proud? That woman thinks she's the queen of the jungle, in her mind. You know the truth is, it's a good thing things didn't work out with that Lord & Taylor of yours. I've got enough with Miz Odessa as it is."

You sound as though you were talking about a daughter, is what Cynthia thinks, among other things, but manages not to say. One of the lessons she has painfully learned in this Southern year has been do not interfere in or comment on their relationships with Negroes. And try to get used to the way they pronounce that word, their "Nigra." They are trying to say Negro; she is sure (almost) that that is what they mean to say.

Still, Cynthia braces herself for further argument. "What I've been thinking," she tells Dolly (and as she speaks she notes the Southern slowness in her own voice), "is that maybe we could have this sort of little shop. You know, downtown. We could drive out into the country and buy stuff. From women like Odessa who make things at home, and we could sell them and divide the money with those women. That way we could all come out ahead."

"You mean things from colored women?" Dolly's round black eyes sparkle, as though with mischief.

"Well, it wouldn't be just colored women. More like just country women. Maybe some who don't have a way to get into town."

Dolly narrows her eyes, speculating; inner conflict is visible on her face. She is first of all dubious about any business arrangements involving "colored." (Cynthia is sure she can see this.) But both Dolly's intelligence, which is considerable, if often submerged in layers of bias and lazy habit, and her greed, also considerable, inform her that this is a good idea. It is something she ought to get in on.

At that moment there is the sound of a heavy car passing by on the road out in front, going fast, too fast, so that both women stare, and Dolly laughs. "We're like two country women ourselves," she says. "Watching cars and keeping track of who goes where."

"I catch myself doing it all the time," admits Cynthia, wondering if Dolly, too, recognized the passenger in Russ's car.

As she might have known, Dolly tells her, "That was that psychiatrist fellow, that Dr. Drake. With Russ. I declare, he's around her all the time! I didn't know those folks made house calls, did you?"

"Maybe he's just visiting. I mean, visiting Russ as much as he is Brett, I mean SallyJane."

Dolly gives her a long look that is full of meaning. "Well, maybe I'd best be getting along now. I'll let you get on with your getting ready for Harry."

Harry is coming home for two whole weeks, arriving that afternoon! Driving down all the way from Washington. Cynthia finds herself quite

151

girlishly excited. As soon as Dolly is gone, she washes her hair in the sink, soaping and rinsing it several times with Drene, then towel-drying and putting it all up in pin curls, with her bobby pins (harder and harder to get these days). How Harry hates to see her like this, she smiles to reflect. She covers it all discreetly with a scarf, although it should be dry before Harry could possibly get there.

"I'm never going to do that to my hair!" says Abby, coming in from school with her books and an apple, which she is eating very loudly. "I'm going to wear it long in a braid, and when I get too old for that I'll wrap the braid around my head."

"Well, I'm glad you've got that all figured out."

"What time is Daddy coming? Do I have to be here?"

"I'm not quite sure; he said he'd try to make it by dinnertime. And you should be here, you know that." She hesitates. "Where were you going?"

"Oh, down to the Byrds'. Some of the kids are doing some stuff down there." Abby scowls. "That doctor's around there again."

"Yes, I know."

"I think Mrs. Byrd must have some kind of a crush on that man." This entirely out-of-character remark comes accompanied by a similarly uncharacteristic giggle, a combination quite shocking to Cynthia. It is as though Abby had added several years to her age all at once.

She wonders: Did Abby think of all that herself, or did someone, some older person, say it to her? She asks her daughter, "Wherever did you get such a silly idea? Or was it your own idea?"

"I just thought of it," says Abby, looking both confused and dishonest. So that Cynthia thinks: Deirdre, I'll bet Deirdre said that to Abby. But what a curious remark for Deirdre to make.

"I have to tell you, I love it. I just really love it," says Esther Hightower, who is at the moment a guest in her own living room.

Esther, as everyone has told her, looks wonderful. She has had her hair cut short and fashionably permanent-waved (Cynthia takes note: How easy and convenient that would be, she thinks). She has also lost weight. She looks very thin and intense. Dedicated. *Young*. In a smart black suit with the new long clinging skirt length. She looks very New York. A career woman.

"These colors are wonderful," she says. "Jimmy wrote me, but I couldn't quite see it in my mind. In my living room, I mean." She laughs. "And actually I love your suite at the Inn."

"Musical houses." Harry laughs, so trim and handsome in his spanking-new Navy uniform. Everyone says this, and Cynthia agrees. He adds, "Maybe people should do it all the time. Or at least more often. We could trade next with the Byrds, don't you think so, Cynthia, love?"

"Oh. No." This came out more vehemently than she had meant it to. "I mean I'm sure it's very nice, but it's more of a house than I could handle. I don't know how SallyJane manages."

"You've never been there?" Esther is curious.

"Well, actually not. You know, Brett— SallyJane—has been sick so much. And I don't think Russ actually likes, uh, much social life."

"You're absolutely right there," Jimmy, the recent Russ Byrd expert, chimes in. "The man really hates it. Interferes with his work, I mostly think. But he seems to pretty much like going round to other folks' houses. I guess then he can leave when he's a mind to."

Jimmy's speech has become noticeably more country, more rural Southern, Cynthia notes, then thinks, Of course, he's imitating Russ. And she thinks again with a stab of what she has to recognize as the purest jealousy of Russ and Jimmy working together on Jimmy's novel—and then she reminds herself, as she has before, that she does not have a novel or even a plan of one that Russ could help her with. She does not have a secret stack of poetry to show him.

What she does have, and what they have all been discussing earlier, is this plan for a country women's store. Which has run up against what has been to Cynthia the most amazing resistance. Which went like this:

It turned out that Dolly had a cousin who lived way far out in the country, a true country cousin, who made "the most beautiful doilies and cocktail napkins you'd ever want to see." Dolly had mentioned the proposed store to this cousin, and had also mentioned Odessa and her work. "You mean a store for colored and white together?" the cousin had demanded.

"Well, not the people together, of course not. Just these things that they make."

"Well now, Dolly, I just don't know. Lem wouldn't like the sound of that, not one bit."

"But that's really crazy," Cynthia had argued. "What does she think, her doilies will be contaminated by possible contact with Odessa's pillows?"

"Now don't you start getting huff-puffy like

154

that, Miss Yankee," Dolly countered. "It's just not the way we do things down here. As I'm sure Willard or Clifton Lee would be the first to tell you. Or Russ Byrd, for that matter. Any of the men around here. It's just not our way of doing things."

And Cynthia was forced for the moment to leave it at that, to leave it exactly nowhere. And to wonder, among other things, just why Willard Bigelow and Clifton Lee or even Russ Byrd were such experts, such judges of "what's right," as Dolly herself might put it.

"Southerners are—well, extremely complicated," Esther tells her. "And absolutely nuts on the subject of colored people, as they call them. It's a little different in Oklahoma, don't you think so, Jimmy? And of course my family is Jewish."

"I would not entirely exonerate Oklahoma from racial foolishness," Jimmy tells her, "but mostly you're right. Although it does seem to me I've heard a certain amount of ugly stuff about what they call 'Indian blood.' Who has it and who doesn't, and who just might." Cynthia notes that he is no longer sounding like Russ.

"If any of them had any idea what's going on in Germany." Esther sighs, with a gesture of hopelessness.

"Your work is good, though?" Cynthia asks.

"It's so exciting, and so frustrating." Esther explains, "We do get a lot of people out of Germany, with sponsors and incomes, places to live and all that. But there's a sort of elitist cast to our operation that's beginning to bother me a lot. We're mostly saving rich people with 'connections.' What about all the others?"

Though she mentions discouragement and frustration, Esther's face is still radiant, and intense. How Cynthia envies that sense of mission. All she has is an idea for a silly store that will probably never work.

Harry seems at least to have been thinking about her problem. "Tell you what," he says, with one of his more charming grins. "Why don't you and Dolly open up two stores, one for colored and one for white? Isn't that the Southern solution?"

Everyone laughs, if a little edgily, especially Cynthia, who then says, "And I'll be the one to run the colored store, and no doubt get run out of town for my trouble."

"I'll run it with you," Esther tells her. "They can't run us both out of town."

The visit with Harry at home has been more than a little disappointing to Cynthia, no doubt at least in part because she so built it up in her mind, a fantasized romantic reunion. Whereas in fact it has been simply nice, or perhaps not so simply; there are certain complexities. But they have been a nice small family all together again.

Abby has been more present than was usual for her in the past year or so.

She has seemed most to want Harry to go for walks with her; she takes him to places that she has especially liked: to a waterfall, a secret meadow, down to the creek and across the bridge to its further bank. They come back from these trips often a little muddy but happy, enthusiastic over wildflowers and new streams. Cynthia notices that Abby is closely observing her father's face as they talk, and she thinks, a little sadly, Oh dear, she really wants him to like it here. She wants us to be an ordinary family in a house, in a settled place. And she thinks, Oh, my dear Abby, you have probably chosen the wrong set of parents for that.

Cynthia herself is experiencing a time of some loneliness. Nothing has improved in her negotiations with Dolly and their projected store; the last word from Dolly was that, according to Willard, a bank would never finance such a project. "He's probably right," was Harry's opinion, when told of this.

Cynthia felt lonely and isolated, even with Harry there. And much worse when he left.

Chapter 21

No one will give a shit for his pig-shit play, thinks Russ, barely managing a smile at his thought. He is limping into the second act; he is sitting at his desk, empty-headed. He is dreaming of everything in the world but the play that he is, in theory, writing. He is staring out the window, watching the squirrels chase each other along a pine bough. He is listening to his houseguest, Dr. Clyde Drake, who is making a lot of phone calls in the next room. He is wondering if Brett—if SallyJane will get up before the kids come home from school. He is wondering if Deirdre is pregnant. Again.

Once he could write no matter what. That was the only thing that never failed him, his work. Once, although out of his mind in love, so crazily wanting Deirdre, and worried and dying of guilt toward Brett and his children, plagued with bills,

157

not to mention some painful problems with his teeth—he still could write. In those days he wrote some of his best poems, and *Restless Omens*, the play that sent him out to Hollywood, to all that money.

But now his mind is hollowed out, his imagination dead. The words that parade through his brain seem to be in another language—or, more precisely, could be the words of someone new to English. A refugee from Europe, or maybe a very small child, just getting the hang of sentences.

"Now, darlin'," he hears dimly, Drake's voice from the room next door. "You very well know…" And then the voice is lowered, so that Russ can hear no more, does not know whatever the other person very well knows.

And what, he wonders, does anyone very well know? He thinks of the three of them under this roof at this moment, himself and Clyde Drake and Brett SallyJane Caldwell Byrd, and of what any of them must know. If he, for example, could entirely know what either of those other two know, he could write forever, could fill volumes, and stages full of actors. He could write the most endless poetry, from one day, even one hour, inside the consciousness of his SallyJane.

Does Drake "see into" SallyJane in this way? Isn't he supposed to? Does he say to SallyJane "…you very well know"? (She wouldn't like that, probably.) Could Drake possibly have been speaking to SallyJane when he was saying, "Now, darlin', you very well know—" No, he couldn't. For one thing SallyJane is here, in this house. In bed. For another that is not a tone that a doctor would take with patients. It is how a man talks to his wife, or maybe a girlfriend who is being a little difficult. Suspicious, maybe, or clinging too long.

Sometime, a long time ago, when SallyJane was Russ's girlfriend, she was a little difficult, but she was also so beautiful then, so golden, her hair and her skin looked like gold, and she loved him so much and she was so—so sexy. As eager for kissing and touching and squirming together as he was. More so, he sometimes thought. Sometimes she scared him a little, when they were both so young and her father was the president of the goddam university. She was always finding secret places for them to be together, and secret times when the parents and the help were all away. Lying together on some bed in a guest room, even though they kept their clothes on, he was scared. And sometimes in the moist between her legs— oh Jesus, she wouldn't let his hand stop. He had to make excuses for not going on.

But she was as vulnerable, as sensitive, as she was sexy, Russ soon learned. It took almost nothing to make her eyes tear up, her voice tremble, although she had a lot of pride, always, and would try to hide how she felt. But especially when she was more eager for love, for kissing and all that stuff, than he was—that hurt her most; he could feel her hurt, along with his own almost killing guilt.

He often thought of leaving her then, and taking up with some more ordinary girl. Some flirt. He imagined this girl, this ordinary girl, as dark and saucy, always laughing. A little like Dolly Bigelow. That type. A girl who would lead him on, the way girls are supposed to do, and then stop him cold, not caring much herself. With SallyJane he felt strange, although he often told himself that of course he felt strange, he was a poet. Like no one else around these parts, and it was not SallyJane's fault. And then at other times he would think it was all SallyJane's fault, the poetry, all of it. With a more normal girl, he could go to business school, or study medicine, for God's sake, like some normal guy.

He gave her the new name, Brett—like Lady Brett in Hemingway's book, of course—in the hope that her character too would change. Not that she would become the Brett of that novel (God forbid!) but that she would be at least a little harder, a little more independent. So that he wouldn't have to leave her, after all. But that did not work. She did not change, and he married her instead. His beautiful, loving, vulnerable, hardworking wife. So often in tears.

And so often pregnant. Holy God! The wonderful new rubber device, supposed to prevent all that, was for Brett an unromantic interruption. A scientific interference. It was anti-love, and if she had to get up for that purpose, love was over, she could not respond.

And then there was Deirdre.

At first, with Deirdre, he felt like a man entrapped in a poem, in one of his own poems, perhaps. He was encased in breathlessness, in desire, in her beauty. He could barely even speak to her, so constricted was all his blood in its turgid veins; his blood was all flowing, he felt, toward his swollen member.

Only gradually did he notice that Deirdre, like Brett, had those heavy, hyper-sensitive breasts, and those vulnerable eyes. She too spoke little and wept easily. And then she was pregnant, too.

Sometimes he crazily thinks that Deirdre could just move right in with them all, Deirdre and Graham. The two women and the kids would all get along; he could be a sort of grandfather figure to them. Between them the women could get the household work done, and keep the children quiet and happy. They could just forget about romance, and love. And he would only think of it in terms of his work. He could write all day, and maybe at night he would read them bits of what he had done. All of them sitting around the fire.

"SallyJane, you have to understand—"

Russ hears this partial sentence very clearly from the next room, and at first he is mystified, until the obvious answer comes to him: of course, SallyJane has come downstairs and is in the next room, talking to Clyde Drake. It seems strange, somehow; on the other hand not strange at all. Though Drake is at the moment a visitor in her house, she is still his patient, after all. Why shouldn't they talk?

But are their conversations still supposed to be intensely private? Should Russ go on into the next room, the dining room, as, bored and stalled in his work, he would like to do, and say hello to them both?

The day outside is gray and cold, spring seems nowhere near. There is even a cold, persistent wind. As Russ enters the dining room and sees SallyJane there in her sheerest, barest nightgown, his first thought is practical; he thinks, Poor SallyJane, she must be cold. His second very quick reaction is one of a strong and peculiar embarrassment: he has interrupted a scene of some sort; he is in a place where he should not be, even in his own house, between his own wife and her doctor. It is not precisely a sexual scene, although SallyJane's nightgown gives it to some degree that aura. Nor is it exactly a medical conference. It would seem some bizarre combination of the two, though Russ is not able until much later to so describe it to himself.

For an instant SallyJane looks at him uncomprehendingly. Who is he? Where does he live? But then she comes into focus, more or less. Her hands rise to her throat, arms protecting her breasts, as she says, "I just came down to see if you-all needed anything."

"SallyJane still needs a lot of bed rest," Clyde Drake in a man-to-man way explains to Russ. Which is actually no explanation at all, but something that needed to be said. Obviously.

"Anything we need we can find for ourselves," says Russ, not exactly addressing either one of them, but understanding that he is aligned with Drake, at least in SallyJane's mind. She feels herself confronted with two men; he can read that in her eyes, and in her posture, which is defensive. (Is SallyJane afraid of men? Of *him?*)

"I just came down to get some tea," she says, a self-contradiction that they all ignore.

Gently, Russ tells her, "I'll tell the girl to bring you up some. You go on back to bed now, honey."

Looking to Drake as though for protection, SallyJane then turns and leaves the room, colliding with a chair on her way, at which she murmurs, "Goddam," and continues toward the stairs. She turns again then, to say to Russ, "I didn't really want any tea. I just thought I did."

"It's okay, honey."

Faced with each other, Russ and Clyde Drake are silent, and then both begin to speak at once.

Russ asks, "Would you like—?"

And Drake, "Do you ever—?"

In a mild way they both laugh, and then Russ asks his guest, "Can I get you some coffee—anything?"

"Do you know what I would dearly love? About this time of the morning I often treat myself to a plain old Coke. Not even spiked with anything, though I have to admit that I have yielded to that temptation on occasion. But just a good old Coca-Cola."

"Sounds real good to me. I think I'll join you."

"Just out of the bottle, please. Tastes best that way to me." Clyde Drake laughs, a sort of apology for crude tastes.

It does taste good that way, notes Russ—who has never had a morning Coke in his life before, much less one out of a bottle. As the two men move into the living room with their bottles, he observes that he feels very young, and remembers his mother saying that Cokes were bad for your teeth, whereas his father said they were a great source of energy. His father was probably right, he thinks. Maybe a Coke every morning is just what he needs for work.

"It takes a long time, depression."

Clyde Drake has spoken so softly that Russ has to replay the words in his mind before he is sure that he heard them right. He mutters, "I guess it does." For an odd moment he has wondered whose depression they are talking about; but then he knows—of course, SallyJane's. He, Russ, is not supposed to be depressed at all, but busily writing away. At a great new play. About pigs.

"Sometimes it can seem like forever," Drake

continues, before taking an enormous slug from his cold green bottle.

"Do you think—" Russ starts to ask; then he hesitates, and gulps in turn from his own cold bottle. "Do you think, this shock treatment you've mentioned—do you think—?"

Clyde Drake slowly composes his face into a frown. "I sincerely hope not," he says. "Had a lady die on me once; of course the truth is she had a weak heart, a condition, but still it was in the course of my treatment that she died."

A somber silence ensues, during which both men consider the prospect of dead women. If SallyJane died, Russ is thinking, I would be more than half dead too; we've become the same person, almost. These days it's her pain I'm feeling. It's like I'm Clyde Drake's patient too, with all her feelings about him.

This last thought is quite new to Russ, and he examines its implications. He has already noticed in himself an unusual, out-of-character impulse to talk to this man, to tell him things, and to try to get his, Drake's, views on life. He would even like to tell Drake about his play. The pigs. Almost at random (he had not meant to say this) he asks, "Do you think a depression could be contagious? Sort of like having a bad cold in the house?"

Drake seems to be mulling this over as again he frowns, and clears his throat. Then smiles. "That would be a little on the order of—what do they call it?—mental telepathy, am I right? The stuff that fellow over to Duke is working on. Dr. Rhine. Extra-sensory perception, I think some folks call it. If you can believe in all that business, then it's easy enough to believe in what you might call depression germs too." His smile broadens.

Russ has in fact been very interested in experiments done on ESP; he might be said to believe in it. He would like to argue the point, but feels that he should not. He only says, "I guess sometimes in a marriage, though, folks get so close that it feels like you've caught what the other person has. Depression included."

After a judicious pause Drake agrees. "That could certainly be. Like when it seems like you've both thought of the same joke at the very same moment. Lucky you if it's a joke, of course." He gives Russ a grin of boyish complicity.

Against some better (older, wiser) judgment, Russ finds this exchange enormously appealing. He feels young, and bad. Not naughty, as his mother used to put it, but bad, really bad. A bad boy who does terrible things to girls, a bad man who cheats on his wife and does not really love his girlfriend. But he is not depressed!

How handsome Clyde Drake is. Better-looking than some of the Hollywood actors Russ has met around the swimming pools out there. He wonders if Clyde can act, and then remembers that he is a *doctor*. Probably doesn't have the slightest interest in acting.

He wonders what it would be like to be a patient of Clyde's. To tell him all your secrets, everything. Like, how much of the time he does not want to make love to Brett. To SallyJane. And sometimes he does not want to do it to Deirdre. Does Clyde ever feel that way, about his wife, the wonderfully named "Norris," whom so far Russ has never met? Would Clyde say so if he did ever feel like that?

For a moment Russ has this most curious sense that he *is* Clyde.

"Say, I've been wondering," Clyde now says, very slowly. "Tell me, Russ, old man—"

I'll tell you anything, Russ thinks, but he only smiles.

"You ever try any huntin' round here? You know go out and shoot up some squirrels and some rabbits?"

And Russ, who has never shot at anything but a large stuffed target, who desperately hates the sight of the smallest amount of blood—any blood, anyone's, anything's blood—Russ says to his guest, "Great idea! We could even go after wild turkey."

Chapter 22

In the early spring of that year, late February or early March, in Pinehill, for no conscious or angry reasons, Abigail Baird begins more or less to avoid the company of adults. Even Deirdre, with whom she used to enjoy exploring the town, and the woods, the creek, and with whom she certainly had no quarrel—she tends to avoid seeing Deirdre, not calling her, and unable to explain when her mother, Cynthia, says, in a hinting way, "We haven't seen Deirdre for such a long time!" Abby even avoids her mother, although with her father gone so much anyone would have thought (Cynthia would have thought) that they would be "closer," they would "do things together." But Abby, in the half-knowing, self-protective way of intelligent children, chooses almost always to be busy, either with other children or with some private project, maybe a long bike ride out to a place called Laurel Hill. Alone. The other kids she sees most often are Betsy Lee, who is not very smart but will go along with almost any project conceived by Abby, or Melanctha Byrd, who is very smart but touchy and unreliable—you can't tell how she'll feel about anything. Or sometimes she sees Billy and Archer Bigelow.

These children touch off nothing complicated or frightening (not yet) in Abby. Approaching adulthood herself, though still distantly, it is adults whom she finds too complex, too intense, and often too unhappy for her to wish to emulate, or just to spend time with, just now. She has never met anyone, any grownup whom she would wish to be, or even to be like, when she grows up.

Deirdre especially has been a disappointment, although Abby would not have put it so. Toward Deirdre she feels a brooding, vague discomfort; what once seemed warm and easy—and remarkable, given the difference in their ages—has become uneasy, and darkened. Put simply, it is harder to talk to Deirdre now than it used to be. Behind all this, or maybe simply involved in the dark, uncomfortable confusion, is Mr. Byrd. Abby has spent just enough time, which is not much at all, five or ten minutes here or there, with the two of them together to feel strong currents, which in a general way she knows to be sexual, although she would not use exactly that word. But even when Mr. Byrd is not around, Abby feels his presence, with Deirdre; or when she sees Mr. Byrd downtown, in the post office, or just driving past her parents' house, she feels the presence of Deirdre—just in the way he looks at her, at Abby, Deirdre's friend.

And—Graham, Abby knows, in the way that most children wordlessly know everything, that Graham is not Deirdre's little brother;

Deirdre does not treat him like a brother. Though how could brotherless Abby know this so clearly? She just does, as she herself might say. Abby almost knows that Graham is Deirdre's son; she is within a hair of this knowledge, although it may not emerge to her consciousness for quite some time.

She also knows that Deirdre is extremely lonely, and sad. And Mr. Byrd is too, though the causes of his isolation and sorrow are more obscure to Abby.

One afternoon, though, for a variety of reasons, among them the facts that she has nothing better to do that day and all the other children are doing something else, like the dentist or piano lessons—on that afternoon Abby goes by Deirdre's house, and finds Deirdre at home (Deirdre is almost always at home), and she asks if Deirdre and Graham want to walk out to Laurel Hill. They do, although Deirdre says they can't be out for too long; she has to be back by five.

The three of them set off toward the long white winding concrete highway that leads down to the creek.

Just before the bridge, they cut off on a small rutted and muddy road, continuing past a couple of small farms, down a red clay gulch of a stream that they have to jump across. Graham, as always, gets his shoes wet. Deirdre (as always) scolds him, gently. "Oh, Graham—" but she sounds a little distracted, and looks apologetically at Abby, as though saying, I know I should be a better mother, I'm just trying.

The road then enters the woods, where it widens, and instead of mud and ruts there is smooth white dirt. On their left, as they walk along, are the thick deep woods, mostly evergreen, pine and cedar, and on the right are bushes and vines, blackberry, honeysuckle, just hiding the creek. Which they can hear, as it rushes and gurgles over rocks and fallen trees. The blue air is full of the tease of spring, rich and promising.

"My dad was down for a week," Abby tells Deirdre. "I brought him out here—he thought it was great."

"My dad really hated it here in Pinehill," contributes Deirdre. "I think he's pretty happy in California, though. But it's tough without my mom."

"I don't think my dad likes Washington much without my mom. I think he wants her to move up there with him."

"But she's crazy about Pinehill, I thought. And now in that house—"

"I don't know." Abby finds that she doesn't really want to talk about her parents; any aspect of them makes her uncomfortable—if and where they are happy, where they might go.

"I think my dad has some lady," says Deirdre, in a discouraged way.

"Does he try to get you to come to California?"

"No, not really. He and Graham—I don't know."

But if he were Graham's father, as he is supposed to be, he would want Graham to be there too, wouldn't he? Abby feels unhappy suspicions confirmed—or, rather, spelled out for her. And she wonders, What did Deirdre and I ever use to talk about? She can't remember. Maybe nothing at all.

They have come to the place where the road ends: a small sandy beach at a wide bend in the creek, where the water is shallow and fast over smooth small rocks. On the other side of the creek huge gray boulders rise, a granite wall, with crevices and caves from which dark feathered ferns peer out in their complex luxuriance. Trees top this wall, pines and cedars, and among them, glossy and dark green, are great bushes of laurel, grown huge and strong. The laurel of Laurel Hill, just now in full bursting bud. About to bloom.

"I know a way to walk so that you end up over there, on the other side," says Deirdre. "We'll have to do that sometime."

"Oh yes, I'd love to." But Abby knows, somehow, that they won't, and she wonders, disloyally, if Betsy or Melanctha knows about this other walk, to the other side of Laurel Hill. The laurel side. Maybe Billy and Archer?

Cynthia is as restless as a high-school girl, her daughter observes. And she is acting all girlish, changing her hairstyles, buying new lipstick. Ordering new clothes from New York and then sending them back. Abby has read about women acting funny in the so-called "change of life." But isn't her mother a little young for that—thirty-five, whatever she is?

When Harry's away, up in Washington, Cynthia has sort of dates with other men. Jimmy Hightower comes over, and Clifton Lee (he just came once; Cynthia seemed not to like him). A couple of other men. But all they do is talk, they never kiss or anything like that: Abby can see the front hall if she leans over from her bedroom door, and she sees them all shake hands, rather formally, as they go.

Cynthia doesn't get particularly dressed up or anything when these men come over. The most dressed up she has been so far was when she and Abby's father, Harry, went down the road to a party at the Byrds'. Cynthia wore a new red dress with a funny fringe across her bosoms; she looked pretty silly, Abby thought. And they can't have had such a wonderful time at the party; they came home early and talked a long time in the kitchen, drinking tea. Abby listened on the back stairs for quite a while.

"...she does look better, don't you think?"

"Truthfully, not a lot, my darling Harry. She looks glazed."

"I thought she looked pretty good."

"You're too kind. I think you just mean not drunk. Poor thing, ginger ale all night."

"What's with that Drake guy? You were talking to him a lot."

"Harry, you're not jealous? Surely. Anyway, he's attractive, obviously, but not very interesting. Sort of a blank. And the most conventional, most Southern attitudes. On everything."

"Seems funny, he's around the house over there pretty much all the time."

"Yes, and never with his wife. I wonder what she's like. It is funny."

"Makes you wonder who his patient is, SallyJane or Russ."

"It's very odd. They're not supposed to be such great friends with their patients. I'm sure of that. Remember, in Connecticut, when Muffy was seeing that doctor—that psychiatrist who was so fat? People had to be very careful not to invite them together."

"Russ seems to find him fascinating."

"And so does SallyJane. It must be a little confusing for the children."

"Those poor little kids. Honestly. More tea?"

"Thank you, dear Harry. Well, I do wonder what on earth Russ sees in that Clyde Drake. Or, for that matter, in Jimmy Hightower's novel."

"Maybe it's good?"

"I hope so. Oh, I don't know. Anything's possible, I guess. How did you feel about Dolly's new black dress?"

"A little tacky, as they say down here."

Cynthia laughs. "Maybe a little. You didn't feel the strong sex appeal?"

"She's not my type, you know that."

"She sure seems to be Clifton Lee's type. Honestly—those two."

"He was drunk. Don't make up stories."

"Well, I just wondered. You know she's still mad at me over the business about Odessa."

"She'll get over it. You know that."

"I hope so. I really like Dolly. In a way."

"As for you, Mrs. Baird, you have lots and lots of sex appeal in that red dress. You really are my type—"

Abby creeps back up to her room.

Chapter 23

Now that SallyJane is well, Dr. Drake—"Clyde"—comes up to see her all the time. He calls her "Sal," another new name. She is not at all sure how she feels about being Sal.

What he says is, he has all these meetings over in Hilton, and there they are, the Byrds, right in— or, rather, *on* his way. Sometimes SallyJane thinks he just wants a free hotel, a guaranteed good dinner (she really fusses over dinner when he comes, uses lots of rationing coupons) and lots of bourbon and a private room. But what an ugly thought! How could she think that of Clyde, who has made her well? Her doctor. At other times she thinks he just comes up to see Russ; he seems terrifically interested in Russ, as though he were a naturalist with a microscope and Russ were some new species of bug that he had never encountered before. Well, that could be true, in a way (just as her ugly idea about the bourbon and the room could be true). It is quite possible that Clyde has never met a poet before, much less one who is also a successful playwright who writes scripts for Hollywood, for a lot of money. Who is now working on a long play about pigs in Kansas. Russ is certainly an unusual man.

But Russ has just begun to lose interest in Clyde, SallyJane has observed, taking note. At first Russ seemed really to take to him, to Clyde, in a way that surprised SallyJane. They were boyish together. They listened to silly stuff on the radio while they drank, and they borrowed *.22* rifles from the boys and went out hunting squirrels and rabbits. But now Russ is quite bored with all that, SallyJane can tell; she hears him making excuses for not doing those things, especially the shooting, which she could have told Clyde would not last long. Russ would like to see less of Clyde Drake, but he does not know how to say so. How can he say, I'd like to see a lot less of you, and still think of himself as a perfect "Southern gentleman"? A considerable problem, for Russ.

There is a secret sad truth about Russ, which possibly only SallyJane knows: he tires of people after not very long, no matter how much he started off liking them. He gets bored silly, and then he does everything so that they will not know how he feels—so that in his own mind, at least, he can be forever gentlemanly. Exemplary. High-class Southern. He tired of SallyJane a long time ago, she thinks, but by then they were married and it was too late to get rid of her, and then they had all those children, none of them terribly interesting to Russ for long, although he is always extremely polite to all of them. Maybe too polite? Would a man who really loved his family be so courteous, always? Maybe he would; SallyJane is not quite sure.

Russ is bored now too with Jimmy Hightower, who at some point quite suddenly became his friend—as though Russ had just noticed him for the first time. And surely he is bored with this novel that Jimmy is writing, supposedly. How will he work that one out? You cannot just ditch a person whose novel is halfway done, or can you? SallyJane does not know, but she feels for Jimmy, whom she likes and perceives as kind, a gentle person. She likes Esther too, but Russ has never been at all interested in Esther. Esther somehow scares him, SallyJane thinks.

Will he ever be bored with Deirdre?

Will he ever develop an interest in Cynthia Baird, who seems in some subtle way to be waiting for him?

These are questions unanswerable for Brett. Sal. SallyJane.

There are also times when she believes that Clyde Drake comes to Pinehill just to see her. And not just as a patient, but as a woman about his age whom he truly cares about. Whom he would like to kiss.

Certainly one of the reasons he comes is to drink a lot, with Russ. His wife does not hold with drinking, SallyJane overheard him saying this to Russ. "Norris doesn't hold with drinking. Irritating for a man my age to have to do his drinking on the sly."

Norris? SallyJane has never heard of a woman named Norris.

And it's ironic: if she, SallyJane, did any drinking "on the sly," she can just imagine, if anyone found out, the shock, the anger all around.

After dinner, when Clyde has come up for the evening, after SallyJane has cleaned up and put all the kids to bed, sometimes she wonders just what she's supposed to do then, especially as she increasingly understands that Russ is bored. He's been bored with her forever—that's nothing new—but he's getting more and more bored with Clyde Drake now; he does not want to sit around at night just drinking and answering questions about himself. She wonders: What would be worse for him, to be alone with Clyde Drake or alone with Clyde Drake *and* me?

Unable to decide, SallyJane settles herself inconspicuously into a chair that is more or less out of their range (she hopes) with her knitting, so that she can at the same time be present, if they need her, and absent, if they just don't want her around, for whatever strong male reasons.

How she loves them both, though—both these men, almost interchangeably. She loves them painfully. If only there were the slightest sign from either of them, then she would be all right. She would be a healthy person if either of them loved her. But of course they do not love her, neither one of them does, at all. Of course not.

Russ stands up. It seems sudden, as though he had been wanting to stand up in just that defiant way for quite a while, but had only then pulled himself together sufficiently to do so. He says, "I think I'll go out for a while." It is absolutely clear that he means alone.

What will happen now?

Clyde Drake leans back heavily in his chair. SallyJane has noticed how large men always pick the smallest Victorian carved chair; she hopes that this will not be the time when it finally falls over and breaks. Clyde closes his eyes as though thinking deeply, but SallyJane, who has been watching him drink all night, is afraid he might fall asleep. (In fact she is afraid of almost everything, it occurs to her just then. Afraid of anything that could happen, at any time.)

Clyde opens his eyes and he comes forward with a bang, quite suddenly. He leans toward SallyJane and he says, "You know, I really love that guy."

Who? She looks her question.

"That Russ. Your man. I really love him too. He's the most exciting, interesting person. It must be thrilling to live with a man like that."

"Well—"

"Love him! I really do. Oh, I don't mean any of that fairy pansy stuff, you know I'm not like that. In fact those guys make me want to throw up, they really do. God help me if I ever have a patient with that problem. But I love Russ like you're supposed to love your brother. With all your heart."

He is very drunk. He does not know what he is saying. Still, it seems extremely strange, and scary, to SallyJane.

He goes on. "And I love you too, little Sal. I love all my patients, they're my true wonderful family. They almost make up for you-know-who, the nympho devil. Pardon my French. But especially I love you and Russ."

And Miss Effington? SallyJane does not ask this, nor does she ask if he really said what she thinks she heard him say about his wife—Norris, who doesn't hold with drinking. A "nympho devil"? Can he have said that?

"I want you to tell me more about Russ," Clyde continues. "You almost never talk to me about Russ, do you know that?" He says some more, but SallyJane has stopped listening to the words, and hears only the sound, which she recognizes as the sound of pain. This drunken man, her doctor, is in the most terrible pain. Is he going to cry? SallyJane believes that he is. She has never seen a man cry, and she knows that she could not bear it.

But at that moment both SallyJane and Clyde Drake hear the back door open, and close, and then Russ's heavy footsteps through the house. With a terrible, anguished parting look at SallyJane, Clyde Drake gets up to his feet, and more quickly than SallyJane would have believed he could manage, he is out of the room, and headed upstairs to his room.

Later, all those moments are very hard for SallyJane to remember; it is as though she, and not Clyde Drake, had been drunk. Which was surely not the case; she does not drink at all, these days. But all the words between them blur, so that she cannot remember which of them said what. Was she telling Clyde how much she loved Russ? That is a large and apparently permanent fact of her life. Or was it Clyde who was saying that he loved Russ? That seems so unlikely; she must be crazy even to have thought of such a thing.

Was it Clyde, so heartbroken-sad that he almost wept—or was it herself, often-weeping SallyJane?

The next morning Clyde is sad and quiet, but that is how he always is, except when he drinks. He has his regular three Cokes, and he even says to SallyJane, "You're sure looking pretty these days, little Sal. I never did care for a skinny woman. Lord knows why I married one."

SallyJane feels she is not looking pretty at all; she has suddenly got so fat. She wonders if it could have something to do with the pills Clyde gave her, not even on the market yet but very effective, he says. How could pills make you fat? And Clyde would have warned her about that, wouldn't he?

She thinks she remembers that Clyde said she should talk more about Russ, but there is so much about Russ she could never, never tell anyone. How she married him, really, because otherwise he would not make love to her: he had to "marry pure." (Russ had grown up a Baptist and that was how Baptists talked, she guessed.) Anyway, he wouldn't do it to her, really, no matter what they were actually doing. Squirming around on the sofa in the game room of her parents' house in Hilton (the president's house). All that touching and kissing, breathing words of love.

But that cannot be the sort of thing that Clyde would like to hear about.

Chapter 24

As Cynthia, at night, looks out her bedroom windows to the garden below, for most of that April before the war she sees only white flowers. Dim white shapes, white clouds of petals, their mingled fragrances drifting on a light evening breeze. White-blossoming trees, beds of white, everything pale and white. She wonders if Esther planned it, either romantically or sadly, for these hours. For whiteness.

Certainly Cynthia's own thoughts, as she gazes there, are both romantic and sad. She misses Harry, and she feels that their lives are separating. He seems increasingly involved in Washington, in the Navy. Doing things, seeing people about whom he is jovially mysterious, smilingly discreet. How men love wars, thinks Cynthia. No wonder we have so many, with them in charge.

She senses that Harry has never been happier in his life, and she wonders if they will ever again converge into a marriage, a family. They should have had more children, she thinks—though at the time, after Abby, their lives were so uncertain economically—Harry with his unsatisfactory job, and she with her stupid shopping debts. But if along with Abby they had had another one or maybe two little children—a boy and a girl, perhaps—at this point Cynthia imagines that she would be both busier and less lonely.

However, just look at poor SallyJane, down the road. Five children and a husband who works at home, and she is very busy. And crazy. Poor SallyJane is clearly crazy, and fatter every day. Cynthia often thinks she should go to see her, but what do you say to someone who is having a "nervous breakdown"?

Cynthia is lonely. Although she hates the word, she has to face it: she is, and even just thinking the word "lonely" makes it worse, and brings her close to tears. A lonely aging woman on an April night, staring out to flowers, inhaling them. Her eyes blurred, her throat tight. Alone.

She wonders a lot about Russ, about the inconclusiveness of their connection. When she remembers her early decision and plans to come down to Pinehill, and thinks of the drive itself, the deep shades of this land, her first sightings of this countryside—she remembers feeling then an infusion of Russ. Lines of his poetry were always in her head, back then. All her fantasies in his direction were basically romantic; they were, she supposes—well, sexy. Something that certainly has not happened between them. But she also feels that there is some more even essential connection missing. Which could be an important conversation that they have never had. It is as though she had come all the way down here for something that never happened. Was that stupid and embarrassing pig conversation to be forever the high point, the most intense moment together? And, come to think of it, that took place in the very garden to which she now looks out with such loneliness.

Cynthia has even worked it out that at the very moment when she and Harry were driving south,

180

her heart and mind so full of James Russell Lowell Byrd, Russ was driving through Kansas. With SallyJane and all those children. Running into the pig. When, in a sense, he should have been running into her. Metaphorically speaking.

Cynthia has never precisely articulated what she "believes," not to herself and certainly to no one else. But she does believe in order, even a universal order. Order is more or less like gravity, she vaguely believes. If there is no order, no reason for the being of everything, then the earth might fly apart, with no center. Gravity gone.

These are not thoughts that ordinarily or consciously occupy her for long, though. She is far more likely to be thinking, in the scented white April night: Why aren't Russ and I at least, or maybe at most, great friends?

The curious fact that she moved to the Hightower house must have had something to do with Russ, she reasons; fate cannot have brought them so close together for no reason. No "order."

Cynthia also sometimes thinks that she misses Dolly. Or she misses seeing her in the old easy intimate way that they had just established when it all went wrong. They do see each other still, but almost always in groups, with Irene Lee, for instance, and other local ladies. But Cynthia catches something in Dolly's eyes, when focused on her, a black gleam of the purest disapproval, as though Cynthia had broken or tried to break certain basic rules. Which, she supposes, she did.

Dolly is funny and smart and very observant, all the Southern nonsense notwithstanding, the layers of bias and worse. She is a truly great gossip; it is this that Cynthia misses, the gossip and what she felt as Dolly's affection for her; Dolly had "taken to" her from the start, as no one else in town entirely had, which made Dolly's current disapproval the harder to withstand.

But one morning "out of the blue," Dolly telephones. Her voice is high, almost breaking with distress. She says that she would really like to see Cynthia.

"*Sure*. Of course. Do you want to meet downtown for a Coke?"

No. Dolly would rather come to Cynthia's house, if that's all right with Cynthia. What she has to say is private. Very private.

Okay. Certainly. Dolly can come right over.

Too much powder does little to hide the fact that Dolly has surely, very recently been crying. Crying a lot, Cynthia would judge, but she admires the visible effort that Dolly has made to pull herself together: the pretty pale pink spring blouse, the careful curls and lipstick.

Dolly even manages a smile as she makes her announcement. Or, rather, her first announcement. "You are not going to believe this," she starts out. "But maybe you will—probably up North folks' help quits them all the time. But down here they don't. We don't fire and they don't quit. It's like a contract you don't even have to sign, everyone just *knows*. But Odessa has done it. She up and quit on me. Says her husband's coming back. Horace. Some husband, that man hasn't been around these parts for it must be nigh onto two years, and he's getting a job over to the defense plant. Odessa's got it in her mind to do some work at the laundry—they're real short of help right now, 'cause of defense. And she and her sister going to put in more time at their dyeing and

182

weaving. Said somebody's been talking to her about the textile mill, over to Boynton. One of them Communist students, I'll be bound."

Cynthia has two reactions to this saga. Even as she is murmuring words of sympathy—of condolence, even—she is thinking: (1) that this is not what Dolly has been crying about; she is not all that emotionally attached to Odessa. And (2) she is thinking, Hurray for Odessa for quitting her job! Three cheers!

Dolly just sits there, staring straight ahead, out into the soft April day, into Esther's garden, until quite abruptly she says, "And Willard won't even speak to me."

Unable to connect this fact with the surely unrelated fact of Odessa's defection, Cynthia looks a question.

At which Dolly looks away, and can be seen to blush under all that powder. After a pause she looks back, and then she says, still not quite facing Cynthia, "The dumbest thing. We were over to the Lees' last night for dinner, and sometime late in the evening—we'd had our wits about us we'd have been home already, in our bed. But we all seemed along about then to need another drink, and guess what, out of ice, so Clifton said he'd take a run over to the storage plant, and didn't I want to come 'long, keep him company. Well, it all took a little longer than anyone thought it would, including me and Clifton, and when we got back, there was this little bitty smear of lipstick on Clifton's collar. Irene, of course, by that time was much too pickled to notice, but old bright eyes, to whom I'm supposed to be married, he noticed right off, and talk about raising Cain!—though at least he waited till we were out of the

183

house, and on our way home. Which was pretty quick, I can tell you that. But then, accusing, accusing, things he said he'd always noticed—" She broke off, sniffling into her handkerchief.

Was it true, though? Cynthia wants to ask, but does not. *Is* there something going on between you and Clifton Lee? That was not a first kiss that got the lipstick on his collar? *What* has Willard always noticed?

Cynthia has not noticed anything at all between Dolly and Clifton. They are always flirtatious with each other, always full of little compliments, all of which Cynthia has assumed were only half meant. That is how both of them are with almost everyone. They are Southern. By Cynthia's social logic, if anything had been seriously happening between them, the clue would have been an absence of just such flirting as she has observed. But undoubtedly the rules down here are different.

Clever, observant Harry once remarked, "Odd, you and Jack don't dance together much anymore. You must be madly in love." Which was not so far from the truth, and partly for that reason, Harry's observation, Cynthia decided that whatever had been going on had to stop; it was dangerous, and not quite all that much fun.

But do Clifton and Dolly actually do it somewhere? she wonders. She finds that she more or less hopes not. Clifton is so red and fleshy; he looks as though he should be a football coach, though in actual fact he teaches business administration.

Because she cares much more for Odessa than she does for Clifton Lee, Cynthia chooses next to ask, "About Odessa, do you think you can get her back someway?"

"Oh, I just don't know. Sounds to me like she's

looking to find her own path." And then, with a perky, upward twist of her chin, Dolly says, "As a matter of fact, which Willard will never in this world believe, I was asking Clifton about the store we had thought about, you know, with the things that Odessa made and all..." She trails off, clearly not wanting to return to that source of trouble with Cynthia, and smiling to indicate that now it's all over, they can begin again.

And then she gets back to the store. "Clifton said nothing easier. We just rent some little old storefront on Main Street—there's several of them going for peanuts these days, he said—and we get this permit from City Hall, and then we go out and collect these pillows and napkins, all hand-made country things, and we fix some sort of a contract with these ladies, and we sell the things. But of course if Willard found out I was in any way involved with Clifton, even in a business way, that'd be just the end of everything—"

She gives Cynthia a ravaged, pleading look, from which Cynthia understands a great deal. What Dolly wants from her is a sort of unquestioning partnership in this project, this little store. Cynthia, of course, will be the one to talk to Clifton, and probably to Odessa too, at first. Thus Dolly's bridges will be mended for her, without any overt, unpleasant effort on her part. Cynthia has to admire, in a way, the simple, almost childlike direct-ness of Dolly's operation.

Cynthia understands too that the whole other, much more painful and difficult issue, the whole problem of Negro and white women both con-tributing to the store, is to be glazed over; it will simply not be mentioned. No more discussion. Just smiles. The Southern way.

185

Surprisingly, though (Cynthia herself is surprised), her instinct is to go along with all this. Not especially liking Clifton, she still does not mind going to him for business advice. She can also ask Harry, and maybe Jimmy Hightower. She knows Harry to be very smart and practical; she believes that Jimmy is too.

She also likes the idea, the possibility of mending her own bridges with Odessa. As she imagines it, she can just go over to the cleaning establishment where Odessa works now (God knows not back out to Odessa's house). And she can talk in a sensible way about the store. Explain about contracts, maybe. The idea of consignments.

For the store, after all, was her idea in the first place. Wings of excitement flutter within her at the thought of this definite, original, and possibly lucrative project. And even in the midst of her excitement, her busy and efficient mind moves forward, moves ahead with plans and designs and calculations.

It is pleasant too to have Dolly returned as a friend. Dolly who even now is more bright-eyed, much more herself, than when she first came in.

Dolly now leans forward. "Something interesting," she says, in her lowest, most excited voice. Her gossip voice. "You know what? We're finally going to get to meet the famous wife of that Clyde Drake. Mrs. Norris Drake is coming up for the weekend, and they're going to give a party. SallyJane swore to me that this was so, this very morning in the drugstore!"

Chapter 25

"Deirdre, thy beauty is to me
  As of yore
  A great bore..."

Russ has scribbled those lines on his writing pad, smiling furtively as he did so—before he quickly tears off and crumples that page. He does not even want to see it again himself, and he does not want that name even written in his house. And besides, it is not true: Deirdre is still the most perfectly beautiful woman he ever saw, with those translucent sapphire eyes—including New York and Hollywood, nowhere a woman as lovely as Deirdre is. Which perhaps is the problem, her perfection. Once or twice he has cruelly thought that she looks like one of those match-cover ads that say "Draw Me." The curves of her forehead, of her nose, and of her cheeks are all perfect curves, and her rich tawny skin is flawless. She is perfect.

He is not so much bored with Deirdre's beauty, actually, as he is unmoved. Never these days stirred, in the old breathless blood-tingling way that he used to be, for what now seems a very long time. These days when he goes to see her, which he does religiously at least once a week, it is almost never to make love (although sometimes it ends up that way), it is just to say hello. To check in, as though they were married. And to see Graham, about whom his feelings are strong, and ambivalent. And though these visits are mostly innocent, they still must be accomplished with the utmost secrecy. Furtive visits, requiring infinite pains and trouble. Sometimes he almost wishes she would leave, go somewhere else. But he hates himself for that thought, especially since poor

Deirdre has no place else to go. Not back out to her furious terrible father, Clarence, in California—and what would she do alone in New York, for example? Thanks to him, she is saddled with a child, and she is certainly bright enough for a job but she can hardly type. What she is best at (Russ is fairly clear on this) is domesticity; she has made an enchanted cottage of that old house, with handmade curtains and flowers all over, and her cooking is marvelous—Graham has never had a storebought cookie in his life. She is wonderful with Graham, a natural mother, Russ thinks, with a heavy sigh. She would make some man a most wonderful wife, but whom can she ever marry?

Russ tries not to think about Deirdre, and for most of the time he succeeds.

Norris Drake has a small dark intense monkey face, or perhaps the face of some exotic cat, with great unblinking yellow eyes. Her features seem all in focus, all concentrated, surrounded by a mass of wild black hair, which is so extremely dark as to be almost blue. And she is a small thin woman, lively, laughing a lot, and talking. She always seems to be moving, doing something—although when she looks at anyone she seems to consider very carefully, to take that person all in. Or if she is only looking at a table, she takes it in, her gaze comprehends the table.

When she first looks at Russ, as they are introduced, he has a sense of never having been before so seen by a woman, or by any person at all. It is not anything as simple or direct as just seeing through him, through all his usual costumes and disguises, his accents. Or not like seeing him naked. Though both these descriptions of her seeing would apply. But it is rather that she seems to see him entirely, all at once, without in any way hinting at her reaction to what she sees. What she has taken in. Although Russ instantly feels certain that she plans to let him know, in one way or another, just what she makes of him.

He is not at all sure how he feels about her.

Before they met, he was sure that the whole thing was just a nuisance—Clyde Drake and his wife coming up for the whole damn weekend, a party. Just when, after long dry weeks and months, his work had begun to be going along almost well. The Kansas play, the pig play, had finally seemed to be moving along, taking on some life; he feels that everything he has seen and thought about for the past ten years or so, the years of the Depression, is contained in this play. He has even been tempted, very tempted, to send a rough draft out to California, to his Hollywood agent, which is something he never does. (His contract specifies that this play, known as "Byrd's next work," go first to Hollywood, rather than starting in New York, as his work more usually did.)

But he knows better, really, than to risk an ignorant agent's look at a rough first draft (they are all deeply ignorant, in Russ's view). Besides, he hasn't even finished that first draft, not really, and he knows what even the most carefully phrased negatives can do to him. And what makes him think that he could count on such careful phrasing? Those guys play rough out there, even rougher than in New York, which is bad enough.

Russ still has a lot of the countryman's distrust of city folk, which is reinforced, much strengthened, by the Southerner's distrust of Yankees, and especially those Yankees in roles of authority: doc-

189

tors, business agents. What could they know, he deeply if half-consciously thinks, about Southern poetry? Which of course would include his plays, essentially.

And then there is Jimmy Hightower's novel, that whole problem. The novel is awful. But Russ is not sure about what kind of awful. If he had written it himself—but that is impossible; he could never in all his born days have written a piece of garbage about early settlers in Oklahoma. Indians. Oil strikes. All that junk. The characters are all one-dimensional, sentimentalized, and, for Russ's money, over-sexed. Which sounds like a surefire best-seller formula, except that it might not be. Russ is not at all sure of his judgment along those lines. And he is certainly not going to voice such an optimistic view to Jimmy, getting his hopes up so cruelly. On the other hand, should he even encourage Jimmy to send it off, to risk a highly possible rejection, and harsh, un-Southern-gentlemanly words?

All that sex. It has certainly made Russ wonder about the actual life of Jimmy. Of course he knows, he would be the first to know, about a writer's fantasies, or actually any man's. Still. He himself, for example, simply does not think all that much about sex; he has never done so, not since he was a boy.

In any case, he does not know what to do about this goddam book, nor about Jimmy himself, whom Russ, despite himself, Russ sort of halfway likes. And the more he likes him, the more tiresome and boring Russ finds him; that is the terrible paradoxical truth of it, a truth indecipherable to anyone but Russ himself (or possibly SallyJane), and even he is not quite sure of its deepest meaning. He is bored by people he likes? It is more interesting to be a little angry, a little disapproving, even?

Does he disapprove of Norris Drake? She walks right in with her case of Cokes, says "Where's the goddam icebox," and comes out of the kitchen swigging from a bottle. As SallyJane later puts it, "She sure gets right down to making herself at home."

Norris stares at Russ again, and she grins her tight monkey grin, and then she says to SallyJane, "Well, I can see from the kitchen that you and me got our work cut out for us. Big party."

As Russ knew she would, SallyJane demurs. "Oh no, I can—I've really got it all organized, much more than it looks." Which Russ also knew was not quite true; poor SallyJane was never organized these days. Their meals were later and later, as SallyJane got slower and more confused. Sometimes his heart could break for SallyJane.

Knowing none of that, though, Norris can be brisk, "No, no, no, I have to help," she says. "Whatever are houseguests for, now I ask you?" And she laughs, low and sexy, a surprising laugh from such a small woman.

And then, according to what SallyJane said later on, she really did help. With incredible speed and efficiency she did everything; she saw whatever was needed to be done and did it, without any directions or any discussion about it.

And the party arrived. All Russ's familiar friends, their familiar smiles and gestures, known voices. Their same old clothes—their costumes. And Russ himself slips back into his part as the host, and

191

his voice takes on his host accents, his hostly laugh, and smile. Genial, very country.

He watches poor pale fat SallyJane taking Norris and Clyde all around, introducing. Poor SallyJane, he can see that she believes herself in love with Clyde, in a sad, defeated hopeless helpless way, and for the first time he wonders: Could SallyJane be truly sick, something organic, not just all that heavy depression in her head? You would think that Clyde Drake would know, or would have noticed if she was sick; he's supposed to be a doctor, isn't he?

Dolly Bigelow, very demure and pretty in pale blue, sits there demurely next to Willard, her eyes dancing along with Clifton, who is getting drunk. Irene Lee is watching Clifton too, for all the good that will do, poor woman. Harry Baird, home from D.C. on a visit, is flirting very unseriously with every single woman in the room, making them all feel prettier, better (how Russ wishes that he could be so light, so unimpeded). And Cynthia Baird, who is beautiful if not exactly virginal in white, is watching, watching everyone and everything that happens. That is a woman whom Russ cannot understand, not at all.

And everywhere there is Norris Drake, flitting through the party like a firefly, in her light yellow silk, cupping her hands with their long crimson nails around the cigarettes that all the men hasten to light for her, her fingers always touching theirs. Observing all this play of fingers, of touches, for no reason Russ shivers.

Norris comes over to him for a drink—she asks for a Coke: why doesn't she drink, or "hold with drinking"? He pours it for her as they exchange an empty look, a smile. But then, just as she is turning to go back to the party, she comes back to Russ, and with no smile at all she stands up on tiptoes, reaching to whisper. Her breath comes silky in his ear. "I want you to fuck me. I really do. You have to."

And then, with a pure social and public smile, she is gone back into the crowd.

Never in his life has Russ heard a woman, any woman whatsoever, utter that word. Its shock is profound, echoing, rippling through his blood. But then he thinks, No, she did not say that. She's a flirt and she teases, but she can't have said *that*. Much less have meant what she said. What could she have said, or meant?

For the rest of that long and eventually drunken party, sober Russ feels a sort of nervous frenzy in his blood, much closer to fear than to desire. But what has he to fear? It is all impossible. What can she do? Besides, she didn't really say that.

For some time now Russ has slept in his study, which is downstairs, almost in a separate wing of that huge house. He sleeps on a narrow cot; its discomfort wakes him from time to time and imparts a sense of monkish virtue, of sacrifice. Upstairs, in their wide deep marital bed, SallyJane sleeps the sleep of the deeply drugged, from which she sometimes cries out, loud and passionate cries, and groans. Impossible now to sleep with SallyJane.

But Russ, all alone, is deeply asleep when at some weird pre-dawn hour he feels again that sultry breath in his ear, and a whisper, "Don't worry, I gave him some of that stuff he fills SallyJane up with—" And then a mouth against his mouth, a small strong tongue forcing it open, darting in.

But not for long—nothing for long. The mouth and the breath move down, slowly down all the length of his naked body, coming at last to his sex—oh Christ! (He has heard about this act, read about it, but no one, not ever...)

Inside her mouth is all wet and slick, and the tongue now moving all around, and back and forth, up and down, until quite suddenly she has moved, changed everything, and is now up and astride him, and it is her place not her mouth that he is inside, her red hot place, as she rides him, rides him, pushing him down, her long nails pressing his arms, until his whole being breaks like a dam, and he is gone.

The silky voice in his ear, louder now, cries out, "*Shit*, I didn't make it, shit, I never do, and it makes me sick, I am sick. I can't even do it to myself." She is sobbing against him.

Russ has never heard a woman say "shit" before.

Chapter 26

"I don't know, honey. I just can't quite seem to get a handle on what Russ thinks I should do."

"But, Jimmy—"

"I know, I'm a grown man and all that. But you know, comes to literature and the publishing business, I'm as ignorant as a field hand. And Russ—well, he was so very helpful. Up to a point. I don't know."

"How's SallyJane doing?"

"I just can't tell you. She sure is putting on weight, and seems to me like a most unhappy lady. She may be a lot on Russ's mind these days. He sure seems, like, distracted."

"And Deirdre Yates too."

"What was that? This long distance, I couldn't hear you."

"I just said, and all those children too. This connection is terrible."

"Anyways, I'm not getting any clues from Russ about how to handle this novel of mine. I just don't know what to do with it."

"Is that psychiatrist still around all the time?"

"Not so much, I don't think. Not since that party."

"Must have been some party."

"Didn't seem like too much at the time. But I don't know. Something's sure changed since then. Up to and including Russ."

"Jimmy, this new friend of mine, this Helen? Her brother's a big shot at some publishing house. I'm just going to ask her what she thinks we should do."

"Well, honey, are you sure?"

"Jimmy darling, good news. I met this brother of Helen's, Stephen Ludwig, and he's real interested in your book. Says he can't promise anything, of course not, not even having seen it. Except a sympathetic reading. Seems he spent some time in Oklahoma a long time ago, and it's my impression he has some romantic memories."

"Must have been a long way back."

"Well, he said why don't you send it on up to him, and then the next time you're up here for a visit you-all could talk."

"Be pretty embarrassing if he doesn't take to it."

Esther hesitates. "I have to admit I thought of that. But you know, he's been in this business all his life. He must have ways of handling situations."

195

Jimmy laughs. "The last thing I want to be is a publishing 'situation.' But I guess I'm old enough to take bad news, if that's how things turn out."

Esther sighs, a sigh that is audible to Jimmy all those hundreds of miles from New York to the middle South. "Things aren't so great around here," she says. "The more it looks like war, the less we think we can get anybody out at all. Already some cities—like Lisbon, for one—are getting totally jammed with folks who want out, and most passages on the big boats are all booked, months ahead of time." She says then, "Jimmy honey, I'm sort of scared. I really wish you'd come on up here, book or not."

"Okay then, that's exactly what I'll do, baby doll. The book's not the most important thing, after all."

But to Jimmy, actually, it is the most important thing. And these two conversations, including his promise to come right on up to New York, have left him uneasy and anxious. Against some cooler and possibly better judgment, he decides to call Russ—who, surprisingly, says why not come over for a Coke later on in the afternoon.

"Things are a little confused around here," Russ begins by explaining. "We seem to have these folks coming up again. Oh, you met them. The doctor Clyde Drake, and his wife, uh, Norris. SallyJane says that she enjoys having them but I'm not at all sure that's true; she just works herself harder and harder, and the maid we've got now is no real help at all. But Ursula, the lady we met in Kansas when I ran over her pig, Ursula's coming out again to stay for a while, and help out—sort of a housekeeper deal. SallyJane's never been able to deal with help and now she's considerably worse. Clyde

Drake says, she doesn't get better soon we'll have to reconsider the shock. But here I am rattling on like a tired old woman about all my personal problems. I guess the truth is, Jimmy, old man, I don't know what to tell you about your novel. These days I can hardly think about my own stuff, much less anyone else's. I've got about as much sense about books as I do about women."

All in all, this was a most remarkable and uncharacteristic speech from Russ, and Jimmy does not know what to make of it. Except to gather that neither Russ nor SallyJane is in very good shape. In different ways, of course. Jimmy senses a certain desperation in Russ; he sees, or hears a man whose life has run out of control, who is helpless among the major passions of women. Helpless and hopeless there in his very large house.

"Well, he can't hurt anything but my feelings, and I'm too old to worry about a thing like that" is how Jimmy put it to Esther, speaking of Stephen Ludwig, the publisher. "So I reckon I'll come on up there, with my manuscript under my arm."

He has not told Esther about his most curious interview with Russ; he will never tell anyone. It occurs to him, strangely, to call Cynthia Baird, and to say that he is worried over Russ, but he decides against it. There are already too many women meddling in Russ's life, Jimmy feels. SallyJane, and this Ursula, coming to be their sort of housekeeper, and now the Norris Drake woman—seems like she's all over the place. He feels that either Esther or Cynthia, or the both of them, would have something sharply accurate to say about Russ, and whatever it would be Jimmy knows that he doesn't want to hear it. Just as he has never even thought of showing his novel to Esther, who reads a lot, and who presumably has good sense about novels, books. As, for that matter, does Cynthia, who also reads all the time. He could not have explained his reluctance to let these women see his book.

Russ was drinking; that was the first surprise, the afternoon when Jimmy went over to see him. Russ was not a drinking man, which was just as well, since he famously had no head for the stuff, none at all. Everyone said that that was one of the reasons SallyJane's father, President Caldwell, did not approve at all of Russ for his daughter. "The man can't hold his liquor, he drinks like a darkie." (He also regretted the fact that Russ was what was called a "self-help" student, which of course meant poor. "You don't have to marry into poor these days," said Ernest Caldwell. "But trust my daughter. Does not have the sense she was born with.") But that afternoon Russ was slopping bourbon into his Coke—sweetening it, as he put it. "You sure you won't have some, Jim, old man?" "I'm sure."

The second surprise was Russ's conversation—or, rather, his monologue.

He was going off to a monastery, Russ told Jimmy, in a blurry, slurred, but intensely serious voice. There was one in California that he had heard about, down near the Mexican border. That would take anyone—"even old sometimes-married Protestants." Just prayers and working in a vegetable garden. Just monks. No women around, not even nuns.

"I have purely and simply got to get away from women. All women. They all play the devil with me, eventually. I can't stand women. They make me crazy. If I could just never see one. The things they say. What they want. Intolerable to a man."

And more like that. Genuinely shocked and upset, Jimmy was relieved to see that no response was expected from him. He was not sure that Russ really knew he was there, or even who he was. He certainly would not have known what to say. "But, Russ, I like women a lot, especially my wife." Under the circumstances that would have sounded ridiculous.

And so, even had he wanted to, which, loyally, he did not, there was no way Jimmy could have described that conversation. To anyone.

Stephen Ludwig looks like a publisher in a movie. Pipe-smoking and handsome, grizzled, ruddy, with the dark red nose of a heavy drinker. And his office is a movie-set book-lined study; in the spaces without books there are etchings, and a few framed photographs of famous writers, just famous enough for Jimmy to recognize their faces.

They shake hands, Jimmy and Stephen Ludwig, and Jimmy is motioned to sit down.

For several moments, which seem very long to Jimmy, they are silent, smiling politely, examining each other. And then Ludwig says something amazing. He says, "To put it mildly, I really liked your book. I think it's—well, terrific. A little work here and there, but nothing major. I hesitate to say this, but I just think we might have a very, very big success on our hands."

Jimmy is there in Ludwig's office for at least another half hour, but that is all of the conversation that he can recall, as he later tries to put it all together and tell Esther.

They are sitting on the terrace of the Hotel Brevoort, on lower Fifth Avenue.

"He said he'd only read it once so far," Jimmy adds to his recital. "But that's going pretty far out on a limb, wouldn't you say? To go as far as he did? I mean, he can't afford to talk like that to every person who sends him in a book."

Even as he says this, though, all these self-congratulatory, self-reassuring sentences, and as Esther responds with a pleasure that is surely genuine, Jimmy has a strong sense of unreality. Even their setting, this attractive restaurant in an expensive neighborhood, where well-dressed couples are out walking their dogs or just walking home, enjoying the warm clear spring night—all this seems as unreal as Stephen Ludwig, with his tweeds and his writer photographs, his pipe and (it seems to Jimmy) his farfetched optimism. None of it quite makes sense; it doesn't mesh with what Jimmy thinks of as his real life, though he would find it hard to define that either; he hasn't been near the oil fields of his young manhood for many years. But all that has happened today has seemed more like a movie, *Jimmy Hightower Goes to New York*, one in which he is not entirely comfortable. It would be better for Jimmy Stewart, Gary Cooper. One of those very tall guys.

He even has this aberrant and quite unusual thought: Do I really want to be a successful writer? Lord, just look at Russ. Russ, who might have been much happier as a small-town college professor, with maybe a play of his put on every now and then by the local company, and poems published in some quiet places, the *Sewanee Review*, the *Virginia Quarterly* (Jimmy can suddenly see this very clearly, as if it were another movie, another life of

Russell Byrd). Does he, Jimmy, want all that money and fame, that kind of success, when he probably should have stayed home and tended his garden, and his investments?

He says to Esther, "It still could all not happen—you know that as well as I do. Just this one fellow's starting enthusiasm."

"Of course. And I think you're very, very wise not to take him too seriously." Esther, despite her new cloche hat over smartly bobbed short hair, and her pretty spring navy silk dress, still seems to mirror Jimmy's own suddenly downward mood; she looks out of place in this handsome, festive, pre-dinner crowd in New York. As out of place as he himself feels.

They talk then for a while about other things, of their daughters and schools, new friends of Esther's here in New York, and Esther's work. But as they talk Jimmy finds himself more and more aware of the mood of the crowd around them, there on the terrace and passing on the sidewalk. It is a festive crowd, on the whole, but Jimmy senses somewhere an edge of panic—or hysteria, perhaps—in the midst of celebration. At first he attributes this insight to his own private mood of joy mixed with apprehension; but then he thinks, No, it's not just me. We're on the edge of a war, and no one knows how it will go, and we're really scared, all of us.

"How did you leave it with Stephen Ludwig, finally?" Esther asks.

"He's going to present it, discuss it with the other editors and the money people, I guess he means," Jimmy tells her. And then, wanting not to talk about all that, he asks, "How about it? Warm enough for dinner out here, do you think?"

"Sure, it's plenty warm. And Helen says the lobster salad here is terrific." She pauses, looking in a questioning way at Jimmy. "Something about the weather, though. It really makes me miss Pinehill, a lot."

Her eyes are so serious, dark and intense.

And knowing that she meant at least in part that she misses him, Jimmy's heart warms to her, and he says what she could never say to him. "I've missed you," he tells her. "A lot."

With a sort of relief, an emotional moment over, Esther laughs, and she asks him, "But how will we ever get the Bairds to leave our house?"

He laughs too, as he says, "It's not funny, really. I've thought about that. It's a funny situation we've got ourselves into. All my fault, actually."

"Very funny. Really not your fault, though."

Jimmy tries: "But maybe Cynthia will end up in Washington with Harry."

"I doubt that. I think she'd rather end up in Pinehill with Russ."

"Esther, whatever—?"

But Esther is given to such gnomic utterances, which he knows that she will never explain. He knows too that she does not mean "end up with Russ" in any ordinary sense.

Now she smiles, still ambiguously, and she says, "It'll be interesting to see how Russ takes all your success."

"Yes—" It had not before seriously occurred to Jimmy that Russ would be anything but pleased, but now he instantly and clearly sees that might well not be the case. Of course not. And he thinks, as he has before, how subtle women are; Esther is an especially subtle woman, he thinks.

He thinks then (another familiar thought) of

how much he just plain likes women (how glad he is to be unlike Russ in that way!). He does not only love them romantically, and for sex, although God knows a lot of that is mixed in usually, but he likes them for friendship and conversation. Talking to a woman is often like reading a very good book. And Esther, thank God, is really the most interesting of all.

But still he tells her, as though in reproof, "We'll see about that when it happens. My big success, and how Russ takes it."

Chapter 27

To Cynthia the Southern spring feels heavy; her blood is turgid, weighted. Such exuberance of bloom, such too rich smells of earth and flowers, and pines—the sweet sharp sun-heated smell of pines is everywhere, as inescapable as honeysuckle vines, and the smells of their sweet small flowers.

New England springs were cleaner, crisper, and more spare. Clean clear fast brooks, translucent, over smooth brown polished rocks, instead of dirty slow mud creeks, bordered with coarse gray sand and carrying heavily their freights of trash.

Almost overnight, it seems to her, a great circle of daffodils has sprung up in the side yard, near the porch, and out in the woods behind her house (which is not her house, of course) the bursting of dogwood seems wild, uncontrolled. Out there in the woods she finds wild iris, yellow dogtooth violets among the thin dead leaves.

Such bountiful activity on the part of nature makes Cynthia feel lonely, somehow. Lonely and also ungrateful: she knows that what she is seeing is wonderfully beautiful, all that generous bloom, at which everyone seems to marvel. "Such a lovely spring, seems like every year it gets more beautiful." That is what everyone is saying, and is probably true.

But I won't be around to see it another year, is Cynthia's involuntary thought—by which she does not mean that she will have died; her revulsion does not go so far. Rather, it expresses the vague thought of her being somewhere else. Maybe Connecticut? Maybe Georgetown, which Harry says she would surely love?

Cynthia wonders: Would Georgetown be as cheap as Pinehill is? In Pinehill they have not felt as rich, as "comfortable," as they had hoped, but at least certain Connecticut expenses are missing: the trips to New York, which, even when they stayed with friends and ate out cheaply, always turned out to be murderous on the budget; club memberships—there are no country clubs in Pinehill; and clothes—both Cynthia and Harry have spent the year in last year's (or earlier) clothes, feeling themselves to be very smart indeed, and Cynthia ordered all Abby's clothes from Best's, the Lilliputian Bazaar, where she had a charge account (if things got really bad, she could always switch to Altman's, Cynthia thought). Georgetown, even with Harry's new paycheck, looked very dear, and some clear instinct informed Cynthia that they could get into familiar forms of trouble there, clothes and parties and a houseful of flowers. Expensive friends. Not to mention clubs and a private school (surely necessary, there?) for Abby.

Harry has pointed out that in Georgetown at least they would not be running two households, not to mention commuting to see each other.

And the long-distance calls. All of which was very logical. Still.

In the meantime Cynthia endures the heady spring, staying mostly indoors.

"How you can stay inside on a day like this just does beat all" is Dolly's opening sally. She has arrived one especially hot May morning for a sandwich and some iced tea. Dolly, in white piqué and perfectly whitened sandals, and stockings; even on the hottest days, Southern women of Dolly's ilk would always wear stockings.

"It is beautiful out," Cynthia murmurs softly. She notes that she is becoming almost as quiet, as compulsively polite as a Southern woman.

Dolly is looking especially pleased with herself. She has an air of someone with barely contained good news. It is impossible, though, to ask directly; as Cynthia has learned, that is simply not done. And so first Dolly admires Cynthia's dress ("That bare-arm look is so young! You could be some Hollywood starlet") and the cut flowers in her house ("Whoever would have thought of putting sweet peas and nasturtiums together in that same little vase?"), and Cynthia in her turn exclaims and admires, and it is quite a while before Dolly gets to it, and says to Cynthia, "Well, I finally saw Missus Odessa Jones. I took myself right over to the laundry."

"Oh, really?" I thought I was the one to see Odessa, Cynthia does not say. "Uh, how is she?"

"Oh, uppity as ever, if not more so." Dolly sniffs. "But I threw out some bait. I said like as how we were going to have this little store and all, and when I said that I could see those old black eyes light up. She really took to that idea, I could tell."

Cynthia's agile mind has begun to race. She can

205

so easily picture the scene between Dolly and Odessa, out on the sidewalk next to the laundry; Dolly would have had to make it look like a casual encounter. "Well, Odessa, for heaven's sake, how're you doing these days? How's your family?" Tall strong awkward Odessa, bending down a little, and small graceful Dolly, looking up and chirping, like a sparrow.

As though to confirm that fantasy, Dolly at that moment says, "...and you know her daughter Nelly? The one she likes so much? Well, Nelly's going to come and work for me!"

In ways at first indefinable to herself, this bulk of news is very saddening to Cynthia. Even as she is saying to Dolly, "Oh, how wonderful" (as though she were as Southern as Dolly), and is listening to plans for the store (of course Cynthia will be a partner, they'll work out all the details on that, and the main thing is "We'll just have the best old time!") and to Dolly's joy and triumph at the acquisition of Nelly ("...she's young but I can train her to do things just my way, she won't be as stubborn as her mother always was. Not that I'm not deeply fond of Odessa. You know that, honey").

At first, introspective and sometimes dark-minded, Cynthia accuses herself of a simple sort of schoolgirl jealousy; plans were made behind her back, reuniting Dolly and Odessa, and Cynthia felt left out. If so, she can accept this possible reaction as being silly, but not exactly reprehensible. In any case, she is aware of other, stronger, and more complex feelings. Which, finally, that afternoon after Dolly has gone, she is more or less able to sort out.

And she sees, at last, how deeply pleased she

was on first hearing about Odessa's defiance of Dolly. Not because of anti-Dolly feelings of her own, but really because of the originality, the sheer *unusualness* of Odessa's act, her quitting her job with Dolly. In a curious way, only half-conscious at the time, she has been cheering for Odessa, and now, to have Nelly, Odessa's youngest and most loved child, thrust back into the mold—it is that that is deeply distressing to Cynthia. And even as she comes to this awareness, she is aware too of a sudden lurking evil thought: she thinks, Maybe it just won't work out. Maybe Nelly won't want to do everything as Dolly says to, and maybe she can get herself a better job somewhere else. Maybe at the defense plant.

"And maybe a Negro woman will be elected our next President," says Harry, later, as Cynthia tells him about the visit from Dolly. The news and her own hopeful speculations.

"Oh, Harry, I know. But still."

"Please be a little more realistic, baby. Most people would say that Nelly's lucky to get the job with Dolly. For one thing, she pays a lot better than most people in that town. Curiously enough."

"Most people down here are Southern too. Oh, it's so odd the way they do things. I mean, all the fuss that Dolly made. It was ludicrous, really. About our store selling things made by both colored and white women. And now, with no conversation about it at all, that's all taken care of. I could have argued until I was blue in the face."

"You're right there, absolutely. They don't believe in discussion. 'Don't hold with it,' as they would say."

"It's so interesting, the difference between Southern and New England reticence," muses

Cynthia. "Southern is so much more intricate, elaborate, don't you think?"

"You might even say hidden."

"Certainly submerged. But I am glad we're going ahead with the store. Or I guess I am."

"You'll need some extra money, won't you, Cyn?"

"Well, I guess—"

"I just happen to have quite a lot. Consider it my investment."

A day or so after Dolly's visit, and her subsequent conversation with Harry, Cynthia decides that she will, after all, venture out for a walk in the woods.

But the very air is too much for her. All the smells hang as rich as honey in the clear blue oxygen, thickening her breath, congealing in her lungs. No wonder everyone down here speaks and walks (it sometimes seems) so slowly, thinks Cynthia. The air is noisy too, as well as over-laden with scent. Everywhere birds sing, leaves rustle against each other, and higher up, in the blue, a light wind sings in the pines.

Somewhere she hears a faint sound of water. And somewhere—people talking? A girl's light laugh?

Not wanting to be seen, nor to see anyone at all, especially anyone she knows, Cynthia slowly and quietly turns and retraces her steps. She has not come far.

But too late.

There on a side path, half hidden by a giant bush of some indeterminate lush white flowers, are Russ Byrd and Norris Drake. The instant before seeing Cynthia, hearing her steps, they have been laughing into each other's faces as he holds a branch for her to pass, thus protecting her smooth white vulnerable bare legs. Norris is wearing very short pale blue shorts, at the bottoms of which can be seen the smallest line of white lace, a hint of luxurious lingerie.

They are all embarrassed. The suddenness of it: there the three of them are, confronted with each other, Cynthia having inadvertently interrupted the walk of the other two. Interrupted whatever they were saying, doing together. And so there is nothing for it but that they all must laugh, as though this encounter were funny, and not an embarrassment.

"We were just—" begins Russ.

"I *would* wear shorts, through all these brambles," Norris manages to say. "Clyde's right, I have no *sense*." Mock despair and hysterical self-approval choke her voice.

"I always forget we live so close together," says Cynthia. And then, "Actually I was just heading home."

"Too hot for you?" Russ asks, with equal emptiness.

"Oh yes, much too hot. You know how we Yankees are."

They all laugh again, and they manage, at that, to separate, Russ and Norris continuing to wherever. And Cynthia back to her house, which of course is not her house but Jimmy and Esther's.

Abby is never at home these days, in the afternoons after school, and Cynthia, who has returned to the house for a glass of iced tea in the kitchen, finds herself wishing that her daughter was indeed at home. The encounter with Russ and Norris has left her uneasy. She needs the corrective of a conversation with Abby about her school. What various other children are doing for the summer; Abby is going up to a camp near Asheville, with Betsy Lee and the Hightower girls, some others.

But Abby is not there, and Cynthia sits alone with her tea. With her puzzled, puzzling thoughts, and with no one to tell them to. Even had she known just what she would say.

Chapter 28

Strangely, since SallyJane is a Southern woman, grew up in the South, and thus should be used to its seasons, she reacts to this particular spring very much as Cynthia does, though more intensely. She feels that it is all too much for her, and she stays indoors. She spends a great deal of time in bed. There seems to be a sort of unspoken family understanding that this is what she does. Ursula copes with the marketing (she very much enjoys the Cadillac) and the meals, and mostly she copes with the children, who from time to time pay small and somewhat perfunctory visits to their mother, in her room.

Melanctha, especially, comes to visit. She complains of her breasts. "Why do I have to get them? They're sore, and the boys all tease me. Abby Baird doesn't have any at all, and Betsy's you can't even see. Why do I? We're all the same age."

Because you're my daughter, you've inherited breasts from me. SallyJane does not say this, but only murmurs comfort. But having always disliked her own breasts, she can hardly bear to imagine Melanctha's life, in a body very much like hers. Though Melanctha now is thin and dark, like Russ—with small but quite visible breasts. She is also brilliant and cross like Russ, thinks SallyJane.

"Boys tease you because they like you and they don't know how else to express it," she tells her daughter. "Men are like that too. It's harder for them to talk. I don't know why."

"Archer Bigelow has a crush on Abby Baird and she can't stand him," Melanctha reports. "Would you like to see a poem I wrote? I got an A."

"Oh yes, I'd love to."

"I'll go get it."

And you'll never be old and terribly fat, and every day more sad and more fat, thinks SallyJane, like a prayer.

On weekends, often the Drakes still come up to visit, and sometimes SallyJane comes down to dinner with them all, sometimes not.

Often, on those weekend afternoons, Russ and Norris go out for a walk somewhere. Probably off kissing in the woods. Maybe more. Thinking of this, and pretty well knowing what they are up to, SallyJane thinks, Well, fine. But she hopes the children don't find out about it. Or Deirdre Yates— she does not want her children to know about Deirdre.

Clyde Drake comes up and into her room to talk, looking sad. SallyJane believes that he is not sad about Norris and Russ; it's all right with him too, she thinks. They both know it will end very soon, and not well. The old phrase "no love lost" between those two applies; without saying it she and Clyde both know this. Norris and Russ do not truly love, nor even like each other.

Clyde talks mostly about himself. "Maybe it's being around Russ so much, and getting to know him," he tells her. "But I do think a lot these days about the book I could write. Or maybe it should be a play. You ever write any poems, SallyJane, or anything?"

She lies. "No, I—" Actually she used to write dozens of poems, all carefully hidden from Russ. From everyone.

Clyde continues. "I have these ideas, a lot of them, you couldn't ever believe." His voice becomes low, confiding. "What I really think about Dr. Freud, for example. An old fake, is what I believe. Drew all his conclusions from these rich Jewish ladies. Viennese, who are crazy. I can tell you that from experience of my own. I've had a couple come down as patients—friends of mine from med school sent them along. You know, the refugees? Crazy women. My impression was half the time they were telling lies. And so hard to understand, with that *accent*. You know what I truly think? All this talking therapy, so-called, this so-called psychoanalytic approach is just not any good at all. What proof does anyone have? I just don't see how a person's childhood has any bearing at all on what that person turns into as an adult. Why, my very own parents did certain things to me, of a personal nature, that no one would ever believe, and that I would never reveal to a living soul, I've got no call to. I certainly don't encourage my patients to talk along those lines, as you very well know, my darling little Sal. To me there's a lot less difference than anyone seems to think between a mental and a physical illness. Your depression, now, has a lot of the very same symptoms as a very bad case of the flu, now wouldn't you say?"

"I don't know. I suppose—" But people do not

get fat with the flu. Or do they? I will have to ask Ursula, thinks SallyJane. She's very good on medical things, and she likes to talk about them.

To SallyJane depression is heaviness, and so it makes a certain sense to her that she should be so fat. So fat and getting constantly fatter. She is too heavy to think; various thoughts, like the thought of Russ, move slowly toward her mind, as ponderous and clumsy as elephants, but they never quite arrive, those thoughts. She thinks, Russ and Norris, but she does not really think of them; the whole thought never quite makes it into her mind. It is not like the stabbing, excited thoughts that she once had about Russ and Deirdre Yates. She is no longer that thin, excited, and exhausted person, so vulnerable to Russ; she is much too fat to be vulnerable these days. And her head feels much heavier than any other part of her, as though it too had gained weight, enormously. She cannot think about Russ, or Russ and Norris. Or Russ and Deirdre. Nor can she think about her children. All their needs.

In the meantime Clyde Drake goes on talking. "That's why this shock treatment we're using now works so well," he says to SallyJane, somewhat out of context. "Fight fire with fire, so to speak. Treat a physical fact with a thoroughly physical fact. A jolt. Jolt it right out of the ring."

He has said more or less this same thing several times. SallyJane understands that he is telling her that he wants her to have shock treatment, but in some way he is afraid to tell her so. Is he afraid of what the shock will do to her, but does not know that he is afraid?

She asks him, "Did it ever kill anyone, this treatment?"

"Of course not. How could it?" He stares at her. "There was one case I heard about up in Boston, but that was a person with a heart defect. Properly administered, no risk at all."

My heart is probably not so good, with all this fat, thinks SallyJane. Very likely the shock will kill me. And then she thinks, Good, that will save me the trouble of suicide.

Which makes her begin to laugh. She laughs and laughs. She is aware that Clyde is staring at her, that he is disturbed, but still she can't stop.

Chapter 29

"Washington's already at war. Last night in the Shoreham, nothing but uniforms. I don't care what Roosevelt says, we're in this war. And I have to admit, it's pretty goddam exciting. Cynthia, you've got to be up here. I miss you terrifically, to put it mildly. I don't want you as my distant pin-up girl, I want you here. And there's some houses in Georgetown, you'd really like them. Lots of style. This is crazy, the way we're living now. We wanted to be young and rich again, and we did get away from all that bad stuff in Connecticut, and now we're almost rich and we're still pretty young, and God knows we're both good-looking, and we're not even living in the same town. Think about it. It does not make sense. Last weekend was terrific, but I don't want you just on week-ends. Christ! you're my wife. I'll bet the Hightowers would like to come back to their house. Just ask old Jimmy. And D.C. is full of good girls' schools, even if it does have to be private. We can afford that now. Please, darling Cynthia.

I'm not dumb enough to give you an ultimatum, but think about it. If this keeps up, we could both end up having stupid love affairs, and wrecking everything. People do. That's not a threat, exactly. But. The real point is that I need you. And you'd like it here. And I love you. I want you. I miss you."

Certainly that very strong missive from Washington gave Cynthia a great deal to think about. And, chiding herself even as she did so, she focused on last points first. "We could end up having stupid love affairs." Did that mean that Harry had someone in mind? Was he warning her, or possibly telling her that he had already fallen in love, or at least had a crush on someone? All these thoughts were quite intolerable to Cynthia. (Although, she had to admit, they were dimly, inadmissibly exciting.) And so she forced herself to hear the more positive notes: I miss you, I love you.

Georgetown, though. For reasons that she cannot entirely fathom, Cynthia finds the idea of a move to Georgetown very frightening. She is filled with a sort of stage fright at the prospect, a fear that she does not remember experiencing on the move down to Pinehill. But that had to do, in part, with a difference in scale: they were moving from the much larger Connecticut–New York arena to a very small town, a pond in which they hoped to be big frogs. And they mostly succeeded, Cynthia felt; they had had a certain impact, that was clear. But to move to Washington would be to walk out onto a very large, very crowded, and important stage indeed.

They could easily get back into some of the same old Connecticut troubles, debts and drinks, and damaging flirtations.

But even as she thinks all this, as she takes these

negative soundings on the move, Cynthia understands that in this curious way she is actually preparing to go. She has to: D.C. is where Harry is, and she wants to be with him, she wants the marriage. She really does not like the time that she spends alone in Pinehill, despite certain friendships (she is thinking especially of Dolly and of Jimmy) and the comforts of their borrowed house. Nor does she like, at all, the idea of handsome Harry alone in Washington.

She does wonder about all these private schools for Abby, who is just beginning to be happy in the local public school. Or so it seems to her mother. She is very involved with friends, and even getting good grades. Such a relief, when the first few months she seemed so lonely and isolated, so angry at her parents for having brought her down there. All that business about wanting to go to a Negro school: Cynthia is fairly sure that there will be no Negroes in the private schools that Harry has in mind.

"I will not move to Washington," Abby is shrieking, her blond face red, tears flying. "I won't! You and Harry go, I'll stay here. I could live with Deirdre and Graham, they have an extra room. Or with Melanctha and her parents, they've got lots of extra rooms."

"But, Abby, we're your parents, we want you—"

"You do not, you're selfish, you don't care where I am. You just want to be together, and you want a lot of money and new friends."

"Abby, you're being extremely unfair, not to mention rude."

"Rude! That's what you say about anything you

don't like. I could be a lot ruder if I wanted to. I won't go!"

Terribly hurt, and almost as angry as she is wounded, Cynthia still manages some control as she thinks: How dare she? What does she know?— this eleven-year-old. She does not cry (Cynthia does not, not until she is alone, later on), she does not yell back in response. She says, "Abby, I think we should discuss this later. Besides, nothing is really decided yet." That is all she says at the time. But in her own voice she has heard the most frightening echoes of her mother's voice, sounds of the late Edith Stone Cromwell, saying to the child Cynthia, about almost anything at all, icily, "We'll discuss this later."

"I'm going over to Melanctha's *now*." And Abby is out the front door, unaware that her mother is running upstairs to fling herself upon her bed.

Half an hour later, her face washed, sitting in the kitchen with a cup of tea, and thinking as rationally as she can about her daughter, Cynthia notes that Abby sounded both much older and much younger than she actually is: she was like a passionate adolescent, shouting for freedom and her own friends, her own school, and at the same time she was like a two-year-old, in a tantrum, protesting life. And that is exactly where Abby is, she reflects; she is poised between childhood and adolescence, and she is stuck there, for the moment. A year or so ago she was a child, in a couple of years she will be an adolescent, dear God, with all those complications.

The phone begins to ring.

"Jimmy, how nice! Well, Jimmy, what great news, that's absolutely marvelous! When does it come out? I literally can't wait. Esther must be thrilled.

Well, of course, in fact Harry and I have been talking about just that. But, Jimmy, anytime you want, you know that. You and Esther have been so terrifically generous. Jimmy, this is crazy but Dolly Bigelow's ringing at the front door. Listen, can I tell? Jimmy, I'll call you tonight. Congratulations!"

And so it is to Dolly, as they drive along in her upright trim green Ford, that Cynthia first tells the great news about Jimmy. "His novel's been accepted by this big New York publishing house. Esther knew someone's brother there. Some connection."

"Jewish people always seem to have these connections. Usually family. Have you noticed?"

"Dolly, really. No. It's got nothing to do with Esther, finally. It's Jimmy's book. I think it's just so wonderful. You know how much he cares about being a writer."

"Well, I don't know as I do. Seems like a big change for an oilman from Oklahoma. Maybe too much of a change."

"I think that's part of the point. He wanted a change." But Cynthia gives it up—hopeless to explain such an impulse to Dolly, even if she were sure she quite understood it herself. However, even not quite understanding, possibly, she has grasped the intensity of Jimmy's wish, his longing to have a published book. A best-seller, he hopes.

Cynthia thinks with great warmth then of Jimmy, her friend. She reflects that it is interesting, their transition from a semi-semi-flirtation to the status and sentiments of old friends. In less than a year.

Partly to punish Dolly (she very much dislikes these small remarks about Jews, and especially now, with Esther, and everything that's happening in Germany), Cynthia continues, "And it looks like Esther and Jimmy are anxious to come back to town. So it looks like it's Georgetown for me and Harry."

"But you-all could just do another house switch, you three Bairds move back to the Inn and Jimmy and Esther and the girls back to their home. Heaven knows you've improved it some."

Looking over at Dolly as she says all this, Cynthia is astonished to see real tears in those bright black eyes, as she is to hear a tremor in that voice. She is touched, and also quite unable to respond in kind.

And so she answers briskly, "Well, it won't be for quite a while. And don't you worry, if we do go, we'll be back to visit all the time. You'll get so bored with us you'll wish we'd never—"

And Dolly recovers, as quickly. "We just might come up to visit D.C. Now, wouldn't that be something? Willard's got a bunch of cousins up there, and we haven't seen them for—oh, forever!"

The weather in the countryside through which they are driving, on their way out to see Dolly's relative who sews, has suddenly changed: what was a clear light May blue has become a heavy dark menacing gray. Storm air.

Dolly asks, "You scared of thunderstorms?"

"No, I never have been."

"I am, I'm here to tell you. I just hope we get there first."

"I read somewhere that a car is the safest place to be."

"It better—"

Because the storm is suddenly upon them. Thick lashing rain across the windshield, and a cover of black clouds across the sky. Heavy thunder growls like jungle animals in the distance, and for an instant a quick streak of lightning splits the sky.

Dolly shrieks, "Oh Lord God!"

"Just pull over, don't try to drive in all this."

Almost as soon as they are halted there, precariously, on the red clay shoulder of the highway, the storm begins to clear. The rain lets up and becomes a gentle patter. The black clouds part, like great bulls moving aside, to reveal a clear blue sky.

"Ooooo-eeeee!" is Dolly's comment. "At least that was a real quick one. I remember some summers down in Mississippi, those great big storms that went on for hours. All of us children hiding under the beds."

The cousin's house, reached shortly after the storm has ceased, is large and spreading, surrounded by a deep veranda on which there are swings and hammocks. The yard is bare, except for a bed of hyacinths next to the house, and a clump of blue hydrangeas at the steps. "Lillian never did know the first thing about flowers," Dolly whispers to Cynthia as together they mount the stairs. "I used to tease her about her black thumb, drives her crazy!" She chuckles with satisfaction.

But: "Your hydrangeas are just the loveliest things!" is the first thing that Dolly says to her cousin. "I never could get mine to grow so full."

The cousin, Lillian, is as tall and pale as Dolly is small and dark. And her house is large and pale and immaculately, shiningly clean; Cynthia finds it hard to believe that children and a working tobacco-farmer husband live here too. Hard to believe in fact that this porcelain woman has ever been touched by the man or by a child, with her perfect skin and long smooth sculptured hands.

Dolly and Cynthia are ushered into what must be the parlor, a shaded room in which all the furniture is upholstered in green velour, like a train. As they sit down, Cynthia observes Lillian taking careful note of the floor behind them, as though they might have tracked in dirt.

Her napkins and doilies are spread out on a card table in the middle of the floor.

Fortunately, since Lillian seems extremely shy of Cynthia, unwilling to smile or to make any sort of contact, Dolly keeps up her steady prattle. "The most wonderful things, honestly, Lil. You must have almost put your eyes out working on these little bitty cocktail napkins. And the lace on these pillow slips! You just don't see this kind of work anymore, not anywhere."

Cynthia reports that night to Harry. "What was so interesting," she tells him, "was not one word about the old sore issue, selling things in the same store with Negro women. Not one word, after all that hysteria."

"Maybe she and Dolly settled that between themselves."

"Maybe, but somehow I don't think so. My hunch is that they just stopped talking about it, and sugared the whole problem over, like frosting on a cake. Southern women!—honestly."

Harry laughs, and then he says, "It could be the money. It really could. The idea of earning any at all. Don't forget, we're still in a depression."

"You're probably right. But her stuff is really incredible. Lillian's. I think my grandmother did things like that. Remember the sets of linen hand towels we used to have?"

"Not exactly."

"Well, good. I felt terrible when they got lost in the laundry. Anyway, it was a very strange day, all in all. But isn't that good news about Jimmy Hightower?"

"Terrific. And the best part is that they want their house back. I'll be down next weekend, and we can start to plan."

"Yes, and you can talk to Abby. Oh, I forgot to tell you the bad news. SallyJane's back down at Clyde Drake's."

Chapter 30

If SallyJane dies, I will marry Deirdre Yates, thinks Russell Byrd, miserably.

If she dies, I will run off to Mexico with Norris Drake.

I will have a terrific affair with Cynthia Baird.

He thinks, If SallyJane dies, I'll die.

I must stop this. It's only the rain, and the blackness, he thinks.

For this is a strange dark rainy day in June, the hot air all stifled with blanketing black clouds, the woods and flowers and even the birds immobilized. If he were in California, Russ imagines, everyone would be saying it was earthquake weather, remembering the big one, in Long Beach, in '33. But here in Pinehill there isn't going to be an earthquake. There's not going to be anything.

Against his better judgment, he has sent off a draft of his long verse drama, the Kansas pig story, to Oscar, the Hollywood agent. Sent it off knowing that he should not. Knowing that nothing good but only destruction will come of Oscar's reading it. And now whenever the phone rings he imagines that it is Oscar, with bad news.

Or Clyde Drake, with bad news of SallyJane.

For that too was against his better judgment, sending SallyJane back to stay with Clyde. To have the shock treatment that Clyde is so confident will work. Finally. Russ does not think it will work; he does not think that SallyJane's huge sorrow, her heavy sadness could be blasted off with shock. He is often tempted to call Clyde Drake and say, Don't do it. You must not tamper with my SallyJane in that way. Let her be as sad as she wants, if that is what is necessary for her now. Besides, it sounds dangerous.

But he does not call Drake, prevented both by his own sad lassitude and by a helpless sense that a doctor must know more than he knows, mustn't he? Otherwise what is medicine all about, anyway? Psychiatry. Healing the mind.

There will not be an earthquake, of course not, but there will be important news today: Russ is suddenly convinced of that.

News to avoid. He is frightened.

He would like to go out now, to walk and walk, out of range of the telephone. Tell Ursula just not to answer. At the very moment, though, when he has half risen to get up from his desk and go out, the rain increases, pounding down on the roof and against the long window-panes, fast and furiously. Russ stands there watching, transfixed, half wondering if the glass might break—as out in the yard the quince bushes flail about, blossoms scattered and mashed to the ground. As the pine boughs sag and moan.

As the telephone rings.

He cannot answer. His heart jumps, missing beats. Panic. He does answer.

"Long distance. A call for Mr. Russell Byrd."

"Yes. Yes."

Then the clear nasal voice of Oscar the agent, from California. "Hey, Russ, ole boy, how're you-all doin' down there? Pretty good? Right fair?"

Oscar prides himself on his repertoire of accents; he especially likes this Southern hick voice, which afflicts Russ like fingernails on a blackboard, or worse: it is horrible. But, "I'm fine," says Russ, who along with repulsion is experiencing a certain relief: it is only Oscar, who can only talk about work, nothing more serious. Nothing about SallyJane. Russ adds, "It's raining."

"Well, like the song says, it never rains in California, and we could sure use some rain. Now, Russ, ole boy, about this play of yours. This pig thing. Boy, I have to give it to you straight. It just won't work. Or not for us it won't work. You might could take it to Broadway and have a big hit on your hands. Maybe set it to music. Americana stuff. It might be the greatest thing since the zipper. But not out here. It won't go."

He talks on for quite a while, and Russ listens with a curious mixture of boredom, irritation, and relief. Relief that he won't, after all, have to go out there and do all that again. Deform his pig play and go to all those drinking-swimming parties (Russ does not swim). Smile and use his accent as a weapon, simultaneously seducing people and fending them off. His play is his again, in no one's power but his own. Too bad about the money, and he needs it, with SallyJane down there at expensive Clyde's. But he can think about money later.

By the time they have said goodbye, and Oscar has hung up and gone off somewhere, the rain has stopped too, and Russ can go out. As he does so, he calls out to Ursula, "Just don't answer the phone, all right?"

Everything is wet: the ground, its detritus of dead leaves and dead pine needles, all soggy, and wet boughs thrust against Russ's shoulders as he moves along the narrow path, in the woods behind and around his house. He is walking fast but aimlessly, with no special direction. The rain will soon begin again. He wants to walk as much as possible before the deluge.

His sense of relief at Oscar's phone call continues, and he regards this sense with wonder and curiosity. I won't be so rich anymore, he thinks, and then he thinks, *Good,* I was never cut out for Cadillacs, all those fancy trimmings. I don't ever want to cross this country again. I don't want to leave here, this tiny little postage stamp of the South. I don't want to see anyone I don't already know. I want everything to be like it always was, with the children. And SallyJane. Everyone in place.

The woods are loud now with rustlings, drippings from leaves and needles, and the sound of brave single emergent birds. The possible scurrying of small animals. Thank God Clyde isn't here, I don't have to shoot them, is one of the things that Russ thinks. He does not really want to see Clyde anymore, it comes to him in the wake of that hunting thought. And then he thinks, Nor Norris either (he shudders involuntarily as he thinks her name). She's a mean woman, and crazy. A witch. Depraved.

Somewhere in the woods ahead of him a flash of yellow sends alarm. He thinks, Could Norris—? He stops in his tracks, and is standing there halted, scowling, when Cynthia Baird walks toward him, in a yellow slicker.

She asks, "Did I scare you? You scared me." There is rain on her face.

He lies, "No, I wasn't scared, just curious." He smiles very slowly, and the smile remains on his face.

"You could have been some man with a gun!"

"I don't ever carry a gun, unless I'm forced to by some damn-fool company. Some man thinks he has to hunt."

"Oh."

Having both stopped for this encounter, automatically they now start up again, only now they move in the same direction. Russ leading, she following. Slowly.

He turns back and says to her, "It'll rain again soon. You want to stop and have a cigarette before it does?"

"Oh yes, I love smoking outdoors. It tastes all different, and the smell."

They go through the business of his taking out cigarettes, her taking one, and his lighting it for her. Her touch on his hands is feather soft, and smooth.

In a conversational way she says, "Odd I should run into you. I was just thinking of you."

"Oh?"

"Actually I was thinking about Southern voices." She laughs, having robbed "I was thinking of you" of romance.

"Oh." Of course he is disappointed, but still wants to know. "Southern voices?"

"Yes. I guess I mean accents. Southern people all seem to have several. Dolly, for instance, has three that I've heard. There's one that she uses with me, for instance, and quite another for Willard, or at parties—that's a younger voice. And then when she talks to Odessa, or some country person in a store, there's still another."

"And I? Do I have a lot of voices?"

"Oh, you have more than anyone," she says, her own voice full of what sounds like love. "But you must know that."

They look at each other for an instant, and then break the look.

Cynthia's slicker must be an old one of Harry's, all belted and twice the size of her thin body, which only serves to emphasize her thinness, like a child dressed up. Her pale face is bare, washed clean; in the strange yellow stormy light she glows, her eyes wide and luminously green.

With no warning the rain just then starts up again, pelting down noisily on the leaves, through branches. Onto the hair and faces of both Russ and Cynthia.

"My house is nearer," says Russ. "Come on."

He grasps her hand, but pulling her along behind him is impossible—there is no room for them both on the narrow path. In a few minutes, though, they have reached his house, gone in through the back door, through the kitchen, and are taking off and shaking outer garments. Laughing together. From another room somewhere they can hear Ursula and the vacuum cleaner.

They go into the living room. His own room, suddenly unfamiliar to Russ, with Cynthia at its center. Cynthia, now in her ribbed white sweater and faded blue jeans, like a skinny sailor. He asks,

"Can I make you some tea?" and he laughs, as he adds, "Ma'am?"

"I'd love that," and she crosses the room to sit down on a cracked red leather sofa, crossing her bare ankles —beautifully.

Russ is staring at her, almost immobilized as, jarringly, the telephone rings.

Russ feels his whole heart shrink, deflate to an empty sack. He knows, as he has known all day, just who would call and what the message would be.

He goes slowly into the next room and picks up the phone. "Yes. Hello. Yes, Clyde. Oh Jesus. Oh. Yes, I see."

Back in the living room he tells Cynthia, "That was Clyde Drake. It's SallyJane. She died. In the shock." He adds, "Her heart couldn't stand it."

They stare at each other. Each empty.

Chapter 31

The summer that follows the rainy June when SallyJane Byrd died, in shock, is later thought of in just that way: the summer SallyJane died. As though the enormity of that event had stilled most of the usual activity in Pinehill, which it indeed had done, along with the unusually heavy heat. No one gave a party, for those several months, certainly not in the circle of people who had known her best. It was too hot, and also all conversations that summer seemed to have a way of getting back to poor SallyJane. The tragedy of what had happened to her.

Dr. Clyde Drake was much blamed, perhaps unfairly: certainly he had not meant to kill her.

He had known about the slight murmur, and had seen how fat she was, but he had no doubt acted in the belief that she would be all right. That she could withstand the shock. In those pre-litigious days doctors were given the benefit of the doubt in most cases; it was not believed or perceived that they could grossly err. Still, the underlying sense in Pinehill was that Clyde Drake had caused her death, and that he should never show his face around town again. It was assumed that that was how Russ felt. Norris too was blamed, with far less reason; no one wanted to see her either. At some point the news got out and circulated that Norris had left both her husband and her children, a real scandal: a woman who would leave her children? She had run off with a man she met in a local nightclub, run off with him to Mexico. Well, if further proof was needed that a couple was crazy, there it was. Later it was ascertained that Dr. Drake had married his nurse, a Miss Effington, which on the face of it sounded like a sensible move, though for all anyone knew she was crazy too, or a drinker, or something.

According to Jimmy Hightower, the only person to see Russ to talk to (this was easy, since the Hightowers were back in their house), Russ was working day and night, revising his Kansas pig play. Ursula was there to help him with the kids, and he could ask her all kinds of things, Kansas things. Presumably, pig things too.

In any case, Russ wasn't talking much, Jimmy said, and he had aged terrifically. "It's like he's the grandfather to those children now," said Jimmy. "He walks slow and he speaks very soft, speaks not much at all. I'd feel better about the man if he took a drink or three, or got himself involved with some pretty girl. He's a young man, speaking relatively, and he's got a whole long life ahead of him, with any luck. I understand his daddy lived to be eighty-nine. And I never would have thought of Russ as a monk, would you?"

Esther, to whom all this has been addressed, says no, she would not have. But Esther these days is preoccupied with getting her house back in order. Some of the things that the Bairds did were very nice, but still it was more their way than hers. And they were clearly not good at gardening, though they meant well, Esther supposes.

Dolly has been busy with their little store, now functioning downtown in a small storefront on Main Street. She is busy with that and with her boys, who were home all summer except for a week at camp. And busy with Willard, who had little to do and became demanding. All the rumors about Dolly and Clifton Lee had quieted down, along with everything else in town. And the Bigelow family was to spend three weeks at the end of the summer up in Tryon, near Asheville.

Cynthia Baird is on the craziest schedule of anyone. Living up in Georgetown with Harry, she still came down to Pinehill every other weekend, since Abigail had chosen to stay down there for the summer, except for her time at camp; Abby did not want to leave her friends, and the Lees had invited her to stay. Cynthia always stayed in what had been their suite at the Inn, usually by herself, since Harry was always so busy in Washington with the Navy. The war. Cynthia has agreed to stay in Pinehill, in Dolly's house, for the three weeks that they are up in Tryon.

She feels herself stretched between the two

places, all that long sultry thick hot summer. She tries, not always successfully, to blot out the long train rides between Pinehill and D.C., the trains with their aisles full of soldiers and sailors, now often young women with babies. Although Cynthia talks to these people, listening to stories, she says very little to them about herself; for what would there be to say about her life at this moment of suspension? She feels herself distant, not seriously involved in the war, as almost everyone is, in some way.

Nor for that matter is she seriously involved in the little store; Dolly is far more active than she.

And Harry takes his work very seriously; at last he is doing something he cares about and respects, but since whatever he is doing is mostly secret, he does not discuss it even with Cynthia. They talk, they go to parties both in Washington and in Pinehill. They make love a lot. But they are no longer concentrated on each other in the way that they once were.

Abigail seems visibly to strain away from her parents, if for the most part politely. At best she is willing to accept them as somewhat distant old friends. It is clear that she regards them both as over the hill, almost decrepit. On the weekends when Cynthia or both Cynthia and Harry are in Pinehill they see each other, but the visits are often cut short. Abigail has some other project or plan, and Cynthia lets her off, not wanting a guilty daughter.

In a few weeks now, the school will start in Washington, the public school that Abigail has insisted on, but sometimes Cynthia in her suspended state has considered their staying on in Pinehill for the school year; she and Abigail could live at the Inn, and Abigail could start at the local high school with her friends, and they—or she alone, just Cynthia—could visit Harry up in Georgetown for weekends, reversing the present process. Sometimes, as she mulls over that possibility, Cynthia believes that it would be romantic, good for their marriage. At other times she thinks, That is really nuts, I'm married to Harry, I love him, and we've rented a whole big house in Washington. In Georgetown—so lucky to find it these days.

Sometimes, when Abby does have another plan that means they won't see each other, Cynthia is really hurt, and she tries hard not to be hurt. To divert herself.

On an afternoon late in August, then, at the beginning of her three weeks at the Bigelow house, when she and Abby had planned a walk to Laurel Hill, Abby calls to say, "Mom, would you really mind? Betsy and some of the kids want to see this new movie downtown—it's called *Rebecca*. Supposed to be really good."

But isn't it a little sophisticated for Abby? Cynthia cannot say that to her daughter.

"You sure you won't mind?" asks Abby. "I'll see you later?"

"Sure, darling. Have a good time."

Cynthia decides that she will walk to Laurel Hill by herself. It's always beautiful, and she needs the exercise. But she has walked this road so often that by now she hardly sees it; dimly her mind registers, as she looks up, the shining rich green of pine boughs against a blue sky. The white rush of the creek over shoals of pebbles. The small gray beach. The huge boulders across the water, and all the laurel there, the dark green leaves with no flowers, in this season before the fall. Growth suspended in the heat, the dead air that follows summer.

A man is sitting on a log that has fallen there on the beach, his back to Cynthia. He is facing the small, shallow rapids in the creek, as it widens. And although he cannot hear her, probably, above the rushing, gurgling water sounds, Cynthia stops. She thinks that she has recognized Russ Byrd.

Although that is impossible. These are not Russ's woods; she only imagines seeing Russ because of the time that she saw him in the rain, in the woods behind his house. The day that SallyJane died. (Or, another day too, when he was with Norris Drake.) Russ would not be over here in Laurel Hill. It is only that she has thought of him all summer, and longed to see him. She has thought of him ever since they moved down to Pinehill.

The man stands up and turns toward her. It is Russ. He smiles, and she smiles too, and they both say at once, "Oh, hello!"

Hesitating for an instant, they then move toward each other, slowly at first, as on a single impulse, but then their bodies collide, and press together. Arms clutching, their mouths devouring. They kiss as though they had kissed before—had been interrupted in a kiss.

"That's why we both walked to Laurel Hill, we knew we'd meet. I *must* have known. Those aren't my woods." Some hours later Russ says this to Cynthia.

"I know. And I came all the way to Pinehill to meet you."

"Should I believe that?"

"Oh, you should. It's *true*."

They both laugh; they have to, to break the tension between them. Although what they are saying actually is true: they both feel that their lives have led them to this moment, to this lying naked together in Cynthia's wide bed. Cynthia and Russ.

Abby fortuitously has called to say that she would like to have supper and spend the night at Betsy Lee's, if that's all right. "Of course it is, darling."

The idea of what she is doing, the fact of it, is almost as exciting as the act itself. Or, acts: they have greedily made love several times. As he enters her, each time she thinks his name. Even, somewhere in her mind, poems of Russ's flutter down to rest as an interior voice repeats: In bed with Russell Byrd, making love with Russ.

"I feel like I'm sixteen," at some point he says to her. "Except at sixteen I sure wasn't doing anything like this. What a wasted life."

"You were an innocent boy?"

"Very innocent. For years."

The small patch of hair on his chest is dark brown silk, and his lower hair is dark, and silk. She asks, "Do you wish we'd known each other then?"

"Lord, no, I'd have been terrified of you. I almost am now."

"Oh no, you can't be." She pauses, then asks him, "Have you had a lot of, uh, affairs?"

From his instant of hesitation she understands that he will be scrupulous. "Only one that counts," he tells her. "The other was nothing important, just something crazy." (She knows that he must mean Norris Drake.) "Just those two," he says.

And the important one must have been with

Emily Yates, the mother of Graham and of Deirdre? Cynthia wonders if he will ever tell her. Or if she will ask.

"I wish you could stay all night," she says to him, nestling close.

"No, I'm so reliable they'd all worry. Besides," he says, "I don't think I could make love to you again."

But, having said that, he lets his mouth find hers, perhaps intending a tender parting kiss, and everything flares between them again. Tongues thrashing, limbs violently entwined. He inside her.

"Now I do have to go."
"Yes—"
"But tomorrow—"
"Yes. Tomorrow."

The next day they arrange to meet at Cynthia's store; Russ can park in back, no one will notice him there. And since it is a Sunday, no one will come to the store.

In the back is a very small room, just a studio couch, a couple of beaten chairs, a cluttered desk. Cynthia, insofar as she had thought at all, had imagined that they would talk there, in that room. In an almost businesslike way they could sort things out between them. Make some kind of plans.

But even as she waits for the sound that will be his knock on the door, Cynthia feels the wings of a panicked excitement within her chest; she is too excited for speech, for conversation. Minutes pass. He is late. Five minutes. Ten. She believes that her heart will burst. And suppose it did, suppose she had a stroke and died right there, who would find her? Russ has no key. He would knock and knock and think she had gone away, changed her mind, gone back to Washington, to Harry. Odessa would find her, but not until tomorrow, when she comes with some bright new bolts of material.

When Russ at last knocks at the door, Cynthia jumps violently at the unexpected sound.

She opens the door, and he comes in, jaunty and grinning, so that in the instant before they kiss she thinks, I am making him young again—already. He is wearing a plaid cotton shirt that smells of smoke, and his mouth tastes of smoke, tobacco.

She tells him, "Oh, I've missed you," and she laughs, they both laugh. It is too ridiculous, at their age. Too ridiculous that in another minute they are making love again, on the narrow battered studio couch.

Do they make love so much precisely to avoid any conversation? Cynthia wonders this, as, the next day, she waits for Odessa in that same small room. (She has sponged off the couch, but still she wonders if anyone could see or smell anything, any trace of her passage there with Russ.) So much of what they might discuss, things that must be on both their minds, hers and Russ's, are excluded. What could either of them say about SallyJane, or for that matter about Harry? This lack of talk tends to make their contact, in retrospect, somewhat unreal: did she really do all that, with Russ Byrd, in this very room? What actually happened between them could as well have been a dream, or one of her old Russ Byrd fantasies, thinks Cynthia.

Odessa, when she comes, has wrapped a band of purple cloth around her head; with her graying hair, her large, strong-featured, and richly brown face she looks wonderful.

But Odessa never seems to want to talk very much—or not to Cynthia. Certainly not to gossip.

That morning Cynthia tries again. "Did you ever happen to know that Miz Emily Yates, the one who died when she was having little Graham, that brother of Deirdre Yates?"

"Yes'm, I seen her a couple of times." She adds, "They didn't have no help, not usually."

"She must have been very beautiful, a daughter like Deirdre, and that Graham's a handsome boy."

"Yes'm, I reckon."

Do we all look alike to Odessa, Cynthia wonders? All us rich white ladies, who don't really work?

It is crazy for her not to talk to Russ, she decides; if we don't talk, it's my fault, really. Women are better at personal conversations than men are.

She remembers then a play of Russ's that she once read, about some people in an unspecified country, devastated by an unspecified war. But the people themselves are not identified either; there are two men, and another person specified as Woman. Is Russ in that way a little like Odessa? Cynthia wonders. Does he see all women as Woman, so that it does not matter what particular women say? (Dear God, are all men just a little like that?) But surely he must have felt that SallyJane, the mother of all those children, was a separate, individual person. And surely Emily Yates, whom he must have loved (or did he?)— the mother of Graham, so clearly Russ's son?

Will Russ ever want to marry *her?* Cynthia wonders. And if he did, and if she accepted, however would she tell Harry, how to explain? And would friends from Connecticut come all the way down for the wedding, or would they choose to boycott it in a group?

And then she thinks, *God*, I have lost my mind. And she laughs at herself. A little.

Harry, unlike Russ, has indeed a most particular sense of her, Cynthia then decides. She is not Woman to Harry. Maybe she should always stay with Harry, as she had intended? She has had all along an odd small wish to tell him all about this thing with Russ. He would find it interesting, as she does, and he would understand what is going on, in ways that she does not. If only it were all about some other people, she could tell Harry, they could talk about it.

"Is Emily Yates very beautiful too?"

"Who?"

This bit of dialogue, which is quite startling to them both, has taken place between Russ and Cynthia in Dolly Bigelow's living room. No chance for making love there, Cynthia believes; perhaps at last they will talk. And so she began what she hopes is a serious conversation, starting with provocation. She in no way expected Russ's genuinely blank note of surprise.

She answers him, "Emily Yates." Not saying, "whom you loved." She adds, "Graham's mother."

There is a long pause, during which he has obviously understood, but still he stares at her, until he says, "Deirdre is Graham's mother. He is her son. By me."

Reeling at first from this new information, Cynthia then thinks, But of course. How dumb of me not to work that out. Probably everyone else in town caught on right away. Of course, Russ and beautiful Deirdre. Parents of Graham.

Very gently Russ asks her, "You didn't know that? I sort of thought everyone did. Just no one said."

"Maybe. I don't know." I'll never understand Southerners, is one of the things that Cynthia is thinking.

"We just worked out that story, when Deirdre's mother died so soon after Deirdre had the boy. So she could come back here with Graham," Russ is explaining. "I hardly knew Emily Yates, and of course she never knew it was me. The father of Graham. She thought some college boy." He sighs. "Of course one risk was that the boy would look like me, and I guess he does. Pretty much."

"Yes."

"I had this unreal idea that if everyone was here, it would be all right. SallyJane and me and Deirdre and Graham, and all our kids. All of us in the town. Lord God, talk about unreal."

"It didn't work?"

"No." He is silent, frowning for several moments. "Brett—SallyJane got so sick, and then that crazy doctor. Everything wrong."

In that case, we had better get married. I'll handle the real parts, Cynthia thinks. She thinks this but of course does not say it, only smiles sympathetically.

They could get married, though. She could simply stay on down here. Abigail could go to this school, as she wants to anyway. Over Christmas, or sometime, she, Cynthia, could fly out to Reno for one of those quick divorces, as several friends from Connecticut have done. And then come back and marry Russ and move into his house. And change it all around, paint everything white and reupholster all the furniture in Odessa's wonderful colors.

She directs strong silent messages to Russ: Please ask me to marry you. Soon. That way I will know that you love me more than anyone. More than Deirdre Yates. As she smiles and she says, "Graham's a lovely boy."

Somewhat wryly (having caught none of her message), Russ agrees, "Yes, I guess he is."

Could she and Harry stay friends? When she thinks of this, when she asks herself this question, Cynthia is forced to answer no; she very much doubts that they would be friends. And as she tries to imagine her life with Harry nowhere present, she feels a terrifying emptiness. She thinks, I can't lose Harry, he's my best friend in the world. And so, only distantly aware of illogic, she concentrates on Russ. Even on Russ's asking her to marry him. She tries not to think of Harry, even though they talk so often on the phone.

"What do you do with yourself all day? You're so often out."

"Oh, not much. I take walks. That's probably where I am when you phone."

"At night?"

"I might be. We're having warm weather. I love these long warm evenings, and Abby keeps spending the night with friends. Harry, you won't believe what Irene said this afternoon, she said—"

They talk with all their old pleasure in each other's conversation, and Harry is not suspicious, really; he is too busy to worry in that way.

Cynthia asks Russ, "You never see Deirdre now?" She has managed to ask it lightly, but the question cost her a lot; she has spent a fair amount of time in jealous fantasies, speculations.

He tells her, "Not since SallyJane died. It wouldn't seem right. I don't know." He adds, in his honest, boyish voice, "Sometimes I phone her. To see how the boy is. All that. If she needs anything."

"SallyJane never knew?"

"Christ, I hope not."

They never talk about Harry, but one afternoon Russ asks her, "You sort of knew Harry all your life?"

"No, but we come from the same place. In Connecticut."

"I thought that. You seem like from the same place."

"Different parts of the same town, though. My family at first had a lot of money, and Harry's didn't. I think that makes more difference in Connecticut than down here. Crude cash."

"I guess so. It's all family here."

"Is that why your parents gave you such a fancy name?"

"Sure is. I don't come from much, is the truth. But my mother had this book of poems, and she liked the name. This classy mouthful I'm stuck with."

They both laugh, and then Cynthia explains a little more. "I'd planned to go to Vassar, where my mother went. I was all accepted and everything, but then I met Harry."

"Don't you ever think about going back?"

Musingly she strokes his bare upper arm, its soft flesh. "You mean, back to that time? Be young and do it all over again, differently?"

"No, silly. Just back to school."

She would not like Russ to know, actually, just how often she thinks of exactly that, although she sometimes mentions it to Harry. School. Studying something. Anything. Maybe even studying for a profession. Law school, even medical school.

She teases Russ. "How'd you like it if I went back to school and got to be a doctor, or a lawyer?"

He laughs, as she more or less meant him to. "I just said school. I didn't say turn into some lady lawyer, with a briefcase. Or a doctor, for the love of God, with the Lord knows what on her arm."

The basic problem with the little store, and the conflicts that have arisen between Dolly and Cynthia all come from divergent visions: Dolly sees a small space into which a great many things for sale are crowded. Whereas Cynthia cherishes a more austere view of the same space containing far fewer but larger, higher-priced objects. But, Cynthia wonders, maybe hers is not a good theory for Pinehill, and for years just emerging from the Depression? She sometimes concedes this to herself, if not to Dolly.

And maybe she should just wash her hands of the whole enterprise, she sometimes further thinks. Just leave it as Dolly's store. But if she does that, still another inner voice argues, she will have almost no excuse to keep coming back to Pinehill. That is, *if* she goes back to Georgetown. To Harry.

Cynthia finds herself overtaken by a curious passivity, though. A lassitude. It must have to do with so much making love, she thinks. Relaxed, she does not force herself toward decisions, although soon it will be time for her to go back to Georgetown. Or not.

When she is actually with Russ, she waits for him to make some move, some speech. But she is still quite uncertain about what her response would be.

She does not know whether Odessa agrees with her or with Dolly about the plans for merchandising in the store, and she finds no way to ask her. Almost never does Odessa say anything to Cynthia beyond a murmured "Yes'm," or "No'm." Cynthia thinks that Odessa doesn't like her, and then she thinks, I'm being ridiculous. Odessa just does not have conversations with white ladies. I must be as mysterious, as opaque to her as she is to me. One difference being that Odessa probably does not give it a lot of thought. She takes things as they are, being helpless to change them.

Helplessly, hopelessly, Cynthia tries too hard with Odessa. She tries to be friends, even just to communicate. She truly likes her, she genuinely admires Odessa's work, the marvelous multicolored bolts of fabric that Odessa has woven and dyed, but when she tries to praise this work she sounds silly—even insincere—to her own ears. "Oh, Odessa, what an absolutely heavenly shade of purple, it's just divine, I adore it!" What idiotic speech! She feels trapped in her own language, stupidly floundering in schoolgirl exaggeration.

Russ still makes his joke about feeling sixteen with Cynthia, and she always laughs and agrees. For her, though, this "joke" has taken on a slightly new meaning, in that she feels that he is indeed less experienced in love than she is. And how can that be, for the truth of it is that her only real (only all-the-way) experiences have been with Harry, years and years of making love with Harry. Whereas with Russ, besides SallyJane, there has been Deirdre Yates, and Norris Drake, and God knows who in Hollywood, or anywhere. But the point is that Russ makes love in a very boyish, straightforward way. A fair amount of kissing and touching, first, and then he enters her. He moves about inside her quite vigorously, and she comes (or sometimes not; Russ thinks she always does, and he never asks), he comes, and everything is over for a while. None of the variations on that theme, the delicious delays, the intensifying side trips, so to speak, that she and Harry took such delight in. Harry, she guesses, is a real sexual adventurer, who has led her on and on.

If she and Russ marry, Cynthia imagines that she will teach him all those things—or sometimes she imagines this. At other times she thinks, Oh no, he'd be shocked to death if I put my tongue or even my finger there (and she longs to do just that, to tongue and finger him everywhere). Or, at other, worse times, she thinks, I could never do that with anyone but Harry.

But she wants Russ to ask her to marry him. If he does not, it will mean that he doesn't love her, that what they are doing is not serious. Although she knows that for both of them it is highly serious.

He says, "I am thinking of you all the time. I mean that literally. No moment that isn't you. If I think I'm working, I'm really just kidding myself." Russ is scowling as he says this, his high white brow deeply furrowed, and his voice is angry. "I have to get over this," he says.

Looking at him then, Cynthia suddenly and completely understands that when he does decide to marry her, and he will decide that quite soon, it will be in order to end his obsession with her. He will marry her to free himself. Marry in order to be no longer madly in love.

But she still does not know how she will answer him.

He says, "If we have a child—I guess I mean if we *had* a child—I think it would be a beautiful blonde girl. Green-eyed. Like you."

She laughs at him. "And a skinny Yankee, to boot. Oh, Russ, I'm too old even to think about more children."

Very seriously he tells her, "No, you're not. You could even have a couple more, if you want to."

In a literal sense he is right, she is not close to forty yet, and women have children even past that age.

He says, "A woman like you, you could manage a couple of kids and take a few courses at the college too."

Is this his version of a marriage proposal? Not quite, Cynthia decides. It is more like a warning signal: Look, this is what I have in mind, I think you should know.

One afternoon, more or less at Russ's insistence, they walk out again to Laurel Hill. Late September, just before Dolly's return. The sky is a pure deep blue, with a few tiny fluffy, cottony clouds at the horizon, and the air is warm but threaded

245

through with lines of cooler air, just the barest suggestion of cool, like the slightest murmuring sound of leaves, or of wind, that signifies fall. The end of summer.

Thinking this, and thinking of autumn, Cynthia further thinks: The end of us, too. She and Russ could never marry—Good Lord, of course not. She sees that now, and sees too that he should be married, he needs a wife. And so it has to be over between them, she thinks, with a sharp-edged, painful thrust to her heart. And at the same time she is aware that she is being sentimental, she must stop this.

But it is Russ, the poet, who says to her, "Does autumn make you sad?—the end of summer? It does me, every time."

"Despite all the mists and mellow fruitfulness."

"Yep, despite all that."

Looking over, she sees that he is smiling, but then the smile stops, and Russ stops too, stops walking and turns to her, first grasping her arm, then taking her into his arms. He says, "I love you too much, I think of you too much. I want us to get married."

So that he will love her less, and think of her less often? Cynthia later decides that he did mean just that; he wants a diminishing of intensity, an end to such an extreme of passion (although he may not have known exactly what he was saying, or meaning). But at the moment, despite better judgment, she thrills to his words: Russell Byrd is asking her to be his wife (later she is to examine that phrase, and to find some interesting implications therein). Her silly, vain heart thrills, even as, intelligently, she is saying, "But, Russ, we can't. I love you too, but it wouldn't work out as a marriage. Not ever."

He almost too quickly agrees. "I guess you're right."

"But we'll still see each other. I'll come down to see you all the time. There's the store for an excuse. We'll see each other a lot." Cynthia says all this with a rapid-fire desperation, knowing even as she speaks that it is not quite true. They will not see each other a lot, much less "all the time." And she is instantly filled with the most terrific and almost unbearable sadness, as though she will be leaving and losing not only Russ but this whole most intricately lovely little town, with its special scents and weathers, its hard white rutted side-walks and desiccated old brick houses. She is losing Pinehill.

All this passes through her mind, a quick vision of loss, as she also thinks, And Russ will marry someone else. He'll have to.

Part 2

Chapter 32

The day in June, the first June of World War II, on which Deirdre Yates and Russ Byrd are married, is a pale blue day, hung with intricate, filmy, and delicate clouds, like white lace. Amazing clouds, as almost everyone remarked; no one had ever seen their like before. The clouds drift through that pale blue sky, above the wedding reception, which takes place in Russ's garden. Now Russ and Deirdre's garden.

"It's like the day was made to go with Deirdre's blue dress, now wouldn't you say?"

"Well, yes indeed. The loveliest day I ever did see."

"And the loveliest bride, or almost. Surely one of them. Those eyes."

"Sort of funny, her not wearing a real white bride dress, don't you think?"

"Not funny at all, it's like she's saying—"

"Well, what is she saying? After all, it's her first—"

"Isn't it wonderful that Harry and Cynthia made it just in time?"

"Just barely, though. I declare, those two are busy as busy in D.C."

"And down here. Their house. Deirdre's old house."

"Cynthia looks absolutely lovely. And so happy."

"Maybe a little too happy?"

"Whatever do you mean by that?"

"You hear they're putting in a swimming pool, the Bairds are, out in back of Deirdre's house?"

"You mean Cynthia's house."

"I guess. Got three colored men out there digging."

"I heard five."

"Where's Abigail Baird?"

"She and Betsy were over there, I just saw them."

"Can you believe these clouds?"

"How many years is it now since SallyJane died?"

"Two, or is it three? I'm so terrible with dates."

"And then there's the war. So much to keep straight."

"How old is Abby by now?"

"Well, I can't keep that straight either. She must be thirteen, or is it fourteen?"

"I just can't recall exactly what year it was they moved down here, those three people."

"Sure made a difference."

"The Baird family. Remember, we used to call them the 'Bads'?"

"Some of us used to. Some never said such a thing."

"Be real nice, having a pool in town."

"Whatever age she is, she looks older. Abby Baird, I mean."

"Well, so does Melanctha Byrd. Kids these days."

"Can you believe it? Them wearing lipstick?"

"I don't think Deirdre's got on one speck of makeup."

"Must be what Russ likes. Remember poor SallyJane never wore any makeup either. Not even any face powder."

"Have to be as beautiful as Deirdre Yates. Oh, I reckon as of today it's Deirdre Byrd!"

"SallyJane once was a very beautiful woman, now don't you forget it."

"Hard to recall her face exactly by now."

"Melanctha's the dead spit of her daddy, wouldn't you say?"

"SallyJane's body, though. She's going to have some trouble with that chest."

"Whatever do you mean?"

"More boys chasing after her than she'll know what to do with."

"Never heard of a girl that minded getting a rush."

"That's all you know. It can go too far, especially when the girl's really young and she gets confused."

"Well, you ladies sure have a peck of problems, I can see that."

"Have you noticed? No one's talking about the war this afternoon."

"Oh my yes, such a relief."

"Well, that's not quite true. I just heard Jimmy Hightower going on about that General Rommel, off in the desert."

"Oh, that Jimmy, with his maps and his flags and his little pointers."

"What do you bet he writes a big best-seller about the war."

"He'll give it a try, that's for sure."

"Can that be Clarence Yates over there, with that big dark-looking woman?"

"It's got to be Clarence Yates, I guess. All the way from California!"

"Well, of course, it's Deirdre's first—"

"You already said that, and it wasn't funny the first time."

"Interesting about Russ's pig play, don't you think?"

"I didn't hear, what happened?"

"Well, that theatre group over to Hilton's going to do it. They're just wild about Russ, always have been."

"No money to it, I hear, but whole lots of prestige, in that world."

"Wouldn't surprise me none if Russ wasn't happier that way. He never really was a one for all that fancy stuff. No more than was SallyJane."

"Or Deirdre either."

"No sir, that girl is not one bit spoiled, for all her being such a beauty."

"I have to go and say hello to Clarence Yates."

"Were you surprised, I mean at their getting married?"

"Not really. Maybe I should have been. It just seemed right, somehow. And Russ was bound to marry someone, sometime. He's a marrying kind of man."

"Me too, I felt the same."

"And her little Graham, he'll fit right in with Russ's kids. Looks like one of them already."

"Sure does. Sure absolutely does."

"The boys all seem to like him fine, but that Melanctha's taken against him, someone told me."

"Why ever would that be?"

"Who knows with kids. Something to do with SallyJane, do you think?"

"I can't quite see how that would be. Did SallyJane ever see that boy, do you think?"

"Must have, one time or another. They're around town a lot, taking their walks. Her and Graham."

"Wonder whatever she made of that."

"Same as everyone else, I reckon."

"Pinehill must seem awful dull to you, after glamorous wartime Washington, D.C."

"Oh no, not at all, in fact I—"

"Well, we sure do miss you-all, all of us did."

"Oh, I've missed you-all. I missed it here, I couldn't believe—"

"Your store, though. If that's not the darlingest little old store I ever did see."

"Oh, but it's not my store at all. Dolly—"

"Dolly always says how you were the start of it."

"Well, I did have this idea, and Odessa—"

"That Odessa! and that Nelly! Turned out just like her momma. You hear about that? Up and quit on Dolly too, gone off to the defense plant."

"I think I—"

"I wonder if Clarence Yates will remember me. We didn't exactly know each other, just hello on the street."

"Cynthia, that is the most beautiful dress."

"Oh, thank you, so lucky, I found this—"

"I'm just going to say hello to him anyhow."

"Darling, no one will let you talk, have you noticed?"

"Lucky thing I don't have much to say. No point in telling about going back to school."

"You seem very much on edge."

"I do?"

"Yes, really. Very edgy indeed."

"Maybe I am, weddings—"

"Irene is looking perfectly lovely, don't you think?"

"Would you say that being a widow agrees with her?"

"It sure doesn't sound right but I guess you might say that."

"Poor Clifton."

"And poor little Betsy, that child really took it hard."

"And Dolly—"

"Don't you say that! Nobody's supposed to—"

"But there they were."

"Oh, I know, everybody knows that."

"Dolly, you're looking pretty as a picture today. Bet you're happy to have your friend back here in town."

"I was just telling Willard, if Cynthia'd stay on here permanently, I'd be just perfectly happy. But their house here is a start."

"I wouldn't be too sure. Stranger things—"

"Were you surprised?—at the marriage, I mean?"

"Well no, not really. It seemed like a natural thing."

"On the face of it such an outlandish idea, Russ Byrd and Deirdre Yates, but it doesn't seem to have surprised one single person. Not at all."

"Cynthia told me she was surprised."

"Were you surprised when Cynthia bought her house? Deirdre's house?"

"Who would have thought that Deirdre could have got even more beautiful?"

"She's a legend in her own time, that girl is."

"Do you reckon that she and Russ might, uh, increase their tribe?"

"Lordy, what an idea! With Graham there's six already. Heavens above!"

"But they just might, don't you think? Matter of fact, Deirdre does have just the faintest look—"

"Well, a girl can gain a couple of pounds for a whole lot of reasons."

"Jimmy says that Rommel could get completely lost in the desert."

"Rommel, is he on our side or theirs?"

"Theirs, for Lord's sake. He's a German. Rommel."

"Doesn't sound all that German to me. Even when you roll that 'R' like that. Could be just a Yankee name, or English."

"Why is Esther still so sad-appearing, do you think?"

"Jimmy said she'd had some bad news about what's going on in Germany."

"But we're fighting Hitler, like she always wanted."

"That doesn't stop what they're doing to those Jews back there."

"Poor Esther."

"Poor Jewish folk. The Lord have mercy."

"I don't think Jimmy's being so successful has cheered her up a lot."

"They were already rich, that's the trouble with being rich. Or one of them."

"Well, I for one would sure like to have a chance to find out."

"Funny, Jimmy being so much more famous than Russ is now. Jimmy going out to Hollywood instead of Russ."

"Makes sense, if you think about it. Russ was never cut out for that stuff."

"Yeah, he's just a simple country boy at heart."

"If Russ Byrd is simple, I'm a monkey's uncle."

"Well, come to think of it—"

"Oh look, there's Abby Baird now."

"She's a real big girl now, isn't she."

"How old would she be—thirteen, fourteen?"

"Well, let's see, they first came here in '38, or was it '39?"

"And she was eleven, or was it twelve?"

"Is that Archer Bigelow she's talking to? What a big boy he turned out to be."

"Lucky thing he took after Willard and not that little old Dolly."

"Does Russ look sort of sad today, or is that just my imagination?"

"The wedding must put him in mind of SallyJane. You know."

"Well, yes, of course it would."

"That Abby Baird's a looker all right. Or give her a couple of years to get to be one."

"Not a patch on her momma, though. She never will be."

"Come on, now. Just a different type, entirely."

"She's different, all right. You hear about that paper she wrote on integration for her civics class up there?"

"Sure did. So proud of it she sent a carbon right down here to her friend Betsy Lee."

"I guess the whole town's heard about that paper by now."

"Yes, since Irene got ahold of it."

"Hard on Irene, when you come to think of it. Having her husband die and then this upstart Yankee sends this paper to her own little girl—"

"Even favored intermarriage, way I heard it."

"Lord God."

"Got a big fat A on it too. Some teachers they got up there."

"Well, Washington. What'd you expect? Mostly Yankees."

"Well, to play the advocate of the devil, just suppose the paper she wrote was real well done? I mean the grammar, the structure of sentences and spelling and all?"

"So what? It's what she says that matters—anyone at all can learn how to spell."

"You hear about the Nigras in the swimming pool over to the college? Just one of them, I reckon, this colored kid's a freshman from over to Hillsboro."

"I did hear about that. Clean cleared the pool out, is that right? All the other boys got up and got themselves right out of there."

"Well now, I don't think that's right. He had a right to go swimming, same as any other student. He's paid his tuition too."

"Yes, but those other boys didn't pay their money to have to swim with Negroes."

"Now, now, this here's a party, remember? A wedding. Let's not get into any arguments today. Leastways not on that subject. God a'mighty."

"Since you mention it, I do think Deirdre's put on a couple of pounds."

"Yes, and all in the front."

"Archer Hightower, I don't care what you say. I am not going off for any walk in the woods with you."

"But you said in your letter—"

"I didn't mean today. Look, my parents are here."

"But you—"

"Well, maybe later."

"Did you notice Russ hasn't left her side for one solitary minute?"

"There's a bridegroom for you."

"You heard about the swimming pool they're putting in? The Bairds?"

"Sure did! Five colored men digging that hole."

"I heard ten."

"Even not looking perfectly happy, there he is."

"Well, who wouldn't stick close to a bride that looks like that?"

"It's nice we don't see those Drake people up here anymore, don't you think?"

"Oh, very nice. You say hello to Clarence Yates yet?"

"You hear she ran off?"

"I did hear. Left him flat, the way I heard it."

"Left her children too. That's a whole lot harder to understand, I think."

"Sure is. Most anyone wants to leave a husband, one time or another."

"Or a wife."

"Or a wife. Sure thing. You think Clarence Yates is married to that woman?"

"Some crazy woman, that Norris Drake."

"You might know a psychiatrist, so-called, would marry just the craziest person he could find."

"A looker, though, you've got to admit."

"I do not! That woman was terrible-looking, looked like a monkey—"

"More like a cat, to my way of thinking—"

"Well, he was certainly no prize. Handsome, though."

"Poor SallyJane, you might say she got the worst of it."

"Indeed you might."

"She could be alive today."

"In that case, I wonder whatever would have happened to Deirdre Yates?"

"Reckon we'll ever get to calling her Deirdre Byrd?"

"And Graham. Whatever's his name going to be?"

"Well, you just can't tell, lest you take to writing novels, like Jimmy over there."

"Or Russ. Don't you forget it, our Russ's the town's real writer."

"Oh, I know that, and Jimmy knows it too, for sure."

"Oh look, they're whispering together, Russ and Deirdre."

"I ask you, is that sweet?"

"And Russ is not drinking one drop."

"But whatever could they be saying to each other?"

"There's going to be an awful lot of food left over, you know that, hon?"

"Not once the kids get into it, you wait and see."

"I feel bad that Ursula had so much to do."

"She likes work, it makes her happy."

"Today makes me happy, I feel—"

"Honey, I'm glad."

"But I'm worried. This dress, it doesn't seem—"

"Honey, don't you worry. You're the prettiest girl in this town, or this state, doesn't matter what you wear."

"But, Russ, I *show*."

Chapter 33

The news of Russ and Deirdre's impending marriage had come to Cynthia not from Russ (they were not in touch) but in a letter from Dolly. With whom Cynthia kept up an active and lively correspondence; Cynthia found that she very much liked and looked forward to the spice of Dolly's letters, and to all the news of Pinehill—with which they overflowed. Dolly always included small reports on weather and flowers, so that Cynthia could see and almost smell the town.

"*Well*," wrote Dolly (she being one of those whose letters are very much in her own voice), "the really big news is that Russ Byrd is marrying Deirdre Yates this very June. Seems to have been decided in one fairly great big hurry, and you can bet how all the local tongues are wagging over that. No one ever saw them together anywhere, and now suddenly they're always together everyplace and *getting married*. They'll live at Russ's, of course, and Deirdre's already put her funny old house up for sale. You remember that falling-down brick place close to where all the colored used to live? She never did anything to it, except for curtains and things on the inside— didn't have the money, is my guess. But somebody surely could. Somebody could just make a showplace out of that old wreck, and I just know they're going to sell it real cheap. Hint hint. Are you interested, one little bit? Wouldn't you and your Harry like to have this sort of what they call in New York a *pied-à-terre?* Down here? There's this great big old vacant lot out in back, you-all could have the most scrumptious garden. You could even put in a swimming pool, like folks out in California! Are you tempted, the least little bit?

"No one seems to be so very, very surprised at this wedding. I guess every single person around here had certain hidden thoughts about those two, that not one person gave voice to, I can vouch for that. Because if they had I surely would have been a one to hear it, you can bet on that. But there was always the boy, looking enough like Russ to be his brother.

"This April has been just the most lovely you ever did see. The roses—the wisteria—and out in the woods, dog tooth violets and anemones you would not believe."

Cynthia, after the first small jolt, and even the suggestion of a private tear, was not deeply surprised by the Russ-Deirdre news. It was much too reasonable to surprise her. With a small ironic smile, she thought that if she were Russ that would be exactly what she would do. It made perfect sense for Russ to marry a beautiful young woman who loved him, who had borne him one handsome child and would probably be quite happy to do so again. She had recognized a large grain of country sense in Russ, a practicality not wholly unlike her own. (Very likely these were among the very qualities that made them finally separate from each other, several years ago.)

And as for his wanting to marry her, his saying that he did, Cynthia wondered if he did not always know that she could be counted on to turn him down. It was only his way of saying that he seriously loved her—but also of saying that it was time they called a halt.

And call a halt was certainly what they did, although as they slowly walked back from Laurel Hill, their last walk, in the drying September heat—even then, even after she had said no so clearly, Cynthia thought that they could still see each other sometimes (meaning, they could still make love sometimes). But after they had parted, and Abby called that very night to say that she was staying at Betsy

Lee's (okay?), Cynthia realized that she would not call Russ, as she earlier would have done, and say to him, "Please come over." She could not. It was truly all finished between them.

Back in Washington, and plunged into domestic and social busyness there, instead of missing Russ, Cynthia found that she really missed the town. Missed Pinehill. With an acute and painful longing she recalled the enormous rolling seafloor shape of the hills around the town, and then its particular shades of green foliage, all those ancient towering trees. Especially the very tall pines—with their scent, and the shining dark rich green of the needles—against the sky.

It must be admitted that sometimes she did have maudlin, sentimental thoughts about Russ himself, but that was usually when she had had more than one martini at a party (or, God forbid, more than one Zombie at the Shoreham). At those moments, though, Cynthia could simply press closer to whomever she was dancing with—it was apt to be Harry, who was still the best dancer she knew. And she might think, wisely, that it was not so much Russ she had loved as the idea of Russ, her poet-lover, whom in so many crucial ways she barely knew.

Partly for that reason, Russ's final unfamiliarity, Cynthia had managed not to feel too guilty toward Harry about Russ. Or not very guilty, and not often. Just as with Russ she had managed not to think of Harry, so now when she was with Harry, Russ was rarely on her mind.

Harry was extremely busy, often leaving home at eight in the morning, sometimes earlier, and not back until eight or so at night—unless, as was frequently the case, the popular Bairds had a dinner date or a party somewhere. They suddenly seemed to know a lot of Washington people; old friends had new jobs there, like themselves. People from Connecticut, from New York. Everywhere.

Cynthia in Washington spent much more time with Abby than she had in Pinehill. Uncertain of new friends in a brand-new school (the public school that Abby had insisted on), Abby had more time for her mother, and together they explored a lot of the city, museums (Abby especially liked the Smithsonian) and monuments, old houses and old gardens. Churches. Department stores. Art galleries.

As Abby became more involved with school friends, though, Cynthia thought that she herself could and really should get a job; however, she soon saw that without either a degree or secretarial skills, what she got would have to be very lowly indeed. And so, somewhat lazily at first, she registered and began a few courses at Georgetown University. She loved it. Enrolled as a special student—which is to say, a student not necessarily headed for any specific degree, although credit would be granted should she so choose—she grazed among courses: history, art history, literature. Psychology, architecture. She found this last, which was called Design and most of which was new to her, especially absorbing. The instructor had wonderful slides of new buildings by Le Corbusier, Erich Mendelsohn, F. L. Wright, and—in Barcelona—Gaudi. "After the war we have to go back to Europe," Cynthia said to Harry. "That trip with my parents doesn't count. I was missing you so much that I didn't see a thing."

"If there's any Europe left. All the bombing, and the talk about more." Harry, like everyone in

Washington, knew much more than he could say, and from time to time he threw out dark hints, dire prophecies—though he was hardly alone in a desperate concern for the architecture, along with the populace of Europe.

When Dolly's letter came, then, it was probably not surprising that Cynthia reacted strongly to the news of Deirdre Yates's house (along with other strong reactions). But since the first time that she had seen that group of clearly once-elegant old brick houses, as she and Jimmy Hightower drove out on one of their early excursions, she had been fascinated by those houses. Later, as Abigail and Deirdre developed their friendship, Cynthia longed to be invited over, or just asked in. And knew that she never would be.

Without too much trouble she talked Harry into a weekend at the Inn. "It's so lovely down there in April, everything's just starting to bloom and we haven't been in such a long time. And I do just want to look at that house. Honestly, Harry, it's an architectural gem, I know it is. Eventually some historical society will get its hands on it, but I want to see the house first."

Deirdre was staying with some cousins in Hillsboro while her house was being shown to prospective buyers (there were very few), and while she waited for her wedding, to be in June. Russ was spending a couple of weeks in New York, conducting some sort of business with his agent, his publisher. All in all, it was a convenient time for Cynthia and Harry to see the house—and so they did.

So far, in the Bairds' scattered Pinehill weekends since moving up to Georgetown, Cynthia had seen Russ only twice, both times a fleeting glimpse across gardens, at large parties. A friendly wave, a split second of smiles exchanged, but enough to break the spell, the wall of no contact at all. Cynthia had thought, So that's how it is to be, we're friendly acquaintances. Well, good. And then she thought, Thank God no one ever knew. That makes it even less real, somehow.

Literally nothing by way of renovation had been done to Deirdre Yates's narrow dark house, except for the most scrupulous cleaning; everything smelled of strong kitchen soap, Oxydol, and floor wax. In the bedrooms upstairs the flowered wallpaper had yellowed in streaks. (And in one of those rooms—in this one?—Deirdre must have been with Russ, they must have made love.) Downstairs dark panelling had long ago been painted over, an ugly brown, now chipped and mottled, discolored.

But: "This could be wonderful!" Cynthia exclaimed to Harry, and to Mrs. Riggsbee, the agent. "The most perfect small house for us, and really not much work. Just some pretty new paper upstairs—a *toile*, I think—and downstairs get someone to strip off that ugly old paint, there may be some really beautiful wood underneath. And look, there really is room for a pool in back, and a little pool house. And if the place doesn't work out for us we can always sell it and make a lot of money."

They bought it.

"Deirdre, I'm just so happy we're getting your house, it's going to be absolutely perfect for small vacations, and just between us I really need to get out of Georgetown more than we do. So does Harry, though I'm not sure he knows it. And it'll be great for Abby—this way she can keep up with

267

all her friends down here. And with a swimming pool! I'm sure she'll have a lot of new friends too. Oh dear, I'm sounding just like Dolly! I think I always do when I'm down here. Anyway, about the pool. Do you think you could do me this terrific favor and let them start digging on it before absolutely everything is all signed? I mean of course Harry gave Mrs. Riggsbee a check, and I *know* it's good, but if they could get started now we'd be that much ahead, I mean closer to having it ready for this summer. It's all going to be so much fun! You and Russ will have to bring everyone over to swim, all your kids. Yes, I really hope we can get down in time for your wedding, we're counting on that. You'll congratulate Russ for both of us, won't you? And, Deirdre, thanks so much for being so helpful, you've made the whole thing so much easier for us. Yes, I'll have Mrs. Riggsbee call you first thing. And Abby's dying to see you—"

"Odessa, if you could just come over for an hour or so. Just to look around and see what ideas you have. You know, like when you and Miz Bigelow came, a couple of years ago, when we were moving into the Hightower house. It's so dark around Deirdre Yates's house, and I thought—well, Odessa can really go to town, in this place. Odessa, how's your daughter? How's Nelly doing?"

Russ's wedding was more difficult for Cynthia than she had imagined it would be. But her upset only lasted for the actual day of it; both before and after she was perfectly all right. But all during the reception at Russ's, in the somewhat straggly but bountiful garden, she felt slightly unreal, an impersonation of herself. She had dressed very carefully, in a dress from the newest shop in Georgetown, recommended by a new friend. The dress was a simple navy silk with white polka dots, but cut most elegantly, and fitted; Cynthia wore it with a tiny navy straw hat and white kid gloves (of course white gloves), patent bag, and shoes. She knotted up her very long blond hair, applied the most discreet but flattering makeup—only the bright slash of scarlet lipstick was bold. She knew that she looked really good—and conspicuous, among all the Southern pastels, the pale dotted Swiss and flowered dimity. (Will Southern women ever learn the chic of dark clothes in summer, especially black? Cynthia doubted that they would.) She had never looked better, Cynthia knew, and she behaved well too; she chattered away to everyone there, she smiled all afternoon. She did not think in any extended or wistful way: That could have been me, I could have been the one in the center of all this celebration. I could have been the new Mrs. Russell Byrd.

For as soon as that voice began to whisper in her mind, another contradictory set of sentences would start, and would tell her very clearly: No, you could not have married Russ. Something always would have happened to prevent it. For starters, neither of you really wanted to marry the other, you were only "madly in love." That was all, and that is all over now. Best forget it and concentrate on who you really are. You are Harry's wife, and the mother of Abigail, and these days you are going to school. In a year or so you will have a degree, if you want to, and then you can do almost anything.

This is true; despite the random nature of her

course work, it has turned out, made clear in a conference with the dean of women, that Cynthia by now has almost the full requirement for a B.A. degree. And then, as the dean points out, she would have an easy shot at almost any graduate school. With so many young men away at war, there are vacancies. All she has to do is decide what she wants to do. She could not get into medical school, no pre-med courses, but then, a doctor is one of the things she has never wanted to be. The two fields that most interest her (curious, their apparent lack of relation to each other) are architecture and the law. With almost equal ease, according to mood, she can imagine herself as either an architect, designing wonderful new "modernistic" houses, or a lawyer, defending poor people (she thinks), maybe Negroes, who otherwise haven't a chance, who need good lawyers.

And how incredulous Russ would be at either plan! She cannot help thinking this, at his wedding, imagining the deeply furrowed high white brow, and the thicker country accent as he might say, "A pretty lady like you with all that schooling? I just plain can't see the point to it."

Harry thinks either choice would be great, but he wishes that she would make up her mind. He likes to plan ahead, to know what's going to happen.

It was very hard, though, at Russ's wedding, to think of herself as either an architect or a lawyer—as Cynthia chatted with Dolly, so lively and pretty in a very bright pink dress, and sad widowed Irene Lee, also pretty in pale blue, and drinking too much. And her old friends, Jimmy and Esther Hightower (they now seemed like very old, cozy friends).

All these people whom she liked and cared about but whom, she often thought, she would never really know. (Perhaps because they are the least "Southern," the Hightowers also seem the least opaque, the least alien to Cynthia.)

From time to time someone would mention Abby: "Where's Abby? Is she here this afternoon?" or "I just caught a glimpse of Abby— my, she's a great big girl now, and just as pretty as she can be!"

No one, that afternoon of the wedding, mentioned (to Cynthia) Abby's Infamous Integration Paper (Harry referred to it in this way), although Cynthia could sense that thought; she could hear it in the voices that asked after Abby, could see it in the eyes of those asking, "How *is* Abby?" She could hear and see the steel-cold sound and look of disapproval.

Cynthia herself felt a huge, heart-swelling pride in her daughter. For one thing, Abby had worked so extremely hard on that paper, hours of research and pages and pages of notes; a meticulous outline, meticulously followed, and three long drafts of the paper itself, with footnotes. And Abby's conclusions seemed (to Cynthia) both logical and moral: the present laws and the customs having to do with Negroes were both unfair and (often) illegal. Of course they should be able to vote, and if people wanted to intermarry, why ever not? Cynthia was quite furious that Abby should be so criticized. (And amazed and moved by Abby's courage.) "Misunderstood" is how she thought of it.

"Yes," Harry had said, "of course I agree with all that, and you know I love Abby too. Unconditionally. But why did she have to send the goddam thing to Betsy Lee, that dumb little Southern twit?"

"Betsy's her friend, Abby thinks, and she still thinks that a friend is a friend all the way. No holds barred. Maybe this was even a way of testing the friendship. She was sort of saying, Look, this is who I am, and what I think."

"Well, if that's the case, our poor little girl. She'll have to learn that many friendships are very partial."

"Oh, I know! Suppose I tried to really talk to Dolly! But Abby just doesn't know that yet."

Sometimes, in her fantasies of herself as a lawyer, Cynthia imagines defending her willful daughter. Along with the rights of Negroes (Odessa! Odessa's daughter Nelly) to vote, and to live wherever they chose to. To go to whatever schools, and marry whomever they wanted to. If she put all her mind and her energy to it, she might get to be a famous, successful lawyer, maybe even a judge (were women ever judges?—she does not remember ever hearing of a woman judge). She could do all that in Washington, and really affect things, and then come back to Pinehill to defend herself, and Abby.

For every reason, then, strong feelings in so many directions, Cynthia was more than a little tense at the Russ-Deirdre wedding. It was hard for her to be there. And although it was too late to reconsider, with the swimming pool already started, all that digging, she even asked herself if they really wanted a house down here, in this extraordinarily pretty town. Among all these exceptionally kind and graceful people, most of whose ideas on "race" and certain other social issues were appalling.

Chapter 34

Abigail Baird is over-sexed, very over-sexed. She will probably grow up to be a nymphomaniac, or maybe in just a few years she will be one. When she goes to college. A boy from her school, Jack Cutter, took her for a walk in Rock Creek Park, and he held her hand and then he stopped and kissed her, standing there, his mouth on her mouth, and she felt insane. Bursting, hot, and weak. And she doesn't even like Jack Cutter. He is not tall or cute, he has ugly little teeth. She never wanted to see him again after that. He's really a dope and gets all bad grades. So this must mean that she is over-sexed.

Of course she knows the mechanics of the sexual act. What grownups do. She has not, though, been able to make the imaginative connection between that, the penis-vagina business, and her own feelings, which she knows to be sexual, but do those feelings mean that she really wants to do *that?* She is not at all sure about the connection between *that* and kissing. It sounds embarrassing.

Her mother has said it feels better than anything, she can't describe how it feels, and Abby is willing to believe her mother. She thinks how lucky grownups are, to be able to get married and do it all the time. Until they get too old for it, as her parents must be by now.

She is not so sure about Deirdre and Mr. Byrd. When she first got to know Deirdre and went over there a lot, she used to catch them kissing sometimes, holding on to each other as though they were drowning. But she does not know if they have done that other thing too. Now that they are married she guesses that they do.

Abby hated the actual wedding. The giggling, snick-ering way all the grownups there behaved; it was embarrassing, awful. And as usual they all drank too much, except for Mr. Hightower, who has stopped drinking; he used to drink much too much. Mrs. Lee, Betsy's mother, really drank a lot, she always does, especially since Mr. Lee died. He died just sitting up in a car with Mrs. Bigelow. Walker Byrd says he thinks they were kissing too—he had caught them a few times parked somewhere near his house. Everyone, all the grownups, made such a fuss about his dying like that, with Mrs. Bigelow, so there must have been something, not just sit-ting in a car. Mrs. Lee didn't speak to Mrs. Bigelow for almost a year after that, Walker said.

Walker thinks they were probably doing it in the car, going all the way. "Grownups don't stop once they start," he says. "Why should they?"

"But in a car?" Abby does not see how this could be done.

"College kids do it all the time. What'd you think they were parked out on Crest Road for, just plain old necking?"

"I don't see how you know that." Abby is find-ing this conversation very disturbing. She frowns uncomfortably, not looking at Walker.

"Well, Miss Smarty Pants, I am sure. Archer and me, we found these things on the ground. Near where the cars are parked. Lots of times. These rubbers. Ick! I'd never touch one."

Abby does not know exactly what he is talking about (*rubbers?*) except in a very vague way. Cer-tainly she knows enough to know that she does not want Walker to explain any further. She suddenly hates Walker. She would never kiss Walker Byrd.

The kids down in Pinehill whom Abby knows, her group, are all about a year younger than those in her class in Washington, and for that reason (partly) they are nowhere near as fast; there is much less sex in the Pinehill atmosphere. In Washington there's so much sex everywhere that it's scary, if you're not used to it. Boys and girls holding hands as they walk down long brown dusty corridors, couples dancing in the gym at lunchtime, very closely, glued to each other. Girls in the washroom crying because of some boy. And items in the school paper about big love affairs at the school. Jokes told that Abby almost but does not quite understand, but that she finds vaguely exciting. Disquieting.

At the beginning she found everything about that school disturbing; she was deeply uncomfortable. In Pinehill the girls were not wearing lipstick yet, but here in Washington they are, and very, very dark red. Dark red nail polish too, a lot of them. The first afternoon after school, last September, Abby went out to the Georgetown drugstore right after she got home and bought a lipstick, and the next day she wore it to school. But she still had those dumb long braids and straight bangs.

"I want my hair cut! I can't stand looking like a Dutch twin, or some *child*."

"But, darling, you look marvelous, and not like anyone else—"

"I want short hair!"

They compromise, Abby and her mother, on hair for Abby that was fairly long but curled, and never braided again. The wedding was the first time that Abby had worn her hair like that in Pinehill, so that some people looked at her twice, seeming for a minute not to know her.

Her parents stayed in the suite at the Inn for Deirdre's wedding, but Abby got to stay with Betsy Lee, whose mother was still very lonely, they all said, and who liked to have company. "It just does me so much good to hear those little girls whispering all night," she confided to Cynthia. Who later confided to Harry, "Well, it does us good not to hear them, doesn't it, darling Harry?"

Betsy's bedroom is all white ruffles and bows, and watercolors of flowers. The twin beds there are separated by a glass-topped, chintz-flounced dressing table, with a fold-out three-way mirror and two lamps with fluted parchment shades. A silver framed photograph of Clifton Lee, Betsy's poor father. In the balmy, cloud-veiled June night, the night after the wedding, the two girls lie there, in their two beds, and they exchange what information they have, so far, about love and sex.

"I have this amazing secret to tell you," says Betsy Lee, to Abby. "Cross your heart never to tell anyone, ever. But I went for this walk in the woods with Walker Byrd, and I let him kiss me! Oh, I feel terrible!"

"But did you like it?"

"Uh, what do you mean?"

"When he kissed you, did it feel good? Did you just want to go on kissing?"

"I don't know! I guess I liked it all right, but it was so quick. And then I was afraid he'd want to do it again, and he did want to, but I wouldn't let him, of course. And then he said that he loved me, he always had, since the first of the year, and I wouldn't dare tell him but I

276

think I love him too! Walker Byrd! I think I love Walker Byrd!"

"Well, that's wonderful. Next year you-all can get married. Drive to South Carolina."

"Oh, Abby, you're terrible."

The two girls begin to giggle, lying there helplessly; the giggles are contagious, out of control, like small fires. As Abby is thinking, What on earth are we laughing about? This isn't even funny. Walker Byrd: I can't stand him, what's so funny about getting married? But she goes on laughing, she can't stop laughing. "And you know what married people do!" she gasps out.

"Abby Baird, you're the most terrible girl!"

Abby is experiencing just then the most tremendous happy excitement. She loves Pinehill so much, the softness of everything, the particular feel of the dark blue and gently clouded night. And the vague white blur that is Betsy's frilly room. She even likes Betsy better than any girl in Washington, she thinks; Betsy is sweet and funny, and if she isn't terribly smart, doesn't read a lot, so what? Does everyone have to be so intelligent? Her mother thinks they do; she always complains, "But they're so stupid, really!" Cynthia especially says that since she's been back in school, and feeling smarter than anyone.

Abby is tempted to tell Betsy about Jack Cutter, and the kissing in Rock Creek Park, but she decides not to.

And then she thinks, Could I tell Betsy about Benny? Benny and *Harvard?* No. No. The integration paper was bad enough.

Instead she says, "What to you think Russ and Deirdre are doing, right this minute?"

They both begin to shriek with stifled laughs.

For the first couple of years that Abby and her parents were in Pinehill and Benny was still up there in Connecticut, Abby and Benny wrote to each other very occasionally: cards, postcards, and cards at Christmas. The only phone call was the one about the chemistry caper, the trick on poor Mr. Martindale. But then during the next year, which was Abby's first in Washington and Benny's first at Exeter, for no reason that either of them could have stated, they began to write more often, so that the letters came and went between them each week, at least. Strangeness in new places, some loneliness on both their parts may to a degree have accounted for this acceleration, but also they were a little older now. And this increase in age may have accounted for the slight shift in their tone with each other.

For one thing, they exchanged pictures. Benny first; with a modest, semi-apologetic note he enclosed a news photo of himself in his football uniform, all helmeted and padded, but recognizably Benny. And so large; he must be over six feet by now. Abby thought maybe that was why he had sent the picture? Sort of saying, Look at me, I'm a football hero now. After that he sent more clippings, accounts of Exeter games in which he always seemed to star. But usually he included some jokey remark: how silly the whole thing was, how boring. Then he sounded like the old mild funny Benny.

Abby in her turn sent him a yearbook picture that she had had to have taken in her new school. It embarrassed her a little, this picture; with her long curled-at-the-ends blond hair and her dark, dark lipstick, she looked like some movie star—or worse, someone trying to look like a movie star. Like she thinks she's eighteen or so and really glamorous. Sexy. Lana Turner. Betty Grable. Ick!

Benny teased her about the picture a little; he sort of had to. But he sounded more pleased than teasing, actually. "Some glamor girl you've turned into," he wrote. "Don't think I haven't got you pinned up like a pin-up where everyone can see. Of course some baboon from Mississippi made some crack about 'black and blonde' but a couple of friends of mine really told him off. There's a fair amount of that stuff around here, but not as much as I expected. Not as much as my folks told me to expect. Anyway you look very sexy, for such a young little girl."

Most recently Benny has written to say that "some guys from Harvard, some sort of scouts" are really interested in him. For the year after next. "Of course I'd have to play ball there too, it's really a football scholarship they're talking about, but they say I could do that and pre-med too. I hope!"

Harvard! Benny at Harvard.

What would kissing Benny be like? In a slow, secret, and excited way Abby begins to wonder. He said she looked sexy in her picture: was that just kidding, teasing, or does it mean that he really wants to kiss her? She thinks of this a lot. Benny looks so tall now; would she have to stand on tiptoe for them to kiss? Unless they were in the backseat (the rumble seat!) of a car. Or sitting down on a couch. Maybe in his room at Harvard, if they let girls go into boys' rooms.

That Benny is a Negro—is "colored," as people down in Pinehill say—does not figure very largely in Abby's fantasies. She is so used to Benny; in a way she has always known him. Other facts to her are more salient, and more exciting: a boy who goes to Exeter. Who is going (probably) to Harvard. To be a doctor. Someone tall and male.

Half-consciously, though, she does keep her Benny fantasies quite separate from Pinehill fantasies. She does not, so far, think of Benny coming to Pinehill for a visit.

Not yet.

She does not mention Benny to Pinehill friends. Not to Betsy or Melanctha, and certainly not to those boys.

Chapter 35

By September, which in Pinehill is still full summer, or almost, the lives of the Bairds have been quite radically changed by two events.

The first is that the pool, as was more or less expected, is completed—but sooner than anyone thought, and more successfully. It is somehow both longer and deeper than they imagined. Harry and Cynthia and Abby smile at each other as they talk about their pool: such a good idea, such fun for everyone, for themselves and for all the friends who warned that it would take forever and not be done right at all (you know how colored help is). But there it is, a long cement oval, shallow at one end, for small children, and much deeper at the other, for grownup swimmers and even for diving.

And the plantings—or, rather, transplantings— that surround the oval are large and healthy; soon they will be very beautiful. Everyone says so. "My, those shrubs and flowers are going to be just beautiful." Dolly especially says, "Never in all my born days did I see such great big bushes dug up and replanted like that, and living to tell the tale. That Horace, he is just a plain old miracle man with plants, with anything that grows. You-all are just so lucky!"

Horace, the once-errant husband of Odessa (apparently this is his pattern; from time to time he simply shows up, neither asked nor answering any questions), has turned out to be, indeed, a genius with plants. He has transplanted some good-sized boxwood and some privet, a couple of nice young dogwood trees, and some Japanese quince ("It'll be lovely in the spring, but Willard says these days to call it 'japonica,' not Japanese," says Dolly, with her laugh). All those plants that are supposedly somewhere between difficult and impossible to transfer. But Horace has done it all, and he came around every day all summer to see how the plants were doing. (Dolly: "He just loves those flowers, pity he doesn't love Odessa a little more like that.") For Horace has gone again, just disappeared.

Cynthia has a secret plan for Odessa: she wants Odessa to move into their house. There's a whole separate private apartment above the garage, and Odessa could live there; she could be a sort of caretaker of their house. Since her children are all grown up and away somewhere and Horace is usually gone, Odessa would be better off in town, Cynthia reasons—she loves the idea of Odessa being there.

The second and most unexpected event is that Cynthia was accepted by the law school at Georgetown. She is much more pleased by this than she can allow anyone to know; even with Harry her tone is offhand, dismissive. "Who'd have thought I'd grow up to be a lawyer? I'll have to get a whole bunch of new hats. Serious black ones." She clutches her own pleasure and her pride to herself, a secret and deeply exciting present. She imagines power and influence, accomplishment. Once she starts to work as a lawyer, all her energies will be focused, directed. How strong she will be! It is almost frightening.

More realistically, she thinks too of the effort required: going to law school, trying to remember all those cases. Taking exams. Writing papers on the law. It is somewhat daunting to consider, but on the whole she feels confident. She has done very well in all her course work so far, and they would not have accepted her in the law school if they were not sure she could do the work, she reasons. And by the time she finishes law school the war will be over, surely, and everyone can get back to better lives. To a better world.

The Bairds decide to have a party in early September, as both an official opening of the pool and a celebration of Cynthia's new life.

"I'm not sure anyone else will think it's so great, though," she tells Harry. "My going back to school."

"I think it's great," he tells her loyally. "I've always said you're a lot smarter than you think you are."

"Well—"

"*I* think it's great," Abby tells her mother. "No one else's mother is a lawyer, not even in Washington. You could get to be on the Supreme Court someday." (There have been recent jokes: FDR might appoint Eleanor to the Court. Well, he already appointed "that Jewish person Frankfurter"—so who knows? A woman might be next.)

"Come on, you two," says Cynthia. "First I have to get through law school."

But she is pleased by what she feels as family support, and agrees to the party.

That September day, even by Pinehill standards, is incredibly hot. Very early in the morning, at dawn, it is already hot. The air seems both heavy and tired. The hours drag along until noon, which everyone imagines will be a turning point. "It can't stay this hot much longer." But by the afternoon it is even hotter—and those who are friends of the Bairds have begun to think, How wonderful, to have a swimming party to go to. Doubts about whether or not to bother undressing and actually going in are easily resolved: no one wants to get dressed up. Bathing costumes are brought out and inspected. Since it is much too hot to drive to Durham to shop, and none of the local stores carry bathing suits, most people decide to make do. Except for Cynthia, who already has a new suit, and for poor Deirdre Yates Byrd, who is far too pregnant for her own or any other bathing suit; also, swimming is looked upon askance for pregnant women, at that time.

As no one has quite remarked, this is the first time that they have all been in swimming together. More to the point, it is the first time that they have all seen each other in bathing suits, have been so nearly nakedly exposed to each other. And there are, of course, several surprises among all those bodies.

One is that Esther Hightower has an astonish-

283

ingly good figure. In an old navy-blue wool tank suit that is just the slightest bit too small for her (it may be even older than she remembered), Esther is revealed to have high, full, and quite amazing breasts ("Rita Hayworth doesn't have a thing on Esther. Lucky old Jim!" one less lucky husband whispered to another). Normally, Esther wears very expensive, very "good" clothes, but they tend to be about a size too large. (Dolly has remarked on this to Cynthia, who has agreed. "I wonder why she does that?" "I don't know, she's just very modest, I guess.") Of course no one can come right out and say to Esther that she has a terrific body; instead many people tell her how well she is looking, which is also true. "My, Esther, you are looking so, uh, *well*."

Conversely, pretty Irene Lee, in her daisy-flowered cotton dressmaker suit, despite the modesty of her costume can be seen to have a very unfortunate little figure. Thick-waisted, flat-chested, and heavy of thigh. It is interesting that all this has been so successfully disguised in all her pretty dresses.

Dolly Bigelow, as everyone already knew, has shapely, small plump legs, now revealed beneath the tiny red polka-dotted skirt of her suit, but there is something odd about her chest, some curious lack of symmetry there. This of course is not remarked upon—not out loud. Cynthia is perhaps the first to work it out, though she does not say anything either, of course not. Except that much later, to Harry, in a tone of semi-triumph she brings out, "Dolly wears falsies! Can you believe it? One slipped, that's how I knew!"

Cynthia herself is wearing her new red Lastex suit. She has never worn such clinging material before. Used to wool or cotton, she feels a little conspicuous, especially since Harry has said, "You look like a movie star!—only better, much more classy."

Willard Bigelow is paunchier than his loose old tweeds and flannels have ever revealed. And Jimmy Hightower is trimmer and much more muscular than one would have suspected.

Russell Byrd. Cynthia manages barely to look at him, at that once-loved and familiar flesh. The shape of his naked legs, and his muscular, smooth back.

She looks instead at far more familiar Harry, and decides, with perfect objectivity, that his is by far the best male body there.

Perhaps in part because of the heavy, unremitting heat, and because, too, people are slightly nervous at being so relatively naked with each other, everyone or almost everyone drinks a very great deal. Harry, tending bar at one end of the pool, where he has set up a table, observes the frequency with which people come back for refreshers, for what the locals call "a little sweetening."

Odessa, coming out from the house with a tray of glasses, also notices how much the folks are drinking. Pouring it down.

She is not at all sure about moving in with the Bairds. Not because of the drinking—they don't drink bad, especially. And in some ways it would be real nice. The warm dry hardwood floors in ugly weather, and the running water, hot and cold both, all the time. The electric stove, and the lights. The lights so easy, turning them on and off. She thinks of the lights and the good smooth floors on the days when she does think, Yes, I'll take this job, I'll take care of their house for them.

But then she thinks, Horace. What will I do all the times when Horace comes home, and I've got no place for him?

How come you let him right back in your door? Miz Bigelow used to ask her that, like it was some of her business. And Miz Baird might ask the same. They is uppity, white ladies. Call colored uppity, it's them. Asking any old questions comes to their minds. What you couldn't answer even if you had a mind to. Like you was their child, and not real smart.

Yankee ladies not quite so uppity, though. Folks grew up around here think they can ask you any old thing got into their heads. Think since you're the colored they really know you. Almost they own you.

So like she told Miz Baird, she'll think about it. She's just studying what to do. What be best for her, and best for Horace, times he come home. Which he always will do, one time or another. He's a wandering man, but he needs a home to come back to, like any other man. No way to explain. No call to either.

Deirdre does not want to name their daughter Ursula. If it's a girl. Russ keeps saying how much he likes the name, and he likes that Kansas woman, the one with the pig who kept coming out to help when SallyJane was sick. But Ursula: that is surely an ugly, odd-sounding name, thinks Deirdre. Kids would tease a child with a name like that.

"What about SallyJane?" she asked Russ. She was serious, she liked that name a whole lot.

"Deirdre!—really. Lord God, what an idea!"

"But it's the others' mother's name. Don't you think they'd like it?"

"No! Lord God," he said again, not looking at her.

Derek. Deirdre is secretly hoping for a boy, whom she would like to call Derek. Once, just for a year, a boy with that name was in her class at school, a boy from somewhere else—Vermont, she thinks. He was tall and very fair, with hair the color of broomstraw, and he was handsome. Then, after that one year, he was gone, and no one had ever really got to know him, but Deirdre never forgot how he looked, with his narrow blue eyes and big shoulders. And he was very smart; he got all A's that year, and played basketball too. She would like to have a boy like Derek, with that name.

She stretches in the sun, which through her thin cotton dress feels really good. On her poor big stomach. She smiles at Russ, who is drinking too much. What she would really like best, thinks Deirdre, is for this moment to go on and on forever. She would like to be pregnant forever, and never deliver. To stay here in the Bairds' back yard, by their swimming pool, and drink this nice sweet lemonade that Odessa made for her. With all the smells of flowers and someone's perfume in the air. And never go home to take care of anyone.

I could really write a book about this town, thinks Jimmy Hightower, who is also drinking Odessa's lemonade—without gin, and thus noticing a lot. He thinks of the Russ-Deirdre story, with Graham—the Pearl of their scarlet letter. And the brief appearances of Clyde and Norris Drake, the two devils, who killed off SallyJane and almost ruined Russ. (Fucking that woman was horrible for Russ;

don't ask Jimmy how he knows—he just does.
And Cynthia-and-Russ, that story.

And then there's the me-and-Russ story, thinks Jimmy. I have to admit it: I had this real old school-boy crush on Russ, who for years would not give me the time of day. And then he did; he got interested in my book (that was just after the trauma of Norris Drake) and turned it into a goddam bestseller. And then turned back into not giving me the time of day again.

Who or what could be next in line for Russ? he wonders. And then, glancing over at Esther, who has never looked better than she does today (Jimmy first met Esther at a swimming party, come to think of it—back in Tulsa, almost twenty years ago), he thinks, If Russ should take a shine to Esther, I'd kill him dead. But of course that isn't Russ's way, not at all. It's other people who take a big shine to him. They come after him. And he just lets them. Sometimes.

Dolly Bigelow is sitting there in the lovely sunshine, among all the wonderful flowers and all her dearest friends, looking just as cute as pie in her red polka-dotted suit (trust Cynthia to wear a red suit too, and such a tight, show-off one), and she thinks: It does not matter one damn without Clifton. She misses Clifton Lee in just the worst way; sometimes she thinks she can't stand her life without him. She needs him for flirting at all the parties, and then, just sometimes, not often—the kissing, off in cars. It was wonderful, that kissing, and wonderful Clifton never, never tried to push it any further. To do anything that would cause her to have to stop him. And oh! that terrible night when he died, just up and *died*, right there in the car, in her arms!—made this funny noise in his throat, and then a sort of shudder, and then he was gone. She knew right away he was dead. No person in that body anymore. She had watched her daddy die—same thing. All heavy and limp. In her arms.

But Cynthia looks so tacky in that little old red bathing suit of hers, like some teenager, just the tackiest thing. Trust a Yankee! (Clifton never took to Cynthia at all. "That bottle-blonde can't hold a candle to you, honey-babe," he used to say.) And Esther Hightower, just busting out of her suit all over the place. Hasn't anyone told her she's too big now for that suit? And Russ, you can see his— well, some of him is hanging out just a little below his suit.

Oh, Clifton, why did you have to *die*?

After the war things will be a great deal worse, is what Russ thinks, sitting there dejectedly in the sun. Thinking: I do not want to get into that goddam lukewarm copper-sulfated water. And also thinking: What an inferior, lowly bunch of so-called humanity gathered here, in this stinking garden. Not a first-rate mind in a carload of these folk. Or a beautiful woman either. Deirdre's so pregnant, and besides he is married to her. There's Cynthia—well, there is Cynthia. He does not want to think about Cynthia today. Looking up, he sees not Cynthia but Esther Hightower. A brand-new person. A goddess, the most beautiful woman he ever saw. A Jewish queen. Biblical, splendid. How come he never saw her before? Oh, how *come!*

That goddam Jimmy, Russ thinks; now he has everything. Success and fame and the most gorgeous living woman, who is probably intelligent too. Intending nothing, Russ smiles in Esther's direction, but his gaze is somehow intercepted by that of Jimmy himself, who is scowling directly at him. And for what? Now what has got into that silly Oklahoma oil-king bugger?

Is it possible that the sun is getting even hotter, this late in the day? Russ feels that it is, or maybe it's all the booze he has drunk. Too much gin, he knows it, and he's got no head for liquor at all. But today it's not making him drunk, just hot. Looking out at the pool, at all that cool blue lapping water into which no one, so far, has ventured—just Abigail Baird, sitting there on the side with her feet in, kicking up little waves—Russ thinks he really should go in swimming, he really should. And, thinking that, he begins to laugh, just quietly, to himself. The joke being that he does not know how to swim. As a kid, afraid of water, he never learned, and now, still afraid, he is much too old to learn.

Dangling her feet in the water, which is really not so cool, Abby thinks of Benny. "Sweltering," he says, in a shipyard job his Uncle Max got for him. Tough work, but he's making good money, and it may keep him out of the draft. He and a friend plan a little vacation trip before fall and back-to-school.

How great if they came down here! thinks Abby, at first, and then she thinks, Would it really be so great? What about—what about his being "colored," as they say down here? Abby can just hear that silly Dolly Bigelow, her mother's friend: "Well, I just never thought I'd live to see the day, that snippy little old Abby Baird has got this *colored* friend, and he's come to stay with them in their *house*, and he's even going into their *swimming pool*." She is not even sure that her own friend Betsy Lee would be so swell about it. Melanctha— well, you can never tell how Melanctha will be about anything. The boys would all be just awful, she knows that. She hates all the boys around here.

Abby recently read an article, though, about Negroes in the armed services. According to this writer, it's been a big success. And so maybe after the war things will be a lot better. Abby is almost sure that they will. This Southern stuff about "colored" is just too dumb, it can't go on forever. So maybe, if not this fall, some other fall soon Benny will come down to visit. When he's at Harvard, maybe. A football star. She smiles with secret delight at this thought, and she kicks her feet harder, sending blue ripples all across the pool.

Watching her feet, and the water, she is not quite aware at first that Deirdre Yates (Byrd) has got up from where she was sitting and is making her way toward Abby, coming to the edge of the pool where Abby sits.

"Come on, take your shoes off. It'll cool you," Abby tells her friend; she feels full of affection for poor heavily pregnant Deirdre, whom she has not seen or talked to for a while.

Awkwardly, slowly, Deirdre lowers herself to the edge of the pool, her body so cumbersome now. Everything she does is slow and awkward. "Lord, that feels good!" she says at last, her shoes slipped off, feet cooling in the water. "I'm hot enough for two people." She laughs. "I guess I am two people."

Abby is unable to imagine being pregnant. Carrying a baby in your stomach. She supposes that someday she will, but for the moment she would rather not even think about it. Instead she says, "Deirdre, I've been reading all this stuff lately, and do you think it's true that things will be a lot better for Negro people after the war?"

Deirdre stares at Abby for a moment, then seems to adjust to this shift in tone. "I reckon they will," she says. "Stands to reason, with all the colored in the service." She adds, "I surely hope so. The way things are now is just so wrong. Unfair. Not Christian."

This opinion comes as a surprise to Abby. They have never before touched on "race" as a topic, and Deirdre after all is as Southern as anyone around. Pleased, Abby tells her, "Deirdre, I'm so glad you feel like that. Me too. And you see, I have this friend—"

No one, still, has really gone in swimming. Everyone seems content simply to contemplate the cooling water.

Hearing what she believes is the ringing of their phone, and momentarily forgetting that Odessa is there at the house and presumably in the kitchen where the phone is, Cynthia gets to her feet. But as she approaches the back door she hears not rings but Odessa's voice, speaking rather loudly.

She seems to be finishing a conversation, which must have been brief. "...that's all right, then," she hears Odessa say, in a warmly welcoming voice. "I see you later. Soon, now. This here is long distance!"

She has not heard this friendly tone from Odessa before (why would she?), nor seen the happy face that she finds, walking in.

"Oh, Odessa, I thought I heard the phone. But it was for you? Well, that's good." She smiles vaguely, noting that Odessa's expression is already fading back to its customary blankness.

But Odessa says (as though she owed an explanation), "That Horace. He back."

"Oh good, that's nice." And then, from some sheer if diffuse goodwill, Cynthia adds, "You know, Odessa, if you and Horace both decide to come and live here, I'd be—well, that would be wonderful."

"That so?" That is all Odessa says, for the moment, but Cynthia is amazed to hear the quick notes of pleasure and surprise in Odessa's voice. And Cynthia thinks, My God, how terrible, Odessa is surprised and even grateful, just because I said her husband could live here too. Her *husband*, for God's sake. How terrible!

"Well, you think about it," she says to Odessa.

"Yes'm, we think."

When I'm a lawyer, thinks Cynthia a little vaguely, a little ginnily, I will really try to change everything. I'll come down here and take cases for Negro people, for free. She sees herself in front of a courtroom, passionately declaiming. Dressed in something incredibly simple and smart—a little black Balenciaga, perhaps. And then she chides herself severely: I'm going to be a lawyer, not a movie star. However, nevertheless, it wouldn't hurt her cause for her to be well dressed—would it, really?

It is interesting, she also thinks, as she crosses the lawn, that almost no one at the party has mentioned her going to law school.

293

Several thoughts arrive at Russ Byrd's mind simultaneously. He thinks, I'll never be able to write a play again, or even the smallest poem. He thinks, I am terribly drunk. He thinks, I must go in swimming.

He slips down to the pool, strangely unobserved. Everyone else is too occupied with drinks and with talk; they are mostly stupefied, and paralyzed by the heat, and the gin.

But Russ feels an instant cool relief as he wades very slowly out into the pool. The water reaches his cock—ah, delicious!

He walks a foot or so more, and then, quite suddenly, as he might have known it would, the floor falls out of the world, and he has slid underwater, to where he cannot see or breathe. Where his mind will explode into a poem.

It is Abby who first sees that Russ is in trouble. That he is in fact about to drown. She jumps in, followed by Deirdre in all her clothes. Then Cynthia, just arrived at the edge of the pool. And the three women, somehow, pulling together, haul Russ out of the pool.

In some later versions it is Deirdre alone—"big as she was, she jumped right in with her dress on"—who saved Russ's life. Other people say it was Cynthia, who, according to legend, "took a shine to Russ the first time she ever laid eyes on him, maybe even before." Others said Abby, "that brave little Yankee girl, and not so little anymore."

It is Harry, though, who gets Russ from the pool's edge to the grassy space at one end, to a spread-out towel. Harry who sits astride Russ's back, rhythmically pushing down on his ribs, then letting go. Repeating as he does so, "Out goes the bad air, *in* comes the good." An old Navy incantation.

As Russ comes back to life, he sees not a poem or a play but a movie in Technicolor. It seems to be about Heaven, with bursting clouds and the most beautiful angels, also golden and very sexy. He believes that he saved his own life, by agreeing to breathe again.

Cynthia thinks that Harry saved Russ, with his artificial respiration. Harry thinks Cynthia saved him, jumping in like that. There is never any general agreement about who or what saved Russ's life, but it is a topic discussed locally for many months.

In the middle of the following November, a brilliant month of blue skies and scarlet and yellow leaves, and blue-gray wood smoke, Deirdre gives birth to a round, very amiable little baby girl. A golden girl, whom she and Russ name, without much further argument, SallyJane.

IF YOU HAVE ENJOYED READING THIS
LARGE PRINT BOOK AND YOU WOULD
LIKE MORE INFORMATION ON HOW TO
ORDER A WHEELER LARGE PRINT
BOOK, PLEASE WRITE TO:

WHEELER PUBLISHING, INC.
P. O. BOX 531
ACCORD, MA 02018-0531